THE
OUTSIDER

ALSO BY ANTHONY FRANZE

The Advocate's Daughter

The Last Justice

THE
OUTSIDER

ANTHONY FRANZE

MINOTAUR BOOKS
A THOMAS DUNNE BOOK
NEW YORK

A THOMAS DUNNE BOOK FOR MINOTAUR BOOKS.
An imprint of St. Martin's Press.

THE OUTSIDER. Copyright © 2017 by Anthony Franze. All rights reserved. Printed in the United States of America. For information, address St. Martin's Press, 175 Fifth Avenue, New York, N.Y. 10010.

www.thomasdunnebooks.com
www.minotaurbooks.com

Designed by Omar Chapa

Library of Congress Cataloging-in-Publication Data

Names: Franze, Anthony J., author.
Title: The outsider / Anthony Franze.
Description: First Edition. | New York : Minotaur Books, 2017.
| "A Thomas Dunne Book."
Identifiers: LCCN 2016044899| ISBN 9781250071668 (hardback)
| ISBN 9781466882843 (e-book)
Subjects: LCSH: United States. Supreme Court—Officials and employees—Fiction.
| Murder—Investigation—Fiction. | Political fiction.
| GSAFD: Suspense fiction. | Mystery fiction. | Legal stories.
Classification: LCC PS3606.R4228 O98 2017 | DDC 813/.6—dc23
LC record available at https://lccn.loc.gov/2016044899

Our books may be purchased in bulk for promotional, educational, or business use. Please contact your local bookseller or the Macmillan Corporate and Premium Sales Department at 1-800-221-7945, extension 5442, or by e-mail at MacmillanSpecial Markets@macmillan.com.

First Edition: March 2017

10 9 8 7 6 5 4 3 2 1

For anyone who's ever been on the outside, looking in

Law clerks are the lowest form of animal life.

—WILLIAM O. DOUGLAS,
ASSOCIATE JUSTICE, U.S. SUPREME COURT, 1939–1975

THE
OUTSIDER

PROLOGUE

When her computer pinged, Amanda Hill ignored it. This late at night, she shouldn't have, but she did.

All her energy was focused on tomorrow's closing argument. Her office was dark, save the sharp cone of light from the desk lamp. She'd waited for everyone to leave so she could run through her final words to the jury. So she could practice as she'd done a thousand times, pacing her office in front of imaginary jurors, explaining away the evidence against the latest criminal mastermind she'd been appointed to represent. This one had left prints and DNA, and vivid images of the robbery had been captured by surveillance cameras.

She glanced out her window into the night. Normal people were home tucking in their children, watching a little TV before hitting the sack. Her little girl deserved better. She should call to check in, but she needed to get the closing done. Amanda's mother was watching Isabelle, and her mom would call if she needed anything.

There was another ping. Then another. Irritated, Amanda reached for the mouse and clicked to her e-mail. The subject line grabbed her attention:

URGENT MESSAGE ABOUT YOUR MOTHER AND ISABELLE!

Amanda opened the e-mail. Strange, there was no name in the sender field. And the message had only a link. Was this one of those phishing scams?

She almost deleted it, but the subject line caught her eye again. Her seven-year-old's name.

Her cursor hovered over the link—then she clicked.

A video appeared on the screen. The footage was shaky, filmed on a smartphone. The scene was dark, but for a flashlight beam hitting a dirty floor. Then a whisper: "You have thirty minutes to get here or they die."

A chill slithered down Amanda's back. This was a joke, right? A sick joke? She moved the mouse to shut down the video, but the flashlight ray crawled up a grimy wall and stopped on two figures. Amanda's heart jumped into her throat. It was her mother and Isabelle. Bound, gagged, weeping.

"Dupont Underground," the voice hissed. "Thirty minutes. If you call the police, we'll know. And they'll die."

The camera zoomed in on Isabelle's tear-streaked face. Amanda's computer began buzzing and flashing, consumed by a tornado virus.

Amanda drove erratically from her downtown office to Dupont Circle. She kept one eye on the road, the other on her smartphone that guided her to the only address she could find for "Dupont Underground," the abandoned street trolley line that ran under Washington, D.C.

Her mind raced. Why was this happening? It didn't make sense. It couldn't be a kidnapping for ransom. She had no money— she was a public defender, for Christ's sake. A disgruntled client? No, this was too well organized. Too sophisticated. Common criminals, Amanda knew from her years representing them, were uneducated bumblers, not the type to plan out anything in their lives, much less something like this.

She checked the phone. She had only fifteen minutes. The GPS said she'd be there in five. She tried to calm herself, control her breathing. She should call the police. But the warning played in her head: *We'll know. And they'll die.*

She pulled over on New Hampshire Avenue. The GPS said

this was the place, but she saw no entrance to any underground. It was a business district. Law firms and lobby shops locked up for the night. She looked around, panicked and confused. There was nothing but a patch of construction across the street. Work on a manhole or sewer line. *Or trolley entrance.* Amanda leapt from her car and ran to the construction area. A four-foot-tall rectangular plywood structure jutted up from the sidewalk. It had a door on top, like a storm cellar. The padlock latch had been pried open, the wood splintered. Amanda swung open the door and peered down into the gloom.

She shouldn't go down there. But she heard a noise. A muffled scream? Amanda pointed her phone's flashlight into the chasm. A metal ladder disappeared into the darkness. She steeled herself, then climbed into the opening, the only light the weak bulb on her phone. When she reached the bottom, she stood quietly, looking down the long tunnel, listening. She heard the noise again and began running toward it.

That's when she heard the footsteps behind her.

She ran faster, her breaths coming in rasps, the footfalls from behind keeping pace. She wanted to turn and fight. She was a goddamned fighter. "Amanda Hill, The Bitch of Fifth Street," she'd heard the defendants call her around the courthouse. But the image of Isabelle and her mother's faces, their desperation, drew her on.

The footsteps grew closer. She needed to suppress the fear, to find her family.

The blow to the head came without warning and slammed her to the ground. There was the sound of a boot stomping on plastic and the flashlight on her phone went out. The figure grabbed a fistful of her hair and dragged her to a small room off the tunnel. She was gasping for air now.

A lantern clicked on. Amanda heard the scurrying of tiny feet. She saw the two masses in the shadows and felt violently ill: her mother and Isabelle. Soiled rags stuffed in their mouths, hands and feet bound. Next to them the silhouette of someone spray-painting on the wall.

Amanda sat up quickly, and a piercing pain shot through her

skull. She averted her eyes, hoping it was all a nightmare. But a voice cut through the whimpering of her family.

"Look at them!"

Amanda lifted her gaze. She forced a smile, feigned a look of optimism, then mouthed a message to her daughter: *It's okay. Everything's going to be okay.*

It was a lie, of course.

A godforsaken lie.

CHAPTER 1

Grayson Hernandez walked up to the lectern in the well of the U.S. Supreme Court. He wasn't intimidated by the marble columns that encased the room or the elevated mahogany bench where The Nine had been known to skewer even the most experienced advocates. He calmly pulled the lever on the side of the lectern to adjust its height, a move he'd learned watching the assistant solicitor generals showing off. He stood up straight and didn't look down at any notes; the best lawyers didn't use notes. And he began his oral argument.

"Mr. Chief Justice and may it please the court—"

He was immediately interrupted, not uncommon since the justices on average asked more than one hundred questions in the hour of oral argument allotted to each case. But the voice, which rang though the chamber, wasn't from a justice of the highest court in the land.

"I've told you before, Gray, you can't be in here."

A flashlight beam cut across the empty courtroom. Gray held up a hand to shield his eyes. He smiled at the Supreme Court Police officer making his nightly rounds.

"Someday, counselor," the officer said. "But for now you might wanna focus on getting the nightlies delivered." The officer swung the ray of light to Gray's messenger cart filled with the evening's mail.

Gray waved at the officer and returned to his cart. The wheel squeaked as he rolled it out of the courtroom and into the marble hallway.

In Chief Justice Douglas's chambers, two law clerks were sitting in the reception area, fifteen feet apart, tossing a football between them. They seemed punchy, wired after a long day at the office, talking about one of the court's cases.

"A high school has no right to punish a kid for things he says off school grounds. The court needs to finally say so," one of the clerks said. He was a stocky blond guy. Gray thought his name was Mike. Mike spiraled the ball to the other clerk, who looked kind of like a young JFK.

"You're high if you think the chief is gonna side with the student," JFK said, catching the ball with a loud snap. "You upload a violent rap song on YouTube saying your math teacher is sexually harassing students, you're gonna get suspended."

"Even if it's true?" Mike said.

The Supreme Court had thirty-six law clerks, four per justice. It was an internship like no other, promising young lawyers not only a ticket to any legal job in the country, but also the chance to leave their fingerprints on the most important legal questions of the day. The current clerks were all in their late twenties, the same age as Gray, but that's where the similarities ended. Like the two throwing the ball, almost all were white, from affluent backgrounds. Gray didn't think there were any Mexican Americans in the clerk pool, and certainly none who grew up in gritty Hamilton Heights, D.C. They'd all gone to Harvard or Yale or institutions that, unlike Gray's law school, had ivy instead of graffiti on their walls. And they certainly weren't delivering mail.

Gray nodded hello as he lifted the stacks of *certiorari* petitions out of his cart and dropped them in the metal in-boxes for the chief's clerks.

Mike looked at Gray. "No, not more petitions, I'm begging you."

Gray smiled, but didn't engage. His boss in the marshal's office had a rule when it came to the justices and their law clerks: *Speak only when necessary.*

The ball whizzed across the reception area again. "Is it printed yet?" JFK asked. "I wanna get out of here." He looked over to the printer, which was humming and spitting out paper. Gray worked two night shifts a week, and there usually were no less than a dozen clerks still in the office. Theirs was a one-year gig, but they worked as if the justices wanted to squeeze five years out of them.

"It won't take long," Mike said. "It's a short memo, and I just want someone who's a disagreeable ass to point out any soft spots before I turn it in to the chief."

"You're wasting your time. He's never gonna side with the student, he—"

"This case is no different than *Tinker v. Des Moines*," Mike countered. "The court said disruptive speech at school could be punished, but not speech made off school grounds. Off-campus speech, including posting a song on YouTube, should be covered by the First Amendment just like everything else. It's none of the school's business."

JFK gave a dismissive grunt. "A rap expert from Greenwich, Connecticut, I love it."

Mike threw the ball hard at his co-clerk.

"Hey," JFK said, shaking off the sting after reeling in the throw. "I'm just saying, the *Tinker* case was decided in the late sixties. You can't apply it in the digital world. You're in an ivory tower if you think the chief will blindly follow *Tinker*."

Gray pretended not to listen, but he lingered, enjoying the intellectual banter.

The ball flew by again. "Ivory tower?" Mike said. "Fine, let's ask an everyman." He pointed the football at Gray. "Hey, Greg, can we ask you something?"

Mike had once asked Gray his name, a regular man of the people.

"It's Gray."

"Sorry. Gray. We have a question: Do you think if a high school student is off campus and posts something offensive on social media a school can punish him for it?"

JFK chimed in: "It's not just posting something offensive. It's a profanity-laden rap that accuses a teacher of sexually harassing students and threatens to 'put a cap' in the guy."

Gray pondered the question as he retrieved mail from the out-boxes. "I agree with what Murderous Malcolm said about the case."

The clerks shot each other a look. That morning the *New York Times* ran a story about the case, in which a famous rapper was interviewed and defended the student's right to free speech. Every morning the Supreme Court's library sent around an e-mail aggregating news stories relating to the court. Gray was probably the only person at One First Street who read them all.

Gray continued. "I think the First Amendment allows a kid who saw a wrong happening to write a poem about it over a beat." Gray wheeled the cart toward the door. "And if the chief justice disagrees, you might mention all the violence in those operas he loves so much."

"That's what I'm talking about," Mike said, spiking the ball, then doing a ridiculous touchdown dance. He strutted over to Gray and gave him a high five.

For a moment, it felt like Gray was a clerk himself, an equal weighing in on the most significant school-speech case in decades.

"Hey, Gray," JFK said.

Gray turned, ready to continue his defense of the First Amendment.

"I've got some books that need to be delivered to the library."

When Gray arrived at the gym two hours later, his dad already had his hands wrapped and was hitting the heavy bag. There was a large sweat stain on his shirt. "You're late," he called out.

"I told you, I have the night shift on Sundays," Gray said.

His dad didn't respond, just pounded the bag.

He wasn't going to get any sympathy from Manny Hernandez about the night shift. This was his father's one night off from the pizza shop. Since his dad's cancer went into remission, they'd been meeting every Sunday night at the old boxing club in Adams Morgan. Gray would have preferred that they spent these times together somewhere other than a smelly gym, but it made his father happy to see him back in the gloves. It was these moments that Gray was reminded that he probably wasn't the man his father had dreamed he'd become. With his books and big dreams, Gray was his mother's boy.

Gray punched the bag, the hits vibrating through him, his thoughts venturing to his encounter with the law clerks. He threw his weight into his right.

Let's ask an everyman.

Then his left.

I've got some books that need to be delivered to the library.

Gray continued to pummel the bag, his heart pounding, sweat dripping from his brow.

"Somethin' wrong?" His father came and stood behind the bag, holding it in place as Gray kept going at it. "Talk to me."

"It's nothing," Gray finally said, catching his breath, wiping his forehead with his arm. "Just work stuff."

"I thought it was going well? You've loved that building since you were a little kid. And now you're working there, helping the justices."

"I don't think delivering the mail is exactly helping the justices, Dad."

"It's a foot in the door. Once they get to know you, see how smart you are . . ."

Things didn't work that way, but Gray wasn't in the mood to argue.

"It'll happen, son," his father added. "You just gotta pay your dues, Grayson."

"I know, Dad, I know."

CHAPTER 2

At seven the next morning, Gray sat at his cubicle, tired and his muscles aching from the workout the night before. He started his day, as always, slugging down a large coffee while reading SCOTUS-blog, a website that covered the court. It was the first day of the new term, and the pundits predicted it would be an exciting year with several landmark cases.

Gray turned when he felt a hand on his shoulder. Shelby, one of the marshal's aides. A mistake he'd made after a night of drinking with the other aides. She made a point of saying she'd never been with "a guy like him," which he assumed meant a poor kid from a sketchy side of D.C. She worked part-time while finishing her senior year at Georgetown.

"Martin wants to see you," she said.

Gray looked across the expansive cube farm. He could see Martin Melnick, their supervisor, through the glass walls of his small interior office in the back. He was eating something wrapped in foil. A breakfast burrito, maybe. Shelby's expression summed up her assessment of Martin: *Ick*. Martin was in his late thirties, ancient by aide-pool standards. Overweight with bad teeth, he was the antithesis of the bright young things who worked at the high court, the butt of many jokes. He was never particularly nice to Gray;

the opposite, actually. But Martin was good at his job and didn't deserve the ridicule, so Gray kind of rooted for him in all of his slobbiness.

Before Gray made his way over to Martin, Shelby said, "Who's that?" She pointed to a photo pinned to Gray's cubicle. It was of a boxer in the ring, bruised and battered, arms in the air, standing over his opponent who was out cold.

"My dad, back in the day." Gray had pinned it up his first day on the job. His own Facebook motivational meme.

Shelby squeezed Gray's bicep. "I see where you get—"

"I've gotta get over to Martin," Gray said, politely extracting himself.

Martin's office didn't help his image. Stacks of papers every-where. Post-it notes all over the place. He glanced up at Gray and handed him an envelope.

"We got a rush delivery for E.R.D.'s chambers."

E.R.D. were the initials for Edgar R. Douglas, the chief jus-tice. In his month on the job, Gray had learned that the Supreme Court was obsessed with abbreviations and acronyms.

"Oral arguments start at ten, so get this to his clerk ASAP. His name's on the envelope."

Gray fast-walked up to the main floor, shuttling through the impressive Great Hall that was lined with marble columns and busts of past chief justices. He nodded at the officer manning the bronze latticework door and made his way to the chief justice's chambers. The chief's secretary, a tough old bird named Olga Romanov, flicked him a glance.

"I have a delivery for Keir Landon."

"The clerks are getting breakfast," she said in her clipped East-ern European accent.

"Do you know where?"

"Breakfast. Where do you think?"

Gray forced a smile, then headed back downstairs to the court's cafeteria. He marched past the assembly line of trays and the pub-lic seating area and into the private room reserved for the law clerks. A group of four were sitting at the long table.

Gray cleared his throat when they didn't look up. When that didn't work: "Excuse me. I have a delivery for Keir Landon."

The guy from last night who looked like JFK popped his head up. He walked over to Gray and plucked the envelope from his hand.

"What's up, Greg?" Mike said from the group.

Before Gray could correct him again on the name, Gray's phone pinged. A text from Martin, another rush delivery.

Gray hurried out, tapping a text to Martin as he paced quickly through the cafeteria. He didn't look up until he bumped into someone. A tiny woman in her seventies. It was only when the elderly woman's food tray hit the floor that Gray recognized her: Justice Rose Fitzgerald Yorke. She looked different without the black robe. Always weird seeing the teacher out of school. Yorke was one of the most beloved members of the court. Gray had read that when Yorke graduated from Harvard in the fifties, the only woman and number one in her class, none of the white-shoe law firms would hire a woman as a lawyer. A few had offered to make her a secretary. Maybe that explained why she ate in the public cafeteria rather than the justices' private dining room, or why she organized the office birthday celebrations for every single employee at the court. She knew what it was like to be an outsider. She brought what some would derisively call *empathy* to her jurisprudence.

Justice Yorke bent over to pick up her spilled plate and silverware.

"Justice Yorke, I'm *so* sorry. Please, let me clean this up." Gray lightly put a hand on the justice's arm.

"It's no problem, young man, I can clean up after myself."

"No, really, it's my fault. Please."

The manager of the cafeteria was standing there now, looking annoyed. He gestured for Justice Yorke to come with him to get a new plate. The manager shot Gray a hard look as he spirited the justice away.

So there he was on the first Monday in October—the opening day of the term—on hands and knees wiping up the floor, the clerks passing by on their way back to chambers.

You just gotta pay your dues, Grayson.

CHAPTER 3

At the end of his shift, Gray headed down to the court's garage to get his bike. In the elevator, he contemplated his dinner options. He wasn't sure if he could take another night of ramen or SpaghettiOs. Maybe he'd go to the pizza shop. Or to his parents' apartment. Mom could always be counted on for a good meal, and he could bring some laundry. The elevator doors spread open to a field of gray concrete. The bike rack was empty but for his beat-up Schwinn. As he unlocked the chain, he heard a commotion. In the back, behind one of the support beams.

Gray stepped toward the sound. Next to an SUV parked in a reserved spot he saw two men: one had fallen on the ground, the other standing over him. The guy must have slipped. Was he hurt? Something about how he didn't try to get up and the stance of the other man didn't seem quite right.

"Everything okay?" Gray said.

The man who was standing whirled his head around. That's when Gray noticed the ski mask.

Before Gray could process the situation, the assailant had kicked the man on the ground and charged Gray.

Gray's father had taught him that when someone is coming at you, in the boxing ring or on the street, time slows. Nature's way to give you a chance to evade the predator. That was how Gray dodged the blade that lashed in a wide arc, grazing his abdomen.

A panic washed over Gray. And when the attacker came at him again, it wasn't one of Dad's bob-and-weaves that saved him, but a crude kick—more Jason Statham than Cassius Clay—that connected to Ski Mask's chest. The guy slammed into a car, but he didn't go down. He roared forward at Gray again. Gray did a bullfighter's move and pushed the attacker past him, but felt a bite in his side. Ski Mask then jammed something into the small of Gray's back. He felt a jolt of electricity burning into him—a shockwave up his spine—causing him to spasm and gasp for air. Gray went black for a moment, then he was flat on the cold concrete.

Gray watched as Ski Mask turned his attention to the other man who was on his feet now. It was only then that Gray got a good look at the victim: Chief Justice Douglas. The chief had scurried behind a car and was frantically thumbing a key fob, his panic button. The elevator dinged and Gray heard the slap of dress shoes on concrete, the court's police.

Still on the ground, Gray shifted his eyes toward the man in the ski mask, but he was gone. Gray's vision blurred. He heard yelling. Then things went dark.

CHAPTER 4

Gray awoke to the scent of disinfectant and the presence of a crowd in the small hospital room. He must've been given painkillers because it was like watching a sitcom, one of those Latino family comedies written by white guys from Harvard. There was Mom, hovering over him, wiping his brow, pushing the giant plastic jug of hospital water at him. Dad, looking tired and too thin, wearing a flour-stained apron, staring at the old box television mounted from the ceiling. And big sis, Miranda, wrangling Gray's seven-year-old nephew, Emilio.

When they noticed his eyes open, they called for a doctor, and soon an intern was checking Gray's pupils with a penlight.

Gray never got into drugs, but as he sat back in the relaxed haze, he started to understand the fascination. And for the next hour, or maybe it was longer, his family kept talking to him—asking about the garage attack—and he gave woozy responses. God knows what he said.

Sometime later, Gray's attention turned to a familiar voice at the doorway.

"Always gotta be the hero."

One of his oldest friends, Samantha. When they were in elementary school, Gray had intervened to save Sam from a schoolyard bully, only to have the kid pummel Gray until Sam put an end to it by giving the kid the worst wedgie Gray had ever seen. Sam *still* gave him shit for it.

As Sam hugged everyone hello, Gray's father shadowboxed and said, "He used the moves I taught him."

Gray didn't have the heart to tell him that most of the credit went to Jason Statham.

Sam came to his bedside and punched him in the arm.

"What was that for?"

"For being so stupid. You're lucky to be alive."

"That's what I said to him," Mom said.

The room grew loud again with his family talking over one another. Gray watched as his nephew reenacted Gray's confrontation with the mugger. He was feeling the pull of sleep, more drugs they'd put in the IV, and closed his eyes. He was just about to drift off when the room went suddenly quiet, a rarity at any Hernandez gathering.

His eyes popped open at another voice.

"I owe you a thank you."

A tall man was standing at his bedside. He wore a sports jacket, shirt open at the collar. It took Gray a moment to realize it wasn't the drugs, it was really him. Chief Justice Douglas.

"It was nothing," was all Gray managed in response.

"No, if you hadn't arrived when you did, then . . ." the chief's voice trailed off.

Gray introduced the chief justice to his family. He noticed the chief hold Sam's gaze a beat longer than comfortable when they shook hands. Sam had that effect on men, and Gray supposed Supreme Court justices were not immune to her beauty. To Gray, she was still the flat-chested tomboy he used to play dodgeball and video games with.

After the introductions, the chief pulled up a chair next to Gray's bed. It was awkward to talk because the room was compact and his family wasn't too subtle about the gawking.

"Someone at the court told me you're a lawyer?" the chief said.

"Top of his class," Gray's mother said.

"Mom, please." Gray felt his face flush.

The chief justice smiled. "The doctors said you'll be out of commission for a few days."

"That's what they said, but I don't think it'll be more than a day. I'm already feeling—" He stopped when he saw the hard look his mother was giving him.

"It's always wise to listen to your mother," the chief said with a dry chuckle.

His mom nodded, giving a satisfied smile.

"But do me a favor, would you?" the chief continued.

"Of course."

"When you get back to work, come by my chambers." Before Gray could respond, the chief added, "You're not gonna be a messenger boy anymore."

CHAPTER 5

"Nothing? They found nothing?" Special Agent Emma Milstein asked. Her partner, Scott Cartwright, stood in front of Milstein's desk in the FBI field office, staring into an open file. Cartwright wore his usual navy suit, white shirt, plain tie clamped around his thick neck.

Cartwright shook his head.

"A guy with a knife strolls into the Supreme Court, attacks a justice, and not one camera catches him, no one knows how he got in or out, nothing?"

"Nada," Cartwright said.

"What about the kid? What's his name again?"

Cartwright flipped a page in the file. "Hernandez. Grayson Hernandez. The Supreme Court's squad interviewed him. Been on the job there for about a month, well liked. They're confident it was just wrong place, wrong time."

"Criminal record?"

"No, he's a lawyer, actually."

"A lawyer? I thought he was a messenger?"

"Yeah, works in the marshal's office. Times are tough in the law business, I guess," Cartwright said.

"I guess so. Our guys agree with the Supreme Court's police? We're sure Hernandez is clean?"

Cartwright walked over and put the open file in front of Milstein. "We don't think he was involved in the attack. He got into some trouble as a kid—joyriding in a stolen car with some friends. But that's like jaywalking in Hamilton Heights."

"He grew up in Hamilton Heights? Don't they call that area 'Afghanistan'?" Milstein looked down at the file, studying the photo of Grayson Hernandez. He was a good-looking kid. Late twenties. Striking blue eyes, unusual for a Hispanic. He had a scar that ran from the corner of his left eye to his ear. Jagged, no plastic surgery.

"Yeah, he's a regular local boy makes good," Cartwright said, heavy on the sarcasm.

"Any criminal associates?"

"He was childhood friends with a real charmer, Arturo Alvarez, who's just out of prison and already at war with a rival sect. But it appears that Hernandez left the Heights and never looked back. The report says no contact with Alvarez in years."

Milstein read through the rest of the file. "Does the press know he was there when the chief was attacked? I don't need reporters sniffing around. If they find out there's a connection to Dupont Underground they'll—"

"They don't know anything," Cartwright interrupted. "The court released a statement about the mugging, but no details. They're pretty tight-lipped up there."

"What's the Supreme Court's police chief saying?"

"Aaron Dowell? He's saying we should mind our own fucking business. They're in charge of protecting the chief."

"Yeah, they're doing a great job."

Cartwright said nothing.

"When can we talk to the chief justice?" Milstein asked.

"They're still stonewalling. I don't think they're taking the connection to Dupont seriously."

"You told them we think it's the same perp?"

"Of course I did. I'm working on it, Em."

"Work harder." Milstein let out a loud, frustrated breath.

"You want me to get you a snack or something?" Cartwright said. "When my kids get a little cranky, I bring them some Goldfish crackers and it—"

"Any luck on getting the wires?" Milstein said, ignoring him.

Cartwright made a sound of disbelief. "Neal says you're crazy if you think you'll get a bug anywhere near that building." As usual, Neal Wyatt, the assistant director in charge of the field office, was being too cautious, playing politics.

"Cowards."

"You need to tread lightly. This is the Supreme Court."

"The Franklin Theater fire was on July fifth. The Dupont Underground murders on August fifth. Now the attack on the chief October fifth. And we now know it's the same perp. What's it gonna take to get the Supreme Court's squad to take this seriously?"

Cartwright shook his head. "Hopefully not another victim on November fifth."

CHAPTER 6

A week after the garage attack, Gray sat in the conference room outside the chief justice's chambers. He'd started his first day back with everyone in the cube farm clapping when he walked into the office. That felt pretty damned good if he did say so. The court's public information officer soon put a damper on it all, however, when she sent an e-mail explaining that the court would *not* be commenting further on "the incident" in the garage, and reminded everyone of their duty of confidentiality. The court's famous omertà. So Gray got back to the grind, rushing around the building delivering interoffice envelopes and briefs.

But at lunchtime he'd received a call from Olga Romanov that Gray should come to the chief's chambers at one o'clock. And here he was, gazing at the long table in the oak-paneled conference room where the justices deliberated in secret. In that very space, justices of the past had voted on *Brown v. Board of Education*, *Miranda v. Arizona*, and virtually every important opinion Gray had read in law school.

At 1:20 p.m., Chief Justice Douglas strutted into the room. "Grayson, I'm so sorry I made you wait." He wore no jacket, white dress shirt rolled at the sleeves, tie loosened. He stuck out his hand and gave Gray's a hard shake.

Before Gray muttered a word, the chief said, "Don't you love this room?" The chief sank back in the high-backed leather chair, his gaze spanning the room and stopping at the portrait of Chief Justice John Marshall above the marble fireplace. "On a tough case, sometimes I come in here and try to imagine what Marshall or Holmes would have done." The chief looked off at nothing. After a long silence, he snapped out of it. "Enough of that. I wanted you to come by so I could thank you again."

"It's really unnecessary, I just—"

"You're feeling better? The hospital treated you well? I called the chief of staff myself to make sure they took good care of you."

"Yes, I'm feeling much better, and the doctors and nurses were terrific. Thank you for asking."

"Your parents were just delightful. They seem like hardworking people. What do your folks do for a living, if you don't mind me asking?"

Gray had been down this road before, but never quite knew how to proceed. Be nonchalant? Defensive? Proud? He opted for being straight. "My mom's a maid, and my dad runs our family's pizza shop in Hamilton Heights."

The chief nodded, not a flinch. He touched his chin. "It's not Ringside Pizza, is it?"

Gray was surprised at that. The Heights didn't exactly seem like one of the chief's haunts. "That's the one."

"I've been there. Good pie."

Gray didn't know whether the chief was just flattering. But his dad did make a great pizza. Not for the drunks who stumbled in for a slice after a night at the bars in the Heights. They got whatever the cheap help put together. But his father personally made the pies for the dinner crowd, mostly local families.

"You're from D.C., then?" the chief asked.

"Not really *from*. We came here when I was a kid—from Mexico. My parents became citizens when I was eight."

"Where'd you go to school?"

"D.C. State for college and law."

Usually the mention of D.C. State, a fourth-tier law school—never mind that Washington, D.C., was not even a state—elicited a sad look. But not from the chief.

"And what's your legal experience since law school?"

"I've done some pro bono work for a housing clinic, some temp work for big firms. Nothing like the experience of the lawyers who work here."

"Nonsense," the chief said. "You've got something far more valuable: life experience outside the bubble of affluence and the Ivy League."

Was it a crime to give the chief justice of the United States an uninvited hug? Gray opted for a thank you. To which the chief justice stood.

"You got time to come by my office? I want to show you something."

Gray followed the chief into his private office next to the conference room. Prime real estate behind the courtroom assigned to every chief justice since the building opened in the 1930s. The chief's chambers did not disappoint. Old law books on tall shelves lining the walls. Oriental rugs. A massive fireplace. The chief walked him to a framed document hanging on the wall. It wasn't an award or diploma or expensive piece of art. It was a wrinkled sheet of paper that had NOT YET! written on it in black Sharpie.

"This is my latest acquisition of Supreme Court memorabilia."

Gray smiled. He recognized the document. "Thurgood Marshall?"

The chief clapped his hands together, pleased. "Ah, you know it! You know the story!"

Lore had it that when the aging Justice Marshall had fallen ill and was in the hospital, Richard Nixon had asked the doctor for a report on Marshall's condition, not out of concern, but with the hope that the elderly justice was dying so the president could replace him with a more conservative jurist. The doctor asked Marshall if he could give the president a report. Marshall said he'd love to give Nixon an update, then took out a pen and wrote NOT YET! on his chart.

"I bought it on eBay of all places. With a name like Douglas," the chief said, referring to the notoriously unpopular Justice William O. Douglas who left the court in the seventies, "I thought it was good to remind everyone I'm not going anywhere either."

Gray laughed at the Douglas reference, which also seemed to please the chief.

"How'd you know the Thurgood Marshall story, if you don't mind me asking? None of my clerks had any idea what the thing was. You a Marshall fan?"

The chief was too polite to ask, but he was wondering how an immigrant from a rough part of the city could become a court watcher. Not unfair. Gray's first memories of America were walking to the run-down public library so his parents could study U.S. history and government for their citizenship exams. That library would later serve as the one place Gray could escape the pressures of the neighborhood. He remembered a judge swearing in his parents, and something about this powerful man in a black robe who made his mom and dad so happy stuck with him. Shortly after they became citizens, his mom took Gray and Miranda on an outing to the Supreme Court. He remembered staring at the gleaming white temple. The marble columns thicker than old redwoods. On either side of the plaza, giant statues of a man and woman, like guardians outside an ancient tomb. The look on his mom's face. Her words: *One day, you could be a justice, Grayson.* She believed it. And secretly, as his classmates spiraled into drugs and crime, he believed it too.

"Oh, I'm no expert, just a history buff. Something my mother got me into."

Justice Douglas spent the next half hour showing Gray his Supreme Court memorabilia collection. "Speaking of history," the chief said as he escorted Gray to the door, "it's interesting that your name is Gray."

"Why's that?"

"The first justice to ever hire a law clerk was Justice Horace Gray back in the 1800s."

That bit of history Gray didn't know.

"I'd like you to clerk for me," the chief added. "And I'd like you to start right away."

Gray had never believed that something could make a person speechless, but there he was, frozen, mouth agape. He felt like he did when the guy in the ski mask had charged him. Heart thumping, time suspended.

The chief studied him, a hint of amusement on his face. "So?"

"It would be an honor. But, I mean, can you do that? The term already started. I never clerked on a lower court. And you already have four clerks."

The chief barked a laugh. "One of my predecessors had a saying: 'With five votes you can do anything around here.' But when it comes to hiring my clerks, I only need one vote. And I just made it."

CHAPTER 7

Gray started the next day. Not much time for it all to sink in. The other law clerks weren't openly hostile to their new colleague, but the reception he got wasn't exactly warm either. He suspected they didn't think he'd earned a position they'd clawed over thousands of Ivy grads to get. But there was more to it than that. He wasn't one of them. Oliver Wendell Holmes once described the justices as "nine scorpions in a bottle," but that seemed a better fit for his co-clerks, whose stingers were pointed in Gray's direction.

There were four of them. Keir Landon, the JFK wannabe, was as dismissive as ever. Mike Dupree was less friendly to Gray than before, but at least he didn't call him Greg. There was Praveen Bhandari, a serious Indian guy. And last, Lauren Hart, a beauty, someone Gray already couldn't stop thinking about. In a stroke of luck, the chief assigned Lauren to show him the ropes.

"All you need to know," Lauren said in her ten-minute orientation, "is that there are five key tasks of a clerk: pool memos, death penalty stays, bench memos, drafting opinions, and the most important task—whatever the hell the chief justice needs."

Helpful.

When he probed, she started with the first task. "Pool memos are short memos we write that are used by all the justices, not just the chief. They summarize each of the seven thousand requests the court gets from litigants asking the court to hear their cases. The justices take only about seventy cases, so the memos are an important part of the screening process."

"We take only seventy out of seven thousand?" Gray asked.

"Yeah, 'We are the one percent,'" Lauren said in her dry way. She explained that the clerks from all nine chambers split up the docket and wrote memos summarizing each case. They even made recommendations on whether the court should accept a case for review—whether to grant *certiorari*, or *cert*. If the clerk recommended that the court deny *cert*, the case ended up on the "dead list." No justice would ever evaluate the case. If a clerk recommended that the court grant *cert*, the case would appear on the "discuss list," which the justices would go through at their secret conferences held about every other Friday.

"So what stops us from ginning up the memos for issues we know the chief wants to hear? Writing the memo in a way that makes the other justices think the case is *cert*-worthy?" Gray asked. "Or making a worthy case look like a dog if we know the chief doesn't want the other justices to mess with the law?"

Lauren shook her head. "You think you're the first person to ever think of that?" When she frowned the dimples on her smooth cheeks were more pronounced. "Every memo we write gets scrutinized by the clerks for the other justices. And we get to read their pool memos. If you slant a memo, the clerks will tell their justice, who will then complain to the chief, and, well, you know what happens next."

Gray nodded.

"Recommending that the court grant review is a huge deal and will get a lot of attention, so be super careful," Lauren said. "In fact, if you're gonna recommend a *cert* grant, you should come talk to me first." It was condescending as hell, but Gray still hoped he'd have a grant so he'd have an excuse to talk with her.

She showed him to his workspace, a second-floor office everyone called "the closet." It was bigger than a closet, but not by much. There was an old metal desk that had two computer monitors. On the wall, a lone picture, the stock photo of the justices. Five seated in the front row, four standing in the back. Like their seats on the bench, the justices were lined up in order of seniority, with the chief justice at the center seat. Black robes against a burgundy curtain.

"Don't worry," Lauren said, reading his thoughts. "We share two other offices on the first floor, one next to the chief's chambers, one down the hall. We're two to an office, and we rotate periodically. It gives each of us a chance to be closer to the chief's chambers. We also get really sick of each other since we've been here working around the clock since the summer. We'll throw the closet into the rotation."

Gray took his seat at the desk. He placed his palms on the desktop, and drew in a breath, taking it all in.

"I don't want to intrude on your moment here," Lauren said, "but do you have any questions?"

Gray felt heat engulf his face, embarrassed. "I think I've got it. Do we meet with the chief or—"

"He left this morning for the recess, but we get together pretty regularly when the court is sitting. He'll be back in a couple weeks for the November sitting."

During those couple weeks, Gray immersed himself in the *cert* petitions, fascinated by the array of legal questions: whether Virginia's anti-sodomy statute was constitutional, whether a state could make it a felony for anyone on a sex offender registry to access social media, whether a ten-year-old could properly waive his rights against self-incrimination without a parent present. Gray read each petition with care, even the unintelligible ones written by prisoners. He then independently researched the questions, and wrote a pool memo for each case. He'd hoped to talk through the issues with his co-clerks—spitball ideas while tossing around the football—but so far none of the others seemed interested or had come up to the closet. Nor had they invited him to lunch or dinner. But he wouldn't let that get him down. He stared at that old photo of his dad in the ring, now pinned on the wall next to the picture of the justices. He'd work hard. He'd prove he was smart. Prove that he deserved to be a law clerk for the United States Supreme Court. Just like them.

CHAPTER 8

Chief Justice Douglas returned from recess on November 1. For the first couple of days, Gray waited eagerly for the chief to call, a summons to chambers to work through a tough case or assist with some research. But his phone never rang. Finally, on November 5, the chief called a meeting of all the clerks. He wanted to talk pool memos, which was just as well because it was the only one of Lauren's "five tasks" Gray had mastered. The five clerks huddled around the chief's antique desk and they went through each memo that recommended that the court grant *cert*, including the memos written by clerks for the other justices.

"Okay, *Toby v. Samuels*," the chief said. "Justice Scheuerman's clerk recommends we grant review. It looks like a clear circuit split to me and I'm inclined to agree, but what do you all think?" Circuit splits, Gray had learned quickly, were the bread-and-butter work of the court. They occurred when two or more circuits in the federal court of appeals made conflicting rulings on the same legal question. The Supreme Court essentially had to break a tie.

The chief looked out at them. Gray was still having trouble adjusting to the idea that the chief really wanted their views. Yet there they were, making recommendations on which cases the Supreme Court should hear. It was as intoxicating as it was troubling.

All the clerks stayed quiet. Gray realized that, as the clerk who'd analyzed the *Toby* memo—double-checking the work of another justice's clerk—they were waiting on him to speak up. He'd wanted to fly under the radar, learn more before sticking out his neck and challenging a more experienced clerk's conclusions. But he felt the stares of his co-clerks. He wondered what they were thinking. Pulling for him? Hoping he'd fall on his face? He got a look at Keir Landon's glare and he knew the answer.

Gray's throat clicked as he swallowed. "I agree there's a circuit split, but I think there's other reasons the court should deny review." It was uttered with the most confidence he could conjure.

Gray held his breath as the chief justice studied the memo. As last, the chief's eyes rose from the document, his expression skeptical.

Keir jumped in. "I disagree," he said. Despite the JFK thing, on closer inspection, Keir was no Kennedy. He had thin lips and his mouth didn't open completely when he spoke. Gray was reminded of those Claymation figures from the *Rudolph the Red-Nosed Reindeer* shows at Christmastime. "I think the memo got it right." Keir flicked a smug glance at Gray. "The case has everything. Not just a split between the Fourth and Ninth Circuits, but also a dissenting opinion. And it's clearly an issue of national importance. The latest challenge to Obamacare."

Gray felt his face redden as the chief scrutinized him. He needed to remain calm, not get defensive. Gray's father told him that at the beginning of a fight, when the boxers would do the stare down and touch gloves, his dad always whispered something to himself: *No fear.*

"I think Keir makes good points," Gray said at last. "There is an acknowledged circuit split and the lower court judges also couldn't agree, so there's a dissent. It's just that the order was interlocutory, so I think there's a vehicle problem." He was proud of himself for using the jargon of the court. "Vehicle problem" meant that the issue in the case was a good one, but something about the procedures made it a poor vehicle for the court to consider it. "The trial court continued the proceedings while the appeal was pending, and it appears that a recent order may render the question presented moot." He'd looked this up in *Supreme Court Practice*, the treatise all the clerks called "the Bible."

"That's not in the petition," Keir challenged.

Keir was right, it wasn't in the petition for *cert.* Gray stood and handed the chief a copy of an order he'd found on the PACER database that contained documents filed in federal courts nation-wide. None of the briefs had pointed out the problem, but on a hunch, Gray had investigated the docket himself.

The chief examined the order. Without further discussion, he said, "Dead list it." He threw the pool memo on his desk, as if dis-pleased. "And Keir, please draft a memo for my signature that I can send to Justice Scheuerman about her clerk's shoddy work." There were really two messages the chief was delivering—one to the other justice and one to Keir.

Gray worked until nine o'clock that night. On his way out, he decided to stop by Keir's office to smooth things over. As he ap-proached the door, he heard several voices.

"You all can invite Snuffy the Seal if you want," Keir said. "But I'm not going out with the guy. He's only here because he's the chief's charity project."

Keir was referring to Gray. But "Snuffy the Seal"? What was that about?

Keir continued. "And did you see that suit he was wearing? He belongs on a used-car lot, not working for the Supreme fucking Court."

Gray lowered his head, examining his suit. He thought back to the night before he'd started his new position. Hard to believe that of all the things he'd been worried about—Was he smart enough? Would he have the stamina for the job? Would the other clerks like him?—his main concern was what he would wear to work. As a marshal's aide he had a uniform. Blue blazer and kha-kis, striped tie. He'd picked up two of each on sale at Lord & Taylor. He had only one suit, a Men's Wearhouse clearance-rack special, ill fitting, shiny at the elbows, and, the worst part, double-breasted. More low-level La Cosa Nostra than power-lunch D.C.

"I think you're just mad because he got the best of you today," Praveen said.

Then Mike's voice: "He did make you his bitch."

Lauren laughed. Was this little gathering just about Gray?

"Do whatever you want," Keir said, "but I've got enough to do without entertaining the chief's new shiny red ball."

Gray took off before he heard more. You can say it doesn't bother you. You don't care if you're not part of the group. That you don't belong. But no matter how old you are, no matter who you are or where you're from, it hurts.

He trudged down to the garage, backpack slung over his shoulder. The officer stationed there, a new security addition since the attack on the chief, nodded hello. Gray felt a stone in his throat. He couldn't let the clerks get to him.

He rode out onto First Street, the only light the glow from the Capitol dome. The windswept streets were empty. During the day, the busy bees of the Hill swarmed around the dome—cabs jettisoned about and tourists wandered with their cheap souvenir shirts and hats bought from street vendors. But at night, it was quiet, tranquil. He saw Vincent, a homeless man who'd taken up residence near the building, setting up camp for the night. With his scraggly beard and distant expression, he looked like Vincent van Gogh, so Gray wasn't sure if Vincent was the guy's real name or just a nickname the cops in the marshal's office had given him. Vincent never bothered anyone, so the officers left him alone. Gray waved at Vincent, but the man ignored him. Not even the homeless guy wanted to be friends.

When Gray pedaled up to his basement apartment, he saw his neighbor Camila on the front sidewalk. She seemed to be having words with Jorge, her ex. Behind Camila, her five-year-old little girl. A U-Haul truck was parked at the curb. Gray shoved the bike in the dank entryway to his apartment.

"You ain't leavin'! You can't take Marianna from me!" Jorge had been gone for a while, but he was back, drunk and belligerent like always. He was the reason Camila was moving away.

"You're not supposed to be near us, Jorge. Don't make me call the cops. I don't want to send you back to jail, but I will." Camila held up her phone.

Jorge slapped the phone out of her hand, and it clattered across the sidewalk. Marianna started crying.

Camila went for the phone, but Jorge grabbed her roughly by the arm. "Don't you threaten me, bitch."

"Hey!" Gray called out.

The man turned, still gripping Camila's arm.

Gray walked over to them. He crouched on his heels, and looked at the little girl. "Hi, Marianna."

Marianna gripped the back of her mother's shirt, tears spilling down her face.

"I have a question for you," Gray said in a soft voice. "Do you still like ice cream?"

Marianna looked to her mother, then to Gray, and nodded.

"How about you go get in that truck, and me and your mom can take you to get some."

She looked to her mother again.

"Yes, Marianna, please go to the truck," Camila said, her voice quivering.

The girl paused for a moment, but released the hold on her mother's shirt and started toward the U-Haul.

"You stay here!" Jorge reached for the girl, but Gray stepped in front him.

"This ain't your business," Jorge said. He let go of Camila's arm and got in Gray's face. His breath smelled of drugstore wine. "A man can get himself killed messing with another man's business." His words were slurred, and he wasn't steady on his feet.

Gray looked back at the U-Haul. Marianna was sitting in the passenger seat now, looking out at them. "Camila, go get in the truck," Gray said.

Jorge reached for her again, but Gray caught him by the wrist.

Camila hesitated, but ran to the U-Haul.

Gray and the man locked eyes. Gray didn't want to hurt him in front of Marianna. "I know you're upset. But you're scaring Marianna. Is that how you want her to think of you? Drunk and scary?"

Jorge tugged to release his arm, but Gray held firm.

Gray looked over to the truck again. Camila was in the front seat, hugging her daughter, stroking the little girl's back.

"I'm going to let go of your arm now, then you're going to leave," Gray said in a calm monotone.

Jorge glowered at Gray, but finally nodded.

Gray released his hold. Jorge then swung at him. Gray ducked, feeling the breeze from the clumsy punch over his head. The momentum nearly spun Jorge around. Gray pushed the back of Jorge's shoulder, kicking his feet out from under him. Jorge was on the sidewalk now.

As Gray walked away, Jorge muttered something, but he wisely stayed down.

Gray climbed into the U-Haul. Camila started the engine and pulled from the curb. In the side-view mirror, Gray saw Jorge ranting at the truck as they drove away. Camila didn't look back.

CHAPTER 9

"Club soda, really?" Scott Cartwright said with a frown as Milstein ordered her drink from the bartender. She was wedged next to Cartwright on a stool at the crowded dive bar near the field office. The place smelled of beer and greasy food.

"It's the fifth of the month," Milstein said. "I wanna be sharp if something happens."

Cartwright hesitated, then said to the bartender, "Cancel the beer. I'll have a Coke."

Milstein stared at the TV mounted to the wall, her thoughts wandering. Why wasn't anyone taking the threat seriously? On July 5, someone had set a fire at the Franklin Theater just outside D.C. in Silver Spring, Maryland. A dozen people were killed from the flames, smoke, and stampede. On August 5, someone killed a lawyer and the woman's daughter and mother at Dupont Underground. And on October 5, a man attacked the chief justice. But it wasn't simply the dates that connected the crimes—they now had evidence suggesting it was the same perp. But for some inexplicable reason, here they were on November 5, and the Bureau, the Supreme Court Police, and Homeland Security acted like she was Chicken Little.

"You really think he'll strike tonight?" Cartwright said. "I mean, the dates could be a coincidence."

Milstein pulled her gaze from the television. "That's what Neal said."

"Let's hope you're wrong." Cartwright superstitiously knocked twice on the bar. "You have Agent Simmons monitoring Metro police for any homicides tonight?"

Milstein nodded. "D.C. Metro, as well as Fairfax, Montgomery, and PG counties."

"Supreme Court Police still being a pain in the ass?"

Milstein heaved a sigh, nodded again. Since the attack in the garage, Milstein had been trying to interview the chief justice and other court employees. The court's police chief, Aaron Dowell, had shut her out.

"Aaron's territorial," Cartwright said. "Has a chip on his shoulder and thinks the Supreme Court's squad gets no respect."

"No, I think he's just a dumb ass."

Cartwright's brow creased into a rail yard of horizontal lines. He looked around to confirm no one was listening. In a quiet voice, he said, "Aaron's no dummy. He's just an inside-the-box guy."

"We can connect all three crimes, and all happened on the fifth of the month, what's so outside-the-box about that?" Milstein was anxious, frustrated that they had so little to go on—that the other agencies were stifling her ability to *get* more to go on. They should be working together.

One of the agents from the field office stopped at the bar and gave Cartwright one of those handshake man-hugs. After the guy sauntered off, Cartwright said, "Oh, I almost forgot." He pulled out his mobile and started swiping at it. "I set up a Google Alert using names and search terms for anything related to the investigation. Look what popped up on my screen today." He handed Milstein the smartphone.

Milstein squinted to see the tiny print on the screen. It was a blog entry or news story, she couldn't tell.

"It's a legal site called Above the Law. Popular with law clerks, law students, associates at the big law firms," Cartwright explained. "It's a story about the guy who helped save the chief, Grayson Hernandez."

Milstein was still having trouble maneuvering the story on the phone. She looked at Cartwright. "They found out he was there when the chief was attacked?"

"No. It's a puff piece, reporting that the kid was promoted to Supreme Court law clerk, which I guess is a big deal. The story says it's highly unusual for a justice to hire someone after the term has started, much less someone who went to D.C. State. There's a lot of speculation about why the chief justice hired him, but nothing relating to the case. Yet, anyway."

"Sounds like the chief justice was grateful to Hernandez."

"I'd say so," Cartwright said. "So you're really sticking around until midnight?"

Milstein nodded. "You don't have to stay."

Cartwright pondered this for a few seconds. "I already told Peggy you're acting crazy, and that I'd be late."

Milstein gave him a long stare. "You can call me crazy tomorrow morning when there's no dead bodies."

CHAPTER 10

Gray had Camila pull into a McDonald's so he could buy Marianna the ice cream he'd promised. The restaurant had only one customer, an elderly black man seated in the back reading a newspaper. Gray bought a sundae and also some hamburgers and fries, food for the long drive to Camila's sister's house in Baltimore where she planned to start their life anew. He saw an ATM machine across the parking lot next to a dollar store. He was making good money as a law clerk—$77,490 a year—so he decided he could afford it. He sauntered over to the machine, took out the $500 maximum allowed, and tucked the bills inside the McDonald's bag.

"You're not coming with us?" Marianna asked as Gray handed her the sundae and fast-food bag through the passenger-side window.

"I'm afraid not."

"I'll miss you," she said in her sweet little girl voice.

Camila mouthed *thank you*, and they pulled out of the McDonald's lot.

Gray contemplated going home, but he wanted to give Jorge time to sober up. Gray sent a text to Sam:

Long day, want company?

It was only a few seconds before Gray's phone pinged:

Come!!

Gray took an Uber to Sam's place. She answered the door wearing a tight top and PJ bottoms, and greeted him with her customary punch in the arm.

Her loft was a large, open space, a former dance studio—tall mirrors, railings along the walls. She was a photographer and the place was both her home and workspace. A section was cordoned off with expensive-looking lighting equipment, tripods, and camera gear.

In the living area, Sam's work hung on the exposed brick. Lots of black and whites of people, working people, living their lives. She had a knack for catching moments, the tiniest gestures or facial expressions. Love. Pride. Disappointment.

As she made them both drinks, Gray casually scanned the latest books on her expansive shelf. Since they were kids she was a reader. There was a new biography of Lincoln, a photography book, and drugstore paperbacks. Sam had once told him that she loved to read anything but what she called RPP fiction (rich people problems)—stories about affluent people finding themselves or twenty- or thirty-something angst. More with the acronyms, she ought to work at the Supreme Court. His eyes stopped at a small framed photo on the shelf. Not her professional work, but a shot of Gray, Sam, and Arturo when they were kids at the rusted playground in the courtyard of the apartment complex. They'd been inseparable. *The three amigos*, as Gray's dad called them, a reference to some dumb old movie.

Sam handed him the glass, noticing him examining the photo. They had an unwritten rule to never discuss Arturo, but Sam broke it. "He got out last month," she said.

Gray didn't take the bait. Whatever Sam thought of him, Arturo wasn't the sweet kid in that photo. And if he was out of prison, it wouldn't be for long.

Sam pulled the sad look she got whenever Arturo came up, and her body gave a small quiver, like she literally was trying to shake it off, and she changed the subject.

"So, is this your new thing, going around starting shit with muggers and drunk neighbors so you can play hero?"

Gray laughed. Sam always kept him grounded.

"So really, what's new?" Sam sat on the couch and gestured for Gray to join her. "How's the job? No one's seen you since you started."

"It's been crazy busy. Intense. And a huge learning curve."

"But you like it?"

"No," Gray said. "I love it. It's probably the most important job I'll ever have."

Sam smirked, which made him feel a little silly. He imagined how he must sound.

"What's the chief justice like? He seemed pretty cool at the hospital."

"I honestly don't see him much. The court runs in a cycle, sittings, so he's there for two weeks during the sittings, then gone two weeks for the recesses."

"They get recess, like school kids?"

Gray laughed again. "Yeah, so most of my time is spent alone in my office writing memos."

"What about the other law clerks? How are they?"

Gray hesitated. "You wouldn't believe their resumes. There's this guy Praveen, his father is chief of staff at the White House, mom is assistant secretary of state. He won the National Spelling Bee *and College Jeopardy*. He's quiet, but ridiculously smart. Then there's Mike and Keir, I think I told you about them. Before clerking, Keir spent two years writing for *The Atlantic* and his dad is a pretty famous court of appeals judge. Mike played college baseball and was the editor in chief of the *Harvard Law Review*."

"Is Mike the JFK guy or the frat boy?"

"Frat boy," Gray said.

"No girls in this star chamber?"

"Just one, Lauren. She keeps things close to the vest. But I heard she's from old, old money."

"Sounds like you fit in perfectly," Sam said.

Gray smiled. He didn't mention that his co-clerks hadn't exactly taken to him. But there must have been something in his voice—hurt, maybe—that Sam picked up on, because all she said was, "You're just as good as them, you know."

When he didn't reply, she added, "And don't let them make you think different."

Everyone should have a friend like Sam. "Enough about me," Gray said. "How are you doing?"

Sam's face lit up. "I'm great, actually." She crossed her legs and nestled her drink between them. "I got a call today. They're giving me my own show." An exhibition at the prestigious Alexander Gallery. She'd been struggling for years. Life was finally coming together for both of them.

"Do you think you'll be able to get away from work to come?"

"I wouldn't miss it."

"You'd better not," she said. "I need to know I'll have at least one person there."

He hated it when she did that. But they'd both developed these defense mechanisms, knee-jerk reactions, to praise or accolades. It was a way to beat the world from pulling the rug out from under them. They'd throw themselves on the floor instead.

"You hungry?" she asked.

Gray thought about it. "Yeah, starving, actually."

"Mr. Fong's?" Their favorite Chinese place. And most important, the only place in the neighborhood—probably in all of D.C.— that was open late for deliveries.

"You don't know how good that sounds," Gray said. Then his cell phone chimed. Sam's gaze locked on the iPhone. She frowned when he tapped its face.

"Hey, Lauren, what's up?" He used his gravelly cool-guy voice, which prompted an eye-roll from Sam.

"You need to get to the court," Lauren said.

"To the court? Now? What's up?"

He listened as she explained. The second task of a law clerk: an emergency petition to stay an execution.

CHAPTER 11

Sakura Matsuka mopped the convenience store's floor. It was almost midnight, so the rest of her shift should be quiet, save the drunks who started rolling in around 3:30 a.m. after the bars closed. She had just two semesters left in community college and hopefully she'd never have to deal with them again. The store would be her family's problem. She'd been an indentured servant long enough. Soon, she'd never have to sell another pack of cigarettes or replace the filters in the filthy coffee makers or smell the aged hot dogs rolling on the mini treadmills.

She heard the chime from the door. With every customer this late came a twinge of fear. A druggie who would pistol-whip her for the hundred bucks in the register. A sicko who would try to rape her. But there was nothing to fear with this one.

Sakura smiled and rolled the mop bucket back to the storeroom.

As Sakura approached the register, she noticed the customer staring out the door, as if looking for someone. There was something unusual about it.

Then a chill ran through her when she saw the gun, and the customer flipped the OPEN sign to CLOSED.

CHAPTER 12

Gray felt an ominous electricity when he walked into the Supreme Court. He was still learning the ropes of the job, including the death penalty stays, but this much he knew: the court maintained a death watch of sorts and even had a "death clerk" whose job it was to track capital cases that may seek high court review. But something unusual happened in the Anton Troy case, Gray wasn't sure what, and everyone was blindsided.

Usually only one clerk from each of the nine chambers would stay late to handle a death stay, but the chief had ordered all five of his clerks to come in. Gray didn't know if that was because of the screw-up or because Anton Troy had become one of those "celebrity" capital cases, garnering national media coverage, complete with finger-wagging movie stars and impassioned pleas from former presidents.

The things they say about the death penalty, that it takes years and years, appeal after appeal, they're true. Anton Troy had been on death row for more than two decades. But it changed toward the end. When a death case arrived at the Supreme Court, the proceedings moved fast and efficiently, like everything else at One First Street.

Gray found Lauren, Keir, and Praveen in the library, the Anton

Troy record spread out on the long wooden table. Mike had yet to arrive.

"The chief has made his views on the death penalty clear," Lauren said. She held up a booklet containing a decision from last term and read aloud from Chief Justice Douglas's dissenting opinion: "The chief wrote, 'There is evidence that innocent people have been executed, that death sentences are imposed arbitrarily, and that the capital justice system is warped by racial discrimination and politics. For these reasons, to paraphrase one of my predecessors, 'I no longer shall tinker with the machinery of death.'"

Keir scoffed. "I'm sure the families of the cop who Anton Troy killed will appreciate the poetry of his dissent."

"If you want to go against the chief," Lauren responded, "good luck with that."

"Give it a rest, Lauren," Keir said.

"Guys," Praveen cut in. "We don't have time for this."

"Can I ask a question?" Gray said.

The three looked at him, impatience in their faces.

"The chief has said he's done with the death penalty, so what's there even to do? He's obviously going to vote to stop Anton Troy's execution."

"I don't have time to babysit," Keir said. "You tell him. I'll try to reach Mike again." Keir marched off, iPhone pressed to his ear.

Lauren exhaled loudly. Gray wasn't sure if the annoyance was directed at Keir or Gray. "It's not the chief we have to convince," Lauren said. "It's the other justices. We need to give the chief information he can use to turn them his way."

Lauren explained that the chief and three other justices had made clear that they were done with the death penalty, so there were always four votes to stop an execution. Three other justices always voted for no stay, so that meant that it usually came down to the swing votes on capital punishment, Justice Wall and Justice Cutler. With five votes needed to grant a stay, the chief needed to convince only one of them. Their best hope, Lauren said, was Justice Wall. He and the chief were best friends, and, in an unlikely bit of history, they'd actually grown up together. Even more unbelievable, they were ideological opposites.

"Is Mike here yet?" Lauren asked.

"Still not responding," Keir said, glancing at his phone.

Lauren then directed each of their tasks. Keir reviewed the case law on the Eighth Amendment. Praveen, background on Alabama's death system. Gray would help Lauren. He should have been insulted that she too thought that he needed a babysitter, but he was happy to be in her orbit. By then it was 1:30 a.m. They had until 2:30 a.m., the deadline the justices had given the clerks to recommend whether to stop the execution.

The case was the latest in the debate over lethal injections. States traditionally had used a three-drug cocktail to execute defendants. But the manufacturers of the drugs—companies headquartered in Europe that found the death penalty barbaric—decided that they would no longer partake in the United States' use of their products in killing. That left states scrambling to find alternative drugs. With those alternatives came legal challenges. In a five-four decision, the court previously had upheld the use of a controversial drug, the sedative midazolam, but Alabama had run out of sources for that drug and sought to use a replacement. The question presented in the Anton Troy case was whether the new drug would cause Troy immense pain, something his lawyers argued was cruel and unusual punishment forbidden by the Eighth Amendment.

Gray and Lauren worked side-by-side in the shallow light of the library. She told him to make a bullet-point list of all the horribles that had occurred in past executions using the same drug, as she pecked at her laptop, putting together a memo for the chief justice. He tried to focus on only the task at hand, but couldn't help stealing looks at her. The intensity in her large eyes. The crease in her forehead when she concentrated.

At 2:20 a.m., Lauren typed feverishly on the laptop as Gray, Keir, and Praveen stood over her shoulder and called out suggested changes to the memo.

Ten minutes later, they gathered outside the chief's office. Gray would never forget the sound of the knock on the chief's carved oak door. *Clunk, clunk, clunk.*

The chief called them in and the four clerks stood at his desk—

opera music filling the air from an iPod docking station nearby—
as he read the short memo.

Without saying a word, the chief pressed a button on his office
phone and dialed. He had it on speaker so the clerks could hear. It
rang several times until finally there was a voice on the other end.

"I was wondering when you'd call," the voice said. It was
Justice Wall. It sounded like he was on a cell phone, driving
perhaps.

"Peter, I have you on speaker, and my clerks are here," the chief
said.

"Wonderful," Wall replied, a tinge of sarcasm.

"I'm hoping you're going to do the right thing tonight."

"Save the cop killer because the needle may hurt a little?"

The chief rolled his eyes. "It's not just 'a little,' and you know
it. And there's credible evidence he's innocent."

Wall guffawed at that.

The chief continued, "Anton Troy's poor, black, and with a seventy IQ. Convicted in a broken Alabama system based on the testimony of a jailhouse informant, who's recanted. His trial lawyer
was twenty-seven years old, and it was his first death case."

"The appeal isn't about his guilt or innocence—or the effec-
tiveness of his counsel—he's had many, many appeals on those issues, and he's lost them all," Wall said. "Every single one over the
past twenty years."

Lauren reached over the chief's desk and pointed to something
on the memo. The chief glanced at the document, then said, "Since
you're mentioning the timing, twenty years on death row—living
two decades with a death sentence hanging over his head—the de-
lay alone should constitute cruel and unusual punishment."

Wall barked a laugh. "*He* caused the delays with all these appeals. Your argument is akin to the man who kills his parents and
then pleads for mercy on the grounds that he's an orphan."

The chief justice looked at his clerks and shook his head.

"I'm sorry," Justice Wall said. "You should call Cutler, maybe
you'll have better luck . . . if I don't get to her first." The phone
clicked off.

The chief massaged his temples as the opera singer's voice rose to a crescendo. Douglas looked at the old grandfather clock in his chambers. "There's not much time. I'm going to try Justice Cutler. Thank you for your hard work." He was politely kicking them out of his office. Gray left chambers knowing that the chief would be fighting for Anton Troy's life. All they could do now was wait.

CHAPTER 13

It was nearly three in the morning, and Gray and his co-clerks went outside for some air. The marble portico was lit up by floodlights built into the facade. Already word had spread, and the protesters were filling the plaza with their candles and singing and cardboard signs. Some disheveled reporters, called in from home, were filming the scene.

It was odd because this case, this terrible event, was the first time Gray felt like he belonged, and some guilt accompanied that. The four of them didn't say much, though Keir griped that Mike had been a no-show. Justice Cutler's clerks were also outside, huddled in a small circle, occasionally shooting glances at them.

Gray and his co-clerks sat on the marble steps, staring out at the warm white glow of the Capitol dome. Should he be praying? Should they be doing something? As a marshal's aide, he'd heard about the death stays, but it was always just an abstraction. He'd assumed, like much of the public, that if the defendant was found guilty, he'd probably done something horrific and deserved to die. In fact, Gray's duties working on the *cert* pool memos analyzing death penalty cases had hardened his views on capital punishment. The petitions contained the stories of monsters. Men who had raped and murdered children. Men who had taken pleasure in the torture of innocents. But the chief's opposition to capital punishment caused Gray to think about the issue in a new light. The chief was the smartest man he'd ever met, and if *he* thought the death penalty should be thrown out, who was Gray to disagree? Yet Anton Troy had received a trial, multiple appeals, and that cop's family . . .

At 3:24 a.m., a cell phone bleated. First one phone, then another, until a cacophony of phones rang out in the night. The final vote was in. Gray stood and stared at the words carved above the portico. EQUAL JUSTICE UNDER LAW. The gravity of the job was hitting him. He wasn't being melodramatic. The next few minutes truly meant life or death for Anton Troy.

They all darted through the six-ton bronze front doors, which the officers had slid open after-hours especially for the clerks, and ran through the Great Hall into chambers.

They knew the outcome by the look on the chief's face.

"I'm proud of you all," he said. "But the vote is the vote."

Gray felt his face flush. It was hard to swallow.

The clerks soon gathered in the courtyard huddled around an iPhone, following tweets of a local Alabama newspaper's live coverage of the execution. It should have taken only a few minutes to kill Anton Troy, but it went on for nearly an hour—an hour in which Troy writhed in pain, an hour of his convulsing and gasping for breath. The final indignity for Anton Troy came at 4:29 a.m.: the world was first informed of his death via Twitter.

Gray didn't remember the reaction of the others. The sound of that knock on the chief's door just kept echoing through his head.

Clunk, clunk, clunk.

Nails in a coffin.

Gray headed to the public restroom off the Great Hall. He went inside the stall and shut and locked the door. He sat on the toilet tank, feet on the closed lid, and put his face into his hands. And he cried. He hadn't let it out like that since his mom had told him about his father's cancer returning. But, unlike for Dad, there'd be no happy ending tonight. He knew it was an overreaction. The stress of the new position, the lack of sleep. He didn't know how long he was in there, but the lights—set on motion detectors—at some point clicked off.

When he finally left the stall, the lights came back on and he caught his reflection in the mirror. Bloodshot eyes, cheeks puffy and flushed. He ran cold water and leaned over the sink, splashing his face. He needed to compose himself. He didn't need to give Keir or the others more ammunition against him. He'd Googled that "Snuffy the Seal" thing. It referred to a commercial for Discovery Channel's Shark Week. The ad was of a fake local news report about efforts to save an injured seal. As rescuers lowered Snuffy back into the ocean, a great white shark jumped out of the water and devoured the seal. Gray was no expert on metaphors, but he got the point.

Ten minutes later, as he waited outside for his Uber, he wondered how many times this very scene had happened. How many Anton Troys denied their last hope? How many law clerks crying in the bathroom? In the two thousand law clerks since Justice Horace Gray hired the first clerk, he couldn't be the only one, could he? A black sedan rounded the corner and pulled to the curb. Gray climbed into the backseat, exhausted. He was startled by the presence of another passenger.

"Sorry, I thought I'd ordered this one. I didn't know——"

"Hello, Mr. Hernandez," the woman said.

That took him aback. Who was she? How'd she know his name? And what was she doing in his Uber? Then he realized that it wasn't an Uber car. The woman held up a gold badge. On its face were three letters: FBI.

CHAPTER 14

Gray was not in the mood for more questions about the attack in the garage. He'd been interviewed by the Supreme Court Police three times already, and now the FBI? And at five-thirty in the morning? No thanks. The car pulled from the curb.

"I'm Agent Milstein." She offered her hand. The agent looked about in her mid-thirties, but she could've been older. She had high cheekbones, no makeup. There were dark circles under her eyes, strands of hair wisping in her face, as if she too had been up all night. She didn't introduce the beefy guy up front who was driving.

"Look, I've already told the Supreme Court Police everything I can remember about the attack, and it's been a long night, so can't we do this some other—"

Milstein held up a hand for him to quiet. She directed his attention to an iPad. Gray wasn't expecting what he saw when she swiped her finger across its face. "What the hell?" he said, looking away. It was a crime scene photo. Three female victims—one old, one middle-aged, one a little girl—lined up. Their skin was gray, each had purple bruises around the neck. He tried to blink away the images. "What's this about?"

The agent met his eyes. "I'm sorry you had to see that. But I wanted you to understand I'm not here about a simple mugging."

Gray just stared at the agent, dumbfounded.

"Those victims," she added, "they were three generations of a family. Grandmother, mother, and a young girl named Isabelle. Strangled. They probably watched each other die."

Gray swallowed. "The Dupont Underground murders?" Gray had seen the media coverage. The lawyer and her family killed last summer, just before he'd started his messenger job at the court. "I don't understand."

"We need your help." The agent held his gaze; there was an intensity to it.

Gray's thoughts jumbled. Had she mistaken him for someone else? Why would the FBI possibly need his help? The photos kept leaping back at him. The little girl, she couldn't have been much younger than his nephew. Who would do such a thing to a child? The headache that he'd felt creeping up on him was pounding now.

"The murders are connected to the Supreme Court," Agent Milstein said. "And we need someone who can look into some things for us."

"Whoa, hold on." Gray raised his palms. "I'm just a law clerk. You need to talk to the Supreme Court's police, I'm not—"

"Grayson," Milstein interrupted. "I know this is unusual, but you need to trust me on this. We need someone like you."

When Gray didn't respond, Milstein pulled up another photo on the iPad and held it out to him.

"If that's more pictures of them," Gray said, "I'm not looking."

"It's not them," the agent said.

Gray dared to glance down. Vomit immediately reached his mouth. He swallowed it back down. "For Christ's sake." The photo wasn't of the family, that part was true. It was of a young woman, she looked Asian, but it was hard to tell because her face was swollen, covered in blood. She was tied to a chair, shelves of food behind her, a grocery or convenience store. Even Milstein swallowed hard at the photo.

"At each crime scene, the killer left something—something he wanted us to find." The agent stared intently at Gray. "Something I think you'll recognize." She swiped the iPad again.

Gray reluctantly followed her glance. He was relieved that the image was not more victims.

"You know what that is?" Milstein asked.

It was a photo of a white goose-feather pen, like the kind from Shakespeare's days.

"It was left at the murders at Dupont Underground. We found an identical pen at a murder scene tonight, a young woman beaten to death at her family's convenience store."

Gray looked at Milstein. He realized that she'd just come from the scene. He was still having a hard time processing.

Agent Milstein furrowed her brow. "You know where those feather pens come from, don't you?"

Gray realized where she was going with this. The Supreme Court gave out feather quill pens as souvenirs to lawyers arguing cases before the court. It was a tradition dating back two hundred years, when Chief Justice John Marshall gave quill pens and ink-wells to advocates. These days, the pens were placed at counsel's table before all oral arguments. A marshal's aide would place two quill pens at each counsel seat, crisscrossed in an X. "The court gives them out, but you can probably buy those pens anywhere," Gray said. "I think they even sell them in the court's gift shop."

Milstein's head snapped back and forth in sharp dismissal. "Not these pens." She tapped her index finger on the screen. Her nails were unpainted, chewed on. "These were handmade. And we found the supplier. She's one of the only people in the world who makes these things. And guess who her biggest customer is?"

"The Supreme Court," Gray said.

The agent gave a little nod.

Gray was quiet for a long time. Then: "So what exactly is it you want me to do?"

"You worked in the marshal's office, which is in charge of the quill pens. You know the people there, know the office. And you're a law clerk now, which I hear pretty much gives you the run of the place. So I'm just asking that if you see anything you let me know." She paused a beat. "And if I call and need something, you'll help."

"I still don't see why you're coming to me. Surely, there's other people with more—"

"You're the only one who's an outsider," Milstein said. "The only employee in the entire building who didn't work at the court at the time of the Dupont Underground murders. And we think the killer is linked to other crimes before you were hired."

Milstein suspected someone at the court. Gray could be trusted because he'd had no access to the quill pens at the time of the Dupont murders. And maybe the FBI wanted to work independently from the court's police force since the court's squad was technically part of the marshal's staff.

"But do you want to know the other reason you should help us, Grayson?" Milstein said. She must have seen the skepticism on his face.

Gray nodded, as the car pulled to the curb in front of his basement apartment. They knew where he lived.

Milstein pulled up another photo on the tablet. Gray hesitantly glanced at the photograph. It was of another quill pen next to a yellow evidence marker on a concrete floor.

"It's from the same supplier. She puts a tiny ID number on each pen so she can authenticate them. This one is from the same set as the one found at Dupont. And at the convenience store tonight. You know where we found this pen?" She gestured to the photo.

Gray shook his head.

"We found it in the garage of the court."

Gray was feeling the heat in his face now. Pulse thumping at his temples.

"Whoever attacked you and the chief justice," she said, "he dropped it."

CHAPTER 15

Gray arrived at the court at 9:45 a.m. the next morning, much later than he should have since oral arguments started at ten sharp. He was exhausted, emotionally hungover, but he shouldn't have slept in. It was the November sitting, so on top of the *cert* pool memos and death penalty stays, there was the third responsibility of a clerk: writing bench memos. Summaries of each case that the chief justice would use to prepare for oral arguments that would occur over the next two weeks. Gray had written the memo for *Jando v. United States*, one of the cases scheduled for argument that morning. He was supposed to attend the arguments for all of his assigned cases, and he didn't want the chief to look out and see an empty seat in the clerk's section.

Gray rushed into his office, his eyes fixed on the old phone on his desk. Luckily, the message light wasn't on. The chief hadn't called needing anything before the argument. He threw his backpack on the floor, gathered up the argument file for *Jando*, and hurried down to the chamber.

Gray slipped into a seat in the clerk's section next to Keir. His co-clerk gave him a dismissive nod.

The court was hearing two arguments that morning. First up was the *Filstein* case, about the president's controversial drone-strike policy; second was Gray's *Jando* case, which involved the scope of the Fourth Amendment's prohibition on illegal searches.

Gray's heart rate was returning to normal. He'd made it just under the buzzer, the chief hopefully none the wiser that he'd nearly been late.

He turned to Keir. "Packed house," Gray said, scanning the gallery.

Keir sniffed. "Of course it is. *Filstein*'s the biggest case of the term. Don't worry, the room will clear out when your case is argued."

Gray ignored him, taking in the scene. The room was encased in marble columns that shot up to a forty-four-foot gilded ceiling. The raised bench stretched nearly the width of the room. In front of the bench were the counsel tables. On the right, members of the solicitor general's office, the government lawyers who represented the United States in all Supreme Court cases. They were considered the best and brightest advocates in the country. Their confidence bordered on the cocky, but it was reined in because they looked silly in their morning coats and striped pants—the getup reminded Gray of old-time wedding outfits—a tradition the SG's office still clung to for some bizarre reason. On the far left, the other advocates appearing for argument with their sweaty palms and well-tailored suits. And the remaining five hundred seats filled with lawyers, the press, dignitaries, and the general public, all perched on uncomfortable pews and creaky old wooden chairs.

When Gray was in law school he'd watched many oral arguments, a hobby his classmates didn't quite understand. He'd read that Chief Justice Douglas once said he got a lump in his throat every time he marched through the heavy curtains and took the center seat. But it wasn't until Gray became a law clerk that he fully understood what the chief meant. Every time Gray entered the chamber now he too got a lump in his throat, realizing he was part of the institution, part of something greater than himself. Had some of that feeling diminished when the court failed to save Anton Troy? Maybe. But he still sat up straight and with pride when he heard the buzz from the ceiling and the marshal cried: "*Oyez! Oyez! Oyez! All persons having business before the Honorable, the Supreme Court of the United States, are admonished to draw near and give* their attention, for the Court is now sitting. God save the United States and this Honorable Court."

The Nine emerged in threes from three openings in the burgundy curtains and took their seats. The chief, looking a little weary from the late night on the Anton Troy case, started the morning by swearing in lawyers who had applied for admission to the Supreme Court bar. Though the certificate looked good on a lawyer's office wall, the requirements were minimal, effectively $200 and a pulse. Nevertheless, the chief treated the occasion seriously. And today was special. A group of deaf lawyers had applied. Always a class act, the chief used sign language to affirm their admission. He then called the *Filstein* case.

The lawyer challenging the drone policy stepped to the lectern. "Mr. Chief Justice and may it please the court. This case isn't about a policy on drones. Drones are just a tool, not a policy. The policy being challenged here is a policy on assassinations. Without congressional authorization or oversight, the executive branch has exceeded its authority in engaging in a drone war, an unlawful license to kill, which according to the government's own secret records kills the innocent in more than ninety percent of the strikes . . ."

For the next two hours Gray took it all in. Few sights were more riveting than watching a skilled advocate thread his or her way through the grilling of a hard case. Responding to Justice Marcus's tangled hypotheticals, avoiding Justice Cutler's hostile traps, going toe-to-toe with the brilliant chief. He'd heard that in the old days much of the advocacy before the court was mediocre. But the past ten years had seen large firms hire away staff from the solicitor general's office, and there was now a specialized Supreme Court bar. Repeat players who knew the game well. The *Filstein* case had the finest lawyers in the country slugging it out. Even *Jando v. United States*, Gray's lower-profile criminal case, brought out the heavy hitters. It was two hours of exquisite advocacy. Two hours of not thinking about the FBI and murdered women.

At noon, the red light appeared on the lectern, the buzzer went off, and the justices disappeared backstage. Supreme Court Police officers in their immaculate dress blues shushed the masses as the spectators made their way out of the courtroom.

The chief usually took a half-hour break after argument, then went to lunch. Gray decided he would approach him then about the visit from the FBI. The agent had warned Gray to tell no one about their conversation, and had made noises about obstruction of justice. But this was the chief justice of the United States. Gray stopped at the closet to drop off his papers, then made his way to chambers. As he headed into the reception area he saw Olga escorting two guests into the chief's private office. One of them, the woman in the group, turned and gave Gray a hard stare.

Agent Milstein.

She held his gaze for a long moment, then she and her partner were whisked inside.

CHAPTER 16

Milstein studied Chief Justice Douglas. He was in his fifties, but had a boyishness to him. The lick of hair that fell on his brow, the earnest smile. He sat back comfortably in the large wing chair in his chambers. Next to Douglas in his own chair was Aaron Dowell, another chief, this one of the Supreme Court Police force. Not so youthful with his paunch, waxy skin, and jowls.

Police Chief Dowell looked at Milstein and Cartwright, who sat across from Dowell and the chief justice. "So what's the fire drill, why the emergency meeting?"

The murder of the convenience store clerk on the fifth of the month—along with the killer leaving behind a quill pen—finally compelled Milstein's boss to get off his ass and demand Dowell to give the Bureau access to the chief.

"There was a murder last night," Milstein said. "It's connected to the others."

Dowell shifted uncomfortably in his chair. He'd previously minimized the connection between Dupont Underground and the attack on the chief justice. Milstein hoped things would be different now.

"I'm sorry," the chief justice said, "but I'm not following." He looked at Dowell. "What's this about, Aaron?"

Dowell swallowed. "You remember we discussed that the

Bureau thought there was a connection between the Dupont murders and the attack in the garage?'"

"Yes," the chief said, "the feather pens left at the scenes. I thought everyone decided that the connection was tenuous? That the feathers might not be from the same stock or that the pen in the garage was already there?"

"We didn't know. There were a number of theories," Dowell said timidly. "Out of an excess of caution, we increased the justices' security details and changed some protocols. But we ultimately concluded that the evidence didn't warrant more."

"And you were wrong, apparently," the chief said pointedly.

"The important thing," Milstein cut in, giving Dowell a lifeline, "is that now we're more certain about the connection."

"How so?" the chief asked.

Cartwright joined the conversation. "Last night, a young woman was murdered at a convenience store in Hamilton Heights. The killer left behind a quill pen. It was from the same batch as the pens at Dupont and in the garage. There's now no question the pens weren't left at the scenes by accident or happenstance. The killer is purposefully leaving them for us to find."

The chief's brow wrinkled. "Why? What's it mean?"

"We don't know. He's also leaving cryptic messages. At Dupont he spray-painted random words on the wall. At the convenience store, he wrote something in the victim's blood. All of it unintelligible, but our people are trying to decipher if it means anything."

"What did he write?" the chief asked.

"I'm afraid we can't disclose that, Chief Justice," Cartwright said.

The chief sighed. "So what can *I* do for you?" the chief justice asked. "How can I help?"

"We just have some questions, if you don't mind?" Milstein said.

"Of course."

"I understand you knew Amanda Hill, the lawyer killed at Dupont Underground?" Milstein asked.

"Yes, Amanda was an old friend. I still can't believe it. And to kill her mother and young child too . . ." The chief held a look of bewilderment.

"Can you think of any reason why someone might target you and Ms. Hill?"

Douglas rubbed his chin. "Like I told Aaron, I hadn't seen Amanda in years."

"You weren't close friends?"

"I'd describe us more as colleagues. From years ago, when I was a district court judge. Amanda was a public defender. She appeared before me regularly back then."

Milstein knew this already, but an interview is a process, she'd learned long ago. "You didn't have a personal relationship with her?"

"No. I saw her in court or at bar functions. Judges have to be careful with such things," he explained.

"Can you think of any cases that could've made you both targets of the same person? Any other connection?"

"No." The chief answered quickly, it seemed too quickly. "She had hundreds of cases before me, mostly plea deals where I simply imposed the sentence, usually what the prosecution and defense had agreed to."

"Did you get any threats back then?"

"All judges get threats. But nothing credible, nothing with any connection to Amanda."

Milstein nodded. "The young woman killed at the convenience store, her name was Sakura Matsuka. Did you know her?"

"No."

"How about a man named Adam Nowak?"

"No, should I?" Douglas said.

"He's a reporter. He used to work at the *Post*, but freelanced for the past several years."

The chief shook his head. "The name sounds familiar, but I don't think I've ever met him."

"Phone records show that he called both Amanda Hill and Sakura Matsuka."

"He called both victims? Did he tell you what about?"

"No," Milstein said. "He's dead too. The Franklin fire."

Even before the convenience store murder, Milstein knew that Adam Nowak had called Amanda Hill, the Dupont Underground victim. But the Homeland team running the Franklin fire investigation thought it was a coincidence. A single call between two victims of separate crimes didn't mean there was any connection. Also, Homeland didn't want Milstein mucking around with its investigation of the fire. But that morning, Milstein's team ran the convenience store victim's cell phone number in their database and got a hit. A few days before the Franklin fire, the reporter had also called Sakura Matsuka, the store clerk. So it was just a matter of connecting the dots. Feather quill pens were left at the Dupont Underground and convenience store murders, which meant the two crimes were linked. And the reporter killed at the Franklin fire had called both victims; the reporter was the tip of the triangle.

"So you think the same perpetrator started the Franklin fire?" the chief justice said.

"It's looking that way. And not just because of the phone call from the reporter," Milstein said. "All of the crimes occurred on the fifth of the month." This time Milstein stared directly at Dowell since he'd been one of the many who'd pooh-poohed Milstein's suspicions that the killer would strike last night, on November 5.

The chief justice let out an exasperated breath, sinking back into his chair. "Do you have any leads on the identity of this man?"

Milstein shook her head. "No. Worse, our behavioral experts say the killer is just getting started." She paused a beat. "And we have less than a month until he strikes again."

CHAPTER 17

Gray spent the rest of the day in the closet working on his pool and bench memos, trying not to think about the FBI. Trying to shake the images from the gruesome photos, but they kept creeping into his thoughts. He assumed someone must have stolen a batch of quill pens from the court because no one at One First Street could be involved, right? He considered the staff at the marshal's office, which was charged with ordering the pens and dispensing them to advocates appearing for argument. Beyond the hundreds of officers on the police force, the marshal's staff was mostly college kids and senior staff. There was his former supervisor Martin, who made the female staffers feel uncomfortable, but the guy who'd attacked Gray and the chief in the garage was svelte, agile, not like doughy Martin. Who else could it be? A voice interrupted his thoughts.

"You notice I didn't mention this office when I offered you the job?" The chief justice stood in the doorway, an amused look on his face. He gazed about the windowless office, Gray at his desk, hemmed in by a small mountain range of legal papers. "I think we need to get you some air. Got time for dinner?" The chief plucked Gray's suit jacket from the hook.

Twenty minutes later, Gray and the chief were sitting in a plush booth at The Palm. Despite the otherwise refined setting, the restaurant's walls were covered with sketches depicting politicians and local celebrities. The chief directed Gray to the unflattering caricature of the justices, which was all giant noses, sagging cheeks, and sinister expressions. "My ex-wife said they captured me perfectly," the chief said.

The restaurant was filled with the glad-handing Capitol Hill crowd, boisterous men and women, most of whom couldn't resist stopping by the chief's table to say hello.

When the salads arrived, Gray waited until the chief picked up his fork. Both because he didn't want to start first and because he needed to make sure he used the correct utensil of the many spread before him. The chief seemed to notice Gray shadowing him. He made a show of selecting his fork.

"So, how's it going?" the chief asked. "You seem to be picking things up quickly," he said, taking a bite.

"I've been lucky to have help from the other clerks." Not entirely true, but always better to be gracious, his mom always said.

The chief gave a fleeting smile, one that suggested he knew better. He seemed to be stealing looks at Gray's tie, stained from lunches past, and his suit jacket, straight from *The Godfather*. They were interrupted by another visitor, the Senate majority leader. Much of the meal went this way, the stop/start of dining with Washington's version of a movie star. The head of the third branch of government.

The chief turned the discussion to work. "What'd you think of the *Jando* argument today?"

In *Jando v. United States*, the court was tasked with deciding the scope of the "exclusionary rule"—the rule that courts have to throw out evidence when the police obtained the proof by violating the suspect's rights. If the cops failed to read a suspect his *Miranda* warnings or searched a house without a warrant, the evidence was excluded and the government couldn't use it against the defendant. But there was an exception, a fail-safe the police often relied upon: inevitable discovery. If the cops would have inevitably discovered the evidence even if they hadn't violated the suspect's rights, then all would be forgiven. The evidence admissible. The case was about the scope of the inevitable discovery rule.

"The argument was strong from both sides," Gray said.

The chief examined him. "But who do *you* think should win, the government or the criminal defendant?"

"Really tough. If the exclusionary rule is designed to deter police from breaking the rules, won't expanding the inevitable discovery exception undermine that?"

The chief thought about it. "It might, but my experience is that most cops are good people. Why should the criminal go free if a good cop would've found the evidence even if the bad cop hadn't broken the rules?"

"But the rule encourages *all* cops to be good. If the bad cops know there won't be consequences, won't they take more shortcuts? Won't even the good cops be tempted?"

"Theoretically. But when I was a district court judge most of my docket was criminal cases, and I saw the realities of the system. It's easy to decide these rules in the abstract—when you read about them in a law school textbook—but it's much different when you see a victim sitting in the courtroom. What if you were the judge who had to let someone you knew was guilty, a violent criminal, go free? Could you do it, Grayson? Even if you knew that, statistically speaking, he'd do it again? Hurt, or even kill, someone else? You'd free him simply because an officer got carried away? Even if they would have found the evidence without the officer's misconduct?"

Gray still didn't agree. In Hamilton Heights, he'd seen good and bad cops. The job was hard enough without giving the good ones excuses to cut corners. But based on the chief's tone, he knew it was time to retreat. "I never thought of it that way."

"Well, you should start thinking hard about it because I need you to write a draft opinion for me. Think you can write something persuasive where the government wins?"

"I'm sure I can."

"That's the spirit."

The waiter arrived with the main course, two New York strips: the menu said corn fed, aged, covered in béarnaise. "I have an unusual question," the chief said, cutting roughly into the slab of meat. "Have you noticed anything out of the ordinary around the building? Anyone acting suspiciously?"

Gray assumed the questions were prompted by the chief's

meeting with the FBI. He considered again telling Douglas about
his own encounter with the agents. But he thought of Milstein's stare
as she went into the chief's chambers. Last night, she'd warned him
to tell no one about their meeting, that it could constitute obstruction of justice. He doubted that, but the agent had pulled the chief
into the loop, so it was better left alone. "Out of the ordinary? No."
True enough. But Gray wondered if the chief was concerned that
someone at the court was involved. "I saw FBI agents visiting today.
Is everything okay?"

"Nothing to worry about," the chief said. "Just more questions
about what happened in the garage."

Gray wondered why the chief lied. The FBI probably told him
to keep things confidential too, though Gray doubted they threat-
ened *him* with obstruction.

"Have the other clerks told you about our 'First Saturday' out-
ings?" the chief asked, changing the subject again.

"No, they haven't."

"The first Saturday of every sitting," the chief said, "Justice
Wall and I have an event. An outing with all of our clerks. Forcing
you out of the office ensures your heads stay clear." The chief dabbed
his mouth with his napkin. "You'll see on Saturday." It was more
of a command than an invitation.

After the chief paid the check, he said, "You have time to run
a quick errand with me?"

"Of course."

A half hour later they were at Saks Fifth Avenue at Mazza Gal-
lerie in Friendship Heights.

"I want to share with you something my father taught me,
Grayson," the chief said, as they browsed through the racks of high-
end garments on the top floor of Saks. "You've gotta look the part
to be taken seriously in this world." The chief tested the fabric of a
suit's lapel with his thumb and index finger, then directed the salesperson to take it and two other suits to the fitting room.

Gray soon was standing on a platform in front of a tri-folding
mirror, a tailor darting around him with a measuring tape. The
chief sat in the lounge area of the fitting room, drinking a cappuc-
cino the salesperson had brought him, occasionally giving the tai-

lor instructions. "More off the jacket sides." "Cuffs on the pants? You can't be serious?"

"I can't accept this," Gray said as the chief handed a gold card to the salesperson.

"Consider it my personal thank you. You did save my ass, after all."

"You've already done so much."

"No, hiring you helped *me*. You're a bright young man, and already a damn good clerk. And you also helped right a problem with how we hire at the court. We all get set in our ways and hire from the same feeder judges, the same schools, which produce the same types of people, usually smart kids born from families that are legacies of those schools."

The whole thing was a bit too *Pretty Woman*. And spending so much, the designer labels, didn't feel right. The Hernandezes weren't poverty-stricken like some of the families in the apartment complex. They were what the media would call "the working poor." That didn't mean Goodwill or Salvation Army. It meant trotting up to the Kmart in Silver Spring at the end of every summer to buy school clothes. It meant wearing your jeans until you could no longer tolerate the *Expecting a flood?* comments from classmates; borrowing a leather jacket from Arturo in the winter, not asking where he got it. And it meant on your fourteenth birthday wanting desperately that expensive pair of sneakers, the ultimate status symbol in your middle school, and getting the Payless version instead. It meant feeling like a jerk when you just couldn't hide the disappointment and you hurt your mom's feelings. Gray was never one for labels on his clothes after that. But what could he do? He couldn't exactly say no to his boss, the Chief Justice of the United States.

"Time for one more stop?" the chief asked.

Gray nodded. It had been quite the excursion. And Gray soon was in the passenger seat of the chief's Mercedes, zipping down Wisconsin Avenue into Georgetown. Gray stared absently out the window at the historic brick town houses converted into boutiques, and wondered where they were going. The chief pointedly didn't say, and Gray decided not to ask.

The chief crossed M Street down a hill to the waterfront, and took a sharp turn into the mouth of a condo building, bouncing over speed bumps and into the basement garage.

Gray followed after the chief to an elevator. He knew the chief lived in McLean, Virginia, so he wasn't sure who they were going to see.

The elevator opened to a long hallway. The chief stopped in front of the only door on this wing of the building, and slid a key into the lock.

Inside was an elegantly decorated penthouse. It had an open floor plan that spread out to floor-to-ceiling windows overlooking the Potomac.

"Wow, this place is incredible."

"Thank you," the chief said.

"It's yours?"

"Yes. This is where I lived after my divorce. Before I realized I'm not cool enough for Georgetown, and I moved to the burbs." The chief looked at Gray. "You really like it?"

"Are you kidding? I've never been in a place this nice." Gray walked to the window and stared out at the view. On the far left, the Washington Monument, a white spear stabbing into the sky. On the right, the lights from the Key Bridge reflecting in the water.

"Glad you like it." The chief removed the key from the ring and handed it Gray.

"I don't understand, I—"

"Aaron Dowell told me about where you live. That you ride a bike there late at night. I can't have you getting mugged again on my watch."

Gray wondered why the chief of the court's police and Douglas had been talking about Gray, much less about where Gray lived.

The chief continued, "My tenants moved out six months ago, and I decided to keep the place vacant for out-of-town guests—or friends in need. It could use someone here for maintenance and whatnot. If you can handle that, the place is yours rent-free for the term."

Gray thought about what his father would say. First the suits, then the condo. He didn't want to appear ungrateful, but no.

"I can't."

"Let's not go through this again," the chief said.

"It's too much."

"Nonsense. The place is sitting vacant. You'd be helping me."

Gray pressed his lips together. The chief was giving him a curious stare. Gray eyed the giant flat-screen television mounted over the fireplace. Maybe it would be okay.

"I could pay rent. I'm not sure I could afford the full—"

"Excellent," the chief cut him off. "We can work out the details later. Also, I keep a car downstairs. My ex called it my 'mid-life-crisis mobile.' You're welcome to use it." He patted Gray on the shoulder. "Come on, let's get a drink. There's a great pub just down the street."

The chief showed Gray the car, a convertible Audi, and then they exited the garage to the street. At nine o'clock, the sidewalks were crammed with pedestrians, none of them seeming to recognize the chief.

"Who do you think was the worst justice of all time?" the chief asked. They'd spent the better part of the evening talking court history and trivia, and the chief couldn't seem to get enough of it.

Gray thought about the question. "I've read that Justice James McReynolds was a pretty awful person; that he was a racist and anti-Semite who refused to speak to the Jewish justices, and that he once turned his back to a black lawyer during oral argument."

The chief nodded. "A lot of the stories about McReynolds are just urban legends, but he was a son of a bitch. I'm still going to rank Justice Cutler as the worst ever."

Gray took in a breath, not sure how to respond. Cutler was a sitting justice.

"She's only on the court because she's a political hack, not because she earned it," the chief said. "And she's nasty as hell."

That was Cutler's reputation around the building. But Gray was not about to denigrate a current member of the high court. This could be a test. Before he responded, a panhandler stepped in front of their path and jangled coins in a cup.

The chief stopped, looked the man up and down. The guy was in his late twenties and appeared well-fed, healthy. "You want some money?" the chief asked.

The man nodded, holding out the cup.

"Then get a fucking job."

Gray did a double take. For the entire outing, the chief had treated everyone with respect. The waiter, the valet, the tailor. But with this man he was harsh. Vulgar, even. Gray started to realize that Chief Justice Douglas had a distaste for the entitled, those who didn't work hard to earn what they had. But he also disdained those who didn't live up to their potential.

No pressure.

CHAPTER 18

Milstein sat in the car waiting for Cartwright to get their coffee and breakfast sandwiches at the Starbucks in Dupont Circle. The sidewalks were filled with well-dressed women carrying shopping bags. Milstein looked at herself in the rearview mirror. When was the last time she'd gone shopping? Or had her hair done? Gotten a mani-pedi? She and Chase had been split up for almost a year now, and she was tiring of dinner alone at her crappy temp apartment, but the idea of dating again made her cringe. Cartwright appeared at the passenger door holding two cups. Milstein reached over and opened the door, and Cartwright handed her the cup then slipped inside.

"Checking yourself out in the mirror?" He looked over at the stores. "You know, Macy's sells makeup."

Milstein gave him a *fuck you* smile.

They drove up Connecticut Avenue and over the border into Maryland, past the pricey neighborhoods, onto I-495, exiting in Rockville. Traffic was heavy and they finally made it to the old apartment complex. Yesterday, the job took them to the majestic Supreme Court. Today, an ugly brick building painted turd brown. They found the ground-floor unit and rang the doorbell.

An elderly woman, Japanese, peeked through the gap in the

door. She said nothing, just stood there blinking, waiting for them to speak.

"We're with the FBI." Milstein held up her badge. "We're here about what happened to Sakura. Can we come inside?"

The old woman opened the door. It was a small, cluttered space. There was the waft of something fishy. Milstein saw a small shrine to Sakura Matsuka, the young woman killed at the convenience store.

"Can we sit down?" Milstein asked.

"I'm Sakura's grandmother. You need to speak with her father. He at the store." She spoke in clipped, accented English.

"One of our colleagues tried to speak with him, but he refused. I don't think he understands, we're here to help. To catch who did this to Sakura. It's important that we get some information from him. Perhaps you could talk to him, tell him that it's okay—"

The woman let out a scoff. "The last time he speak to you people, what good it got him. He lost everything."

Milstein and Cartwright met eyes. "I don't understand—"

"*Hmpft.*" The old woman narrowed her eyes to almost nothing. "He want nothing to do with F-B-I." She accentuated each letter with distaste.

"If there's something he's afraid of—his immigration status— or something else. We don't care about any of that."

"He a citizen just like you," the old woman said, insulted.

"Then why doesn't he want to help us catch Sakura's killer?" Milstein said, her tone incredulous.

The old woman's face hardened.

Cartwright jumped in. "What about *you*? Will *you* talk to us?"

"I don't know anything. She went to work like always. Police come to apartment, say she dead."

"We have her phone records. She was speaking with a reporter. Do you know what it was about?"

The old woman shook her head. Another long silence.

Milstein pulled up a crime scene photo on her phone. Before Cartwright could talk her out of it, she showed it to the woman. Sakura Matsuka, tied to a chair, her face swollen, awash in red. The CSU determined that the killer had taken a shopping bag, one of the green reusable ones, and filled it with canned goods. He then used it to club the woman. For some reason, they hadn't determined why, he'd strangely cut Sakura's long hair into a short jagged mess. He'd used scissors sold at the store. And he'd taken the hair clippings with him. The killer was smart: he'd also taken the digital security recorder, doused the area with bleach, and left behind no other evidence.

The old woman pushed away the phone. "We know how you operate. Nothing will bring her back." She shepherded them to the door.

Cartwright pushed on. "Did Sakura go by the nickname 'Kora' or does *Kora* mean anything to you?" The perp had written KORA MATSU on the floor in the young woman's blood. They theorized that the killer may have been interrupted, since he wrote only the first five letters of Matsuka's last name. But they didn't know what "Kora" meant.

The old woman shrugged.

Cartwright looked at Milstein, who gave a defeated shrug of her own.

"Can you ask Sakura's mother to speak with us?" Milstein asked.

"She died long time ago."

Milstein let out a loud breath. They were wasting their time. She pulled out a card. "If you think of anything that might help, or if your son would be willing to talk to us, please call."

The old woman took the card—Milstein could tell it would soon be in the trash—and said nothing as she shut the door behind them.

In the hallway outside the apartment Cartwright said, "What was that about? It's her granddaughter . . ."

Milstein shook her head in disgust.

Cartwright washed a hand over his face. "The Supreme Court still won't give us access to their people. The vic's family won't talk to us. And the perp is toying with us. Could this case get any fucking weirder?" Cartwright looked at Milstein. "So what now?"

"I think we need to find out why Sakura's pops won't talk to us. What he's got to hide."

CHAPTER 19

Gray drove the chief's car—top down, to hell with the fact that it was November—to the "First Saturday" event, zip-lining in Sandy Spring, Maryland. He sped along the rural roads lined on either side with white horse fences. In his sunglasses and mussed hair, he felt pretty cool if he did say so. It had been a strange week, with the Anton Troy execution, the outing with the chief, and an encounter with the FBI. Now, a weird zip-lining excursion, and tonight his first law clerk happy hour. The chief justice was right about one thing. With the new clothes and new place, Gray felt different, more confident. More comfortable in his new life. He followed the GPS onto a bumpy dirt road, a cloud of dust trailing the Audi.

After parking on a grassy field near a sign that said ADVENTURE PARK, he found Justices Douglas and Wall and their law clerks getting a safety orientation from a teenager. Gray didn't think he was late, but everyone was already suited up in their nylon harnesses, gloves, and helmets. Gray looked up at the platforms in the trees, the ropes and cables of the zip-line course. The branches were filled with colorful leaves, casting a shadow over the bottom of the forest.

"Let's get moving," Chief Justice Douglas shouted to him.

Gray raced over to the check-in station, signed a stack of release forms, and climbed into his gear. He caught only the tail end of the safety briefing before the others climbed up to the main platform. Gray introduced himself to Justice Wall's clerks. He'd seen them around the building but had never spoken with any of them. There was Sven, the only male clerk, and three women: two named Heather, the other Audrey.

The chief and Wall stood near two rope ladders. "The rules are pretty simple," the chief said. "We'll start at the top on the parallel courses, and the first team to the ground wins."

Gray stared into the treetops, trying not to swallow. The chief and Justice Wall then climbed their respective ladders, their clerks following behind. Gray went last, his muscles contracting as he tried to balance on the rope ladder. The knife wound on his side from the attack in the garage had healed, but the skin was still tender.

When Gray reached the wooden platform, he dared to look down. He clutched the safety rope, and tried to steady his breathing. He watched as the chief sprang from the platform and flew down the zip line. The chief shouted something to Justice Wall, who was zipping down the parallel line. And so began the race. Team Douglas versus Team Wall.

The others must have seen the fear in Gray's face, because they let him cut in line, helping him attach his pulley to the steel cord. He tested the line with a yank, then closed his eyes, and jumped. He dipped for a moment, the straps biting into his thighs, then started his descent. Once the initial fright wore off, it was surprisingly exhilarating. The scent of the forest, the breeze in his face, the adrenaline rush. He swooped in with both feet on the wooden platform, grabbing the safety line, excited for the next run. It went like this for some time, the clerks tearing down each zip line, landing on the platforms, and connecting to the next run on a course that spiraled to the ground. Trying to stay ahead of Justice Wall's team on the other trail. Walls's clerk, Audrey, froze up on one of the runs. A worker at the park called out to Justice Wall, questioning whether Audrey should leave the course, but Wall barked him away.

Given that they'd grown up together, the chief and Justice Wall were quite the contrast. Douglas exuded charm, one of those men who guys wanted to hang out with but the ladies liked even more. He could kick back with a game or watch a rom-com with equal intensity. Wall, by contrast, had an aristocratic air. He looked buttoned-up even on the zip-line trail.

The race intensified as each side got more proficient with the equipment, more confident. Was Gray crazy for wanting to win so badly? He didn't know, but his natural skill on the course had not gone unnoticed by his team. Soon, he was the anchor, helping his co-clerks click the safety lines off and on and glide to the next run. By the last line, they had a good system, a seasoned pit crew.

The chief and Keir were first to the ground, followed soon by Justice Wall and one of the Heathers. Mike was next, then Praveen, but the other Heather and Audrey soon joined them. Lauren gave Gray the eyes when he attached one of the metal hooks, their bodies close, which only emboldened him. Her hair danced in the wind as she flew to the ground.

Finally, it was down to Gray and Sven. The others on the ground cheering. Sven looked like he belonged on the Norwegian Olympic Zip Line team if there were such a thing. Gray could hear the Heathers and Audrey shouting for Sven. Gray's co-clerks were not so loud, but even from this height he could see the chief justice was getting red-faced. No humor in it.

"Let's go, Grayson, bring it home!" the chief yelled.

Justice Wall was not so encouraging to Sven. He gave hoarse commands. "What are you doing? . . . Get a move on! . . . You don't have time for that . . ."

Gray realized that this wasn't just about winning the race. It was about years of competition between these men. He recalled the night of Anton Troy's execution, Wall's smug call with the chief, treating the stay petition like it was a game.

Gray looked across the trees to Sven, who was just seconds behind. Gray shimmied around the wooden platform and connected the slider, the little wheel used to roll down the line. He latched the safety clip—he thought the instructor had called it a tweezle. All he had to do now was hold on and the last run would take him to the ground, just ahead of Sven. He was about to jump when he realized that the slider wasn't rolling. He ripped off his gloves and tried to adjust it.

Jammed.

The cheering from the ground grew louder as Sven attached his pulley. Gray called down about the equipment failure, but they couldn't hear him.

Gray was dripping with sweat now. Sven was about to make the jump.

Gray unclasped his safety harness, straps of leather and nylon, and pulled his feet out of the holes. He wrapped the harness around his right hand, draped it over the line, then grabbed the other end with his left. Before he could talk himself out of it, he took a deep breath and made the leap.

At first, he didn't travel very fast, his makeshift pulley dragging against the line. But then the contraption started to work, and he accelerated, the swish of leather and nylon burning into the steel cord. He looked across the course and Sven was racing down the other line, behind Gray but gaining on him.

About midway down, Gray was still ahead, but his heart dropped when he saw that his harness was starting to tear.

The cheers grew even louder as he got closer to the ground, but his attention was fixed on the harness. More tearing.

Another wave of applause from Team Wall. Sven must be getting closer, zipping down the other line.

At thirty feet, the harness's nylon straps were now threads. The leather parts started to burn through.

Twenty feet.

Gray's hands were slipping now, but it wouldn't matter if the thing snapped.

Ten feet.

The harness broke. Gray landed hard, but fell into a roll, which probably spared him a shattered tibia.

Team Douglas roared. You'd have thought that he'd caught a Hail Mary in the last second of the Super Bowl. The chief justice did an embarrassing victory dance and literally got in Justice Wall's face.

Gray picked himself up off the ground. He bent over, a hand on each thigh, catching his breath. When he looked up, Lauren was standing there.

She arched a brow. "Got any more moves like that?"

Later, as Gray drove to the Supreme Court building for the

law clerk happy hour, he thought of all the cool things he wished he would've said to Lauren instead of just standing there with a dopey look on his face, happy to be alive.

At eight o'clock, Sam arrived at the Supreme Court building for the clerk happy hour. Like so many things at the court, they were a tradition; each justice's clerks hosted one and invited clerks from across chambers. One of the few events where outsiders—spouses, significant others, and friends—were allowed to attend. Gray had invited Sam as an apology for bailing on her the night of the Anton Troy case.

He gave Sam a tour of the building. The usual spots—the spiral staircase, the conference room, and, of course, the courtroom chamber. He even let her sit in the chief justice's tall leather chair at the center of the raised bench.

As Sam looked out across the gallery, Gray pointed up to a frieze that adorned the wall just below the ceiling. It depicted a mythological battle. "It's supposed to represent good versus evil," he said. He was disappointed when Sam didn't seem all that impressed.

"I heard a few years back, some clerks took pictures of themselves sitting naked on the bench," Gray said. "It somehow made it on Facebook and they got in some serious shit."

Sam twirled around in the chief's chair. Finally, she said, "What's gotten into you?" She gave him a hard glare. "You're acting like a teenage girl at a boy-band concert."

He shook his head. Sam instinctively disliked anything too Washington. Why should he have expected this to be any different? He released a weary breath.

"What?" she said.

"Nothing."

"Say it."

"It's just that I'm always open to your *we're artistes* crowd who think they're too cool for everything, I just thought you would—never mind, just forget it."

"Thought what? I'd be cool with your boss buying you clothes like you're a fucking Barbie doll? With him letting you stay in his apartment? The car?"

"I'm just there until the end of the term. And what was I supposed to do? Turn down a free place in Georgetown? A free sports car?"

"What do you think your father would—"

They were mercifully interrupted by one of the clerks who popped his head in and asked if they were coming to the happy hour.

In the courtyard, a crowd soon gathered around them. Gray because he was still a curiosity around the building. Sam, well, she got attention because she was Sam. It was only in these moments, when he saw her through other people's eyes, that he got what all the fuss was about.

"*That's* your best friend?" Mike said.

As the night went on, the clerks for each justice circled with their own. Gray glanced across the courtyard and saw Sam surrounded by a group of male clerks who were obviously showing off. They didn't realize that name-dropping and mentioning their Rhodes Scholarships was like spraying Sam-repellant all over themselves.

"To the best zip-liner in the history of the high court," Mike said, raising a plastic cup of beer. Lauren, Praveen, and even Keir raised their cups. "There are few things the chief likes more than beating Justice Wall, so here's to a job well done, man."

Gray took a gulp of beer. "I was surprised about how competitive they are," he said.

"Boyhood rivalry, I guess," Lauren said.

Mike said, "Yeah, they should just get a ruler and measure their dicks and get it over with."

The others ignored the comment, like they expected as much from Mike.

"The chief's had a good week all around," Keir said. "Not only beating Wall, but the chief talked Justice Cutler into coming over to our side in the *Filstein* case. It's gonna be five-four, and I'm gonna write the majority opinion for the biggest case of the term."

"Good for you, jackass," Mike responded. "No more shop talk. And Praveen, go work your magic on that hot blonde over there."

Praveen rolled his eyes in distaste. He took the last sip of what looked like Pepsi in his cup. "I've actually got to head out."

"Ah, come on, Pravie," Mike said. "I was just kidding. Hang out, it'll be fun."

"Grayson, well done today," Praveen said. "Tell Samantha it was nice meeting her."

"Thank you, Praveen."

"Killjoy!" Mike shouted as Praveen threaded his way through the crowd. Mike and Keir then wandered off.

"Is Mike always like this?" Gray asked Lauren.

"You mean the misogyny and vulgarity? Let's put it this way, do *not* ask him about his vacation in Thailand."

Gray laughed. He looked over at Sam across the courtyard again.

Lauren followed his glance. "Your girlfriend doesn't look like she's having a good time."

Gray could swear he heard a hint of jealousy. He considered playing coy, letting Lauren think that beautiful Sam was one of his many playthings, but quickly decided against it. "She's not my girlfriend. We grew up together. She's one of my oldest friends."

Lauren pondered this. "I don't know too many guys who would just want to be *friends* with *her.*"

Gray emitted a dry laugh. "We kissed once in sixth grade, you know, to see what it was like. I swear it nearly turned us both off of kissing forever."

"I'll have to remedy that." Lauren's lips curled to a mischievous smile.

Gray was trying to think of something clever to say in response, when he felt a tap on the shoulder.

"Hey, I think I'm gonna take off," Sam said.

"Already?"

Sam looked about, made a face.

"Come on, Sam. Give it a chance," Gray said.

Sam didn't respond.

"Did you tell anyone about your show?" Gray asked. "I think you've got some potential customers here."

Sam sniffed. "I want people to buy my work because they like my art, not because they're trying to hit on me."

"I think you need to lighten up."

"I want to go."

"Really?" Gray said, thick with exasperation.

"I can find my own way out."

He was a jerk to stay. But he was fitting in—really fitting in. So he closed down his first clerk happy hour. After nearly everyone had cleared out, Gray saw Mike sitting on the ledge of the court-yard fountain looking a little sloppy. "I should probably help him home," Gray said to Lauren. "I shouldn't drive, though. Want to share an Uber?"

The three soon piled into the car. Lauren's place was on the way, so they dropped her first.

"You want me to walk you up?" Gray said. She wasn't the kind of girl who needed an escort. "I thought you might want to see the rest of my moves." He smiled, referencing her remark at the zip-line course.

Lauren stared deep into his eyes again. Her gaze then moved to Mike, who was slouched in the backseat, head back, eyes closed. "Rain check," she said. She turned, walked up her front steps, and disappeared inside.

Ten minutes later, Gray helped Mike to the front door of his brownstone. After fumbling with the keys, Mike staggered to his couch, mumbling something. Gray took it as a thank you. The place had hardwood floors, expensive-looking furniture. Probably cost a fortune in Dupont Circle. Mike had stacks of briefs on the coffee table.

The Uber driver honked, letting Gray know he was tiring of waiting.

"You gonna be all right?" Gray asked.

"I'm good, man," Mike slurred.

On his way out, something caught Gray's eye. On the table, next to the briefs.

A feather quill pen.

CHAPTER 20

On Monday morning, Gray trudged up the escalator at Union Station. It was 5:00 a.m., and only a few weary commuters milled about. He bought a Starbucks, left the station, then walked under the purple sky down First Street. About halfway to the court building was a guard shack stationed next to barricades jutting from the street, hinged contraptions that came down like drawbridges, allowing only authorized vehicles to park near the Senate office buildings. The sidewalks were empty, and he made his way through the plaza and to the side entrance of the Supreme Court. The officer stationed at the door waved him through.

In his office, he found a new pile of briefs filling his in-box. A foot-tall stack of the blue, red, gray, green, and white booklets. He loved the job, but he sometimes fantasized about the colorful bonfire the briefs would make. In addition to the pool and bench memos, he was onto the fourth task of a clerk: writing the first draft of a decision, the chief's majority opinion in the *Jando* case. He'd started the draft over the weekend, and was struggling to write a persuasive opinion that was at odds with his personal views, a decision watering down search-and-seizure protections for defendants. He knew he couldn't pull any punches. The chief wore the black robe, not him.

The trill of his office phone broke the quiet. It couldn't possibly be his sister calling this early, could it? Over the past two weeks, she'd left several messages. They always started with an exasperated, nasally "This is your sister," and ended with some passive-aggressive reference to whatever family event he'd missed that day.

"Gray Hernandez," he said, trying to sound wide awake.

"Good morning, Grayson," the chief justice said. "I'm preparing for the *Union Health* argument and wanted to look at a couple cases cited in the blue brief."

Gray wrote down the citations and placed the phone in the cradle. He was pleased with himself. Who wouldn't be if the boss called at five-thirty in the morning and you were at your desk? He pulled up the cases on Westlaw, printed them, then paced quickly to the justices' private dining room where the chief was eating breakfast. His mind drifted to his time as a marshal's aide, where he'd learned the shortest route to virtually every spot in the building. How things had changed. He was getting into the groove as a clerk. He understood the job, was speaking the court's language, had friends.

And then there was Lauren. She'd definitely been sending him signals on Saturday night. His good mood crashed to earth, however, when his thoughts jumped to Mike's feather pen. The quill pen was now in the bottom drawer of Gray's desk. Why had Gray taken it? And what should he do now? Call that agent? Tell the chief?

He turned the corner quickly, bumping into someone. There was a gasp, and the woman tumbled to the floor.

Holy shit.

It was Justice Cutler. What was it with him bumping into Supreme Court justices? On their outing, the chief justice had intimated that Cutler was the worst justice in history.

Gray began helping her to her feet but she swatted him away.

"I'm so sorry, Justice Cutler," Gray said.

"What are you even doing here?" she spat. "This is the *private* dining area."

"The chief justice asked that I bring him some materials for the argument."

She glared at him, then shifted her gaze to the dining room door. "Wait here."

She stormed inside. All Gray could hear was "incompetent" and "charity project," but he knew how it was going.

Justice Cutler emerged from the dining room and gave him the eye. The chief, loud enough for Cutler to hear, called for Gray. The chief's tone was stern, prompting a satisfied smirk from Cutler, who stomped off.

Gray walked on the red Oriental rugs to the long table where the chief had his breakfast and briefs spread out in front of him. The chief took a sip from a teacup.

"Making new friends, I see."

"Chief Justice Douglas, I'm so sorry, it was an accident. I was rushing to bring you the cases. I should've slowed down, I should have—"

The chief held up a hand. "Let me give you some advice, Grayson." He folded his napkin and placed it on the table neatly. "I don't care how much you screw something up, in this town you never apologize. Never. The sharks smell weakness like blood in the water."

Gray's thoughts flashed to Snuffy the Seal being devoured by the great white. He nodded. His Washington education continued: *No apologies.*

"Do me a favor," the chief said.

A pause. "Anything. Of course."

"Call Aaron Dowell. See if he caught what happened on the security footage."

Gray got a hard lump in his throat. This was getting more serious than he expected. The chief wanted to involve the Supreme Court Police.

The chief's lips held the hint of a smile. "Seeing that woman fall on her ass sounds like the only entertaining thing on the docket this week."

Gray just stood there expressionless as the chief plucked the case law out of his hand. Before leaving the dining room, the chief handed Gray an interoffice envelope. It was marked CONFIDENTIAL and had a sticker over the little red string that tied it shut.

"Deliver this to Justice Wall's chambers, will you?"

Gray handled the envelope as if it contained nitroglycerin. As silly as it sounded, "envelope duty" was a big deal. The envelope contained the private—paper copy only—communications between the chief and the other justices. It was as environmentally unfriendly as it was an antiquated method of communication. But the practice left no electronic footprint, allowing the chief to speak freely to the other justices without fear that sensitive notes or memos would ever wind up in his Library of Congress papers after he died. The other clerks bragged when the chief assigned them envelope duty. It wasn't that they relished being a messenger, it was the unwritten expression of trust. Despite the importance, Gray's co-clerks also had fun speculating about what was inside the business-sized envelope. Lauren thought it contained the final votes on all cases from the term. Mike thought it had nude shots of Justice Wall's sexual conquests. Keir thought it had a football pool the justices were rumored to participate in. And Praveen said it was none of their business and they should all get back to work.

Whatever was in the envelope, Gray was about to make the most important delivery of his many at the high court. Would he guard the envelope with is life? Right now, having received another small validation that he was a real clerk, not just some "charity project," he just might.

CHAPTER 21

"You want the good news or bad first?" Agent Cartwright asked.

Milstein was hunched over the investigative file spread across her desk. She took a bite of her breakfast, a bruised apple. "Bad," she said, with a mouthful.

Cartwright nodded, like he expected as much. He paced about her office, seeming to contemplate the bare walls and dust on her bookshelves. "Neal says Aaron Dowell is making a play for the Supreme Court's squad to take over the investigation since it involves the safety of the justices."

"And?"

"And Neal said Aaron's going over his head. Said the Director of National Intelligence is using the dreaded T-word."

"Not a fucking task force." Milstein had been through this before. She'd never been a believer in task forces. Too many bodies added more politics than breaks to an investigation.

"Aaron refuses to give us access to the justices or their clerks until it all shakes out. And Neal said we need to stay away from SCOTUS for now."

Milstein shook her head. "The good news?"

"Wait, I got more bad."

Milstein coughed out an exasperated laugh. She tossed the apple core across her office to the small trash bin, making the shot.

"I asked my buddy over at Homeland if we could have access to their intel on the Franklin fire. He said Aaron is making a play for their case as well. Said he can't share the file right now. I reminded him that we could connect a Franklin victim, the reporter, to both Dupont Underground and the convenience store—the reporter had spoken to both victims. He said no file until the politics are resolved. He did tell me something off the record, though." Cartwright's glance turned serious. "The reporter's home was broken into—his computer taken and possibly his work files."

"If someone went to the trouble to break in and steal his research and interview notes," Milstein said, "the murders may be connected to a story he was working on."

"That's what I said to him," Cartwright said.

Milstein pondered this for a while. "If you wanted to find out where someone lived to break into their place, how would you do it?"

"If I was a civilian?" Cartwright said. "Easy: I'd Google their name."

"How many people do you think could've possibly Googled this reporter's name in the last few months? I mean, if you date restrict it before the Franklin fire?"

Cartwright shook his head. "I'll get Simmons on it. She can reach out to our contacts at Google. Could be some red tape, though."

"So can you get to the good news now?"

"Speaking of Simmons, she went banging on some doors near the convenience store again looking for any witnesses."

"Yeah?"

"Don't get excited, she'd didn't find any. But a guy who works at the liquor store down the street has some information. He didn't feel comfortable talking to the feds at his store—thought it could be bad for business."

Milstein cocked her head to the side: *And . . .*

"I called the guy, asked him to come to the office." Cartwright looked at his watch. "He's supposed to be here in ten minutes."

It was another twenty minutes before Bob Jankowski ambled into the field office. He was a large man, Milstein guessed about three hundred pounds, and had thin hair pulled into a greasy ponytail.

"Thanks for coming in, Bob," Cartwright said.

"Call me Blaze, man, everybody does." He had a smooth voice, the cadence of a California surfer. Based on the faint waft of marijuana from his jacket, Milstein understood why people called him "Blaze."

Cartwright gave a faint smile, amused.

Blaze looked about the conference room. "The fricking FBI, this is a trip."

"I wish it were under better circumstances," Cartwright said. Without saying so, he reminded Blaze that this wasn't a social visit. Milstein always admired how Cartwright connected with people. He could be tough without using force, kind without appearing weak, and scold without an explicit reprimand. Milstein's more blunt approach had its efficiencies, but also tended to push people away.

Blaze shifted in his chair, his ruddy face more serious now. "Yeah, she was a sweet girl. She didn't deserve that. I heard the guy beat her so bad you could barely recognize her."

"You didn't see anything suspicious that night?" Cartwright asked.

"I own a liquor store in Hamilton Heights," Blaze said, "there's something suspicious *every* night. But no, I didn't see anything. We close at nine o'clock."

"You told our agent that you might have some information."

"She was asking me why the girl's family wouldn't talk to you all. And I told her it could be because of what happened with the Feebies and her dad back in the day."

"What do you mean?" Milstein asked. Maybe this wouldn't be a complete waste of time after all.

Blaze adjusted his bulky frame. "I was just a kid," he said. "My dad ran the liquor store back then. The convenience store was off-limits to us kids. Dad told me that something happened over there. And that the FBI nearly beat the store's owner to death."

Milstein and Cartwright exchanged a glance.

"You're saying an FBI agent beat Sakura Matsuka's father? When?" Cartwright said.

Before Blaze could answer, Milstein turned to Cartwright and said, "Wouldn't this have come up in our files?"

Cartwright shrugged.

"I may know why nothin' came up." Blaze smiled, displaying yellowed teeth. "Dad said that they changed their name. The Matsukas used to be the Yoshidas or something like that. Dad said the old man sued the FBI, there was some scandal, and that's why they changed their name."

"Do you know what it was about?" Cartwright asked.

Blaze leaned back in his chair and cracked his neck. "Can't say that I do. My dad told me to stay away from the shop, so I did. I own the store now, and I deal with Mr. Matsuka on neighborhood merchant stuff. Never had a problem with him."

"Do you know anyone who would want to hurt Sakura? Anyone who had a beef with the family?"

Blaze folded his arms across his flabby chest. "Like I told the other agent, I can't afford any trouble with these people."

"What people?"

"You run a store in the Heights, you don't just pay the tax man, if you know what I mean."

"Actually, I don't," Milstein said.

Blaze let out a loud breath. "If you want to make sure no one sticks a gun in your face every night or breaks in and steals your inventory, people need to know you're protected. And protection ain't free."

"And you think Sakura's family was paying protection to someone?"

Blaze directed his glassy eyes at Milstein. "The old man was getting fed up with payin'. He got all Norma Rae, and tried to get me and other stores on the block to refuse to pay when the boss got out of the joint and raised the monthly protection tax."

"And I take it you didn't sign on to the rebellion?" Cartwright asked.

"My dad didn't teach me much, but he once showed me the burned-out storefront of the last guy who didn't pay for protection. Cost of doing business."

"So, who's this 'boss'?" Milstein asked.

Blaze shook his head, like he was disappointed in both of them. "Name's Alvarez. Arturo Alvarez. And I do *not* want to get on the wrong side of that guy."

CHAPTER 22

After delivering the envelope, Gray stared at Mike's feather pen intermittently as he worked all morning and through lunch on his draft opinion. He tried to stay focused, but his thoughts wandered back to the night of Anton Troy's execution, the same night the woman at the convenience store was killed. The same night Mike was a no-show at the court. He should call that agent. She'd given him a card, but he didn't have it with him. He checked the FBI website, but it didn't give direct extensions for particular agents. Maybe he'd just call the main line and the operator would patch him through. No, he was being paranoid. This was stupid. His hand-wringing was interrupted by the chime of his iPhone. The Caller ID was blocked.

"Hello," he said.

"Hi, Grayson. This is Special Agent Milstein."

"Funny," Gray said, "I was just thinking of calling—"

"I'm across the street. At the Capitol Visitor Center. Can you come over?"

"Meet? Like, right now?"

"I won't take much of your time."

Gray eyed the feather pen again. "Where are you, exactly?"

"Just walk across First Street. You'll see me." She ended the call.

Gray pulled the feather pen from the drawer. He should bring it with him. He found a Redweld folder and slipped the pen inside. He headed downstairs and out the court's front doors.

Standing at the top of the marble staircase, he gazed across the street. He didn't see Agent Milstein in the small crowd milling about at the mouth of the incline that led down to the visitor center. Gray walked quickly down the famous forty-four steps. An officer who stood at the bottom nodded at him. Only a few people wandered about the plaza. Mostly tourists taking duck-face selfies against the backdrop of the court. The oral arguments ended at noon, so the protesters and reporters had mostly cleared out.

Gray crossed the street and proceeded down the hill to the visitor center. A large group huddled near the entrance, but still no Milstein. He thought he heard someone call his name. He turned around, and there she was. On the bench, eating the last bite of a hot dog from a vendor. She gestured for him to sit, then wiped ketchup from the corner of her mouth with her hand.

"Thanks for coming," she said, dusting off her hands.

Gray nodded. He wasn't sure what she wanted, so he started by handing her the folder.

Milstein's eyes flashed when she looked inside.

"I found it at Mike Dupree's house. He's one of my co-clerks," Gray said. "I'm sure it's nothing, but—"

Milstein shushed him with a waving hand as she carefully removed the feather pen. She examined its stock, holding it up to the sky for light. Disappointment rolled across her face.

"It doesn't have the identification mark." She placed the feather pen in her lap and pointed to a crevice near the tip. "The real ones have a tiny ID right here. I'll have this analyzed, but it looks like it's from the gift shop."

"But still, this seems pretty important, right?"

"Actually, when we found out Mike Dupree didn't show up at the court the night Sakura Matsuka was murdered, we looked into it. He was at a bar from ten o'clock until three in the morning. Credit card charges and video footage. But I appreciate you keeping your eyes open."

Gray felt a weight lifted from his chest. He was being paranoid. So why did she want to meet?

"I actually asked you here for something else—unrelated to the court." Milstein pulled out her smartphone and tapped its face. Reading Gray's expression, she said, "Don't worry, no dead bodies."

Gray glanced down at the device. It showed a mug shot. A Hispanic man.

"Know him?"

"You know I do or you wouldn't be here."

Milstein gave a *fair enough* shrug. "You know how we can find him?"

"No idea. I haven't spoken to Arturo in years. I heard he's just out of prison. Doesn't he have to check in with a parole officer or—"

"We kind of thought of that," Milstein said.

"You tried Madison Towers? That's where he used to run his crew."

"Yeah. But they've got lookouts and escape routes. The moment someone like me shows up . . ."

Gray gave the slightest nod. That much he remembered from when he was a kid.

"I spoke to the Metro cops who cover the Heights. Alvarez is cautious, hard to get to, since some rival gang is gunning for him. The Ortiz family."

Gray's chest heaved at the mention of the Ortiz crew. He shrugged, pretending he knew nothing of the feud. "What did he do this time?" Gray asked. "More drugs? Guns?"

"I'm sure all of the above, but I have no interest in any of that," Milstein said. "Apparently, the convenience store owner wasn't paying your friend his monthly protection."

"You mean the girl who was killed? No way, that's not Arturo's style."

"How do you know? You said you haven't talked to him in years."

"Because I know. He'd never hurt a woman. Ever." Gray's mind flashed to Arturo's mother, the black eye peeking out from behind the big sunglasses. Arturo's disdain for his father.

"How are you so sure?"

"Because I am."

"Would Alvarez have any reason to go after *you*?"

"Me?" Gray said, surprised. "No. Why?"

"Look at it from our point of view. You're attacked and the perp drops a feather quill pen. Another feather is left at a store your boy terrorizes."

"He's not 'my boy.'"

Milstein gazed at him a long beat.

"Look, if you wanna waste your time focusing on Arturo, be my guest," Gray said. "I don't know how to find him, if that's why you called me over here."

"To be honest, I don't think he has anything to do with this. He's got a rock-solid alibi for the Dupont Underground murders: he was locked in a cell. I'm just dotting my i's and crossing my t's. I just need to talk to him, to rule him out."

Gray didn't know if he believed that, but she couldn't be this desperate for a lead, could she?

"I don't know how to find him."

"Can you think of anywhere he liked to go, people he liked to see? I honestly couldn't give a shit about his little criminal empire."

Gray thought for a moment. "I don't know where he is, but I know somewhere he might be next week."

CHAPTER 23

The following week, Gray strolled the rooms of the elegant Alexander Gallery, Lauren at his side, looking fetching in a simple black dress.

"Thanks for inviting me," Lauren said. She tilted her head to the side, examining one of Sam's black-and-white shots hanging under the soft lights of the gallery. "She's really good." The photo was of a little girl. She was clutching a dirty rag doll and standing in line at a soup kitchen. Gray looked over at Sam, who was surrounded by admirers. He caught her eye, and she gave a fleeting smile. They hadn't spoken since their tiff at the clerk happy hour, but the best of friends know the look: *I'm still pissed at you, but I'm glad you're here.*

From behind them, a familiar voice. "Well, look who decided to grace us with his presence."

Gray turned to find his sister. She also looked lovely in her floral dress. She'd always struggled with her weight—she went up and down—and she'd lost quite a bit since he'd last seen her. When was that? It couldn't have been at the hospital, could it?

"Lauren, this is my sister, Miranda." Gray gestured to them both. "Miranda, this is Lauren, one of my co-clerks." He resisted calling her his date, since he wasn't sure that's what this was.

"So nice to meet you," Lauren said, sticking out her hand.

"Nice to meet you too. Glad you could get this one"—Miranda poked Gray in the chest with a finger—"out of that building he loves so much. It'd be nice if you could return a call."

"Would you tell my sister how much work we have to do?" Gray turned to Lauren. "That this is the first time I've been out *anywhere* unrelated to work."

Lauren said, "I don't know what he's talking about. I have plenty of free time." She smiled and took a sip from the champagne flute.

"Just as I suspected," Miranda said. She then sidled up to Gray. In a more serious tone, she said, "Mom mentioned that you've missed every Sunday at the gym with Dad since you started."

It wasn't a question, just an observation. A passive-aggressive observation. They were thankfully interrupted by the sound of someone tapping a glass. The gallery owner—a woman with large-framed glasses and ruler-straight short black bangs—continued tinging until the room went quiet. The owner gave a short talk about Sam's work, calling her one of the most talented artists on the scene. Sam, never comfortable with compliments, blushed and fidgeted. Gray felt a wave of pride for her. He scanned the room and didn't see Sam's mother. He realized that Sam's expression wasn't embarrassment about the accolades. He'd seen the look many times. The one when her mom hadn't shown up to the elementary school play when Sam was the lead. The one where Sam sat alone at the middle school banquet when she'd won an award for her art. The one when she looked out at the crowd at their high school graduation.

"Are Mom and Dad coming?" Gray asked Miranda, hoping at least his parents would be there, the usual stand-ins for Sam.

"No, but they sent flowers. They're watching Emilio." Miranda lifted another drink from a silver tray. "Mommy needed a night out."

"Gray showed me a picture of Emilio," Lauren said. "He's adorable."

Gray could tell Lauren already was winning over Miranda, not an easy task.

"Yeah, he's a pretty adorable little guy—when he's not crying himself to sleep missing his uncle," Miranda said, piling on.

"All right, all right. I get it," Gray said.

Sam finally made her way over to them. She hugged Miranda and then offered a handshake to Lauren.

As Miranda and Lauren continued to gab, Gray turned to Sam. "I'm really proud of you."

"Don't speak too soon. We'll see if any of them sell," she replied.

"I don't think that will be a problem," Gray said, looking about the crowded gallery.

A photographer came over and gestured for the four of them to get closer together for the shot. As the flash went off, Gray imagined the photo: Gray in his expensive new suit, a sophisticated woman on his arm, alongside the other favorite women in his life. At an art show, no less. It was one of those perfect moments from the movies where the photograph freeze-framed and you knew something ominous was coming.

With perfect timing, Gray saw Agent Milstein across the room. She too wore a dress, which showed more leg than he would have expected from a G-woman. She caught his eye, and motioned with her chin to the back of the place.

Sam shuffled off to work the room, and Gray turned back to his sister and Lauren. Miranda apparently was talking about him. "He slept with a stuffed animal, a giant Smurf, until he was fourteen," Miranda said.

"Really?" Gray said.

Lauren laughed and reached for his hand. Gray didn't want to let it go. But then he saw Milstein again, her chin gesture for him to come to the back of the gallery now more stern.

"If you'll excuse me for a moment, I need to use the restroom."

Miranda mocked his voice. "Mr. Manners. You are excused."

Gray heard Lauren laugh again as he negotiated his way through the crowd. The place was filled with a mix of professionals and artist types. He found Milstein in a small side room.

"I thought you said Alvarez would come?"

"I thought he would."

Milstein sighed, then took a sip of red wine.

"There are worse ways to spend an evening," Gray said. "And, like I said, you're wasting your time."

Milstein shrugged, as if he'd made a good point. A couple strolled into the room. "If you see Alvarez," Milstein said in a quiet voice, "text me."

"I don't have your number," Gray said. "When you called me, the number was blocked. And I lost your card."

Milstein handed him another card. She then fished out her phone, tapped on it, and Gray's phone pinged.

"You've now got a card and my personal cell."

When Gray returned to Lauren, Miranda had stepped out to call home to check on Emilio. The gallery was even more crowded now. "Want to get some air?" Gray asked.

Lauren grabbed his arm. "I'd love to."

The night was balmy, fall stubbornly refusing to show itself. The sidewalk in front of the gallery bustled with young Washingtonians, the vocal minority who cared more about the arts than partisan politics. Lauren led Gray past two smokers getting their fix, to the covered doorway of one of U Street's trendy shops. She stopped and turned toward him. She gently touched his face, tracing her finger along his scar. Gray leaned in for a kiss, but the spell was broken by the rumble of a motorcycle that jerked to a stop in front of the gallery.

Gray gave an annoyed look to the biker, who was unbuckling the straps on his helmet. Then he noticed the tattoo on the guy's neck. A scorpion. Not that original, but the ink was distinctive, designed by Sam when they were kids. He'd been right. Arturo, one of "the three amigos," wouldn't miss Sam's big night. Gray turned away, pretending he didn't see him. He quickly tapped a text to Milstein. The bike unexpectedly roared loudly. Gray turned and saw Arturo racing down the street. A car, a souped-up Chevy, jumped from the curb, did a screeching U-turn, and tore after him. Another car, this one a Mustang, went in the other direction, like it was going to cut Arturo off at the pass.

"What was that about?" Lauren said.

Gray shrugged. He then saw Milstein coming out the gallery door. She mouthed to Gray: *What the fuck?*

Gray turned his attention back to Lauren. "Hey, you want to go for a walk?"

She smiled and took his arm again.

They strolled along U Street past the closed shops and then a parking lot surrounded by a tall chain-link fence. The area was gentrified, safe by D.C. standards, but still had pockets of danger. Gray grew less comfortable as the landscape turned more depressed, the street lights more distant. But Lauren continued to walk confidently.

"Your sister is funny," Lauren said.

"I'm not sure I agree with that, but she is sweet."

"Is she raising Emilio on her own?"

"Yeah, though my parents help a lot."

"It's great your family is so close."

Gray nodded. "How about your family? You close?"

"Both my parents passed away."

"I'm sorry."

"It's okay. They got a really late start to having kids. They were already retired when they adopted me." Lauren walked quietly for a long moment, then changed the subject. "Thanks again for inviting me. This was really fun."

"I'm glad you could come. I'm so proud of Sam. You don't know how hard she's worked to—" Gray stopped midsentence, when a car raced around the corner and stopped abruptly at the curb. The Chevy from earlier, the one that had gone after Arturo.

"Let's go," Gray said, taking Lauren's hand. He tried to sound calm, but he could hear his heartbeat and blood whirling in his ears.

The man stepped out of the car and under a cone of lamplight. He stared at Gray for a long moment. There was something familiar about him. Then Gray saw the tattoo on his neck. In gothic script, the word RAZOR. He knew the name. Ramon "Razor" Ortiz. Arturo was in a blood feud with the Ortiz clan. Razor thought Arturo had killed Razor's older brother. It hadn't been the FBI in the cars chasing Arturo, it was Ortiz's crew. Three other men got out of the car. Gray stepped in front of Lauren.

"We follow Alvarez and looky who we found." The man flashed a grin to the others, then turned back to Gray. "What's the rush,

Hernandez?" Razor remembered Gray too. Gray supposed that he would. He'd been only two years behind Gray in school.

"We're leaving." Gray's voice was composed, though he felt the sweat beads on his forehead. He whispered to himself. *No fear.*

A bottle smashed near them. Lauren wriggled her hand free. She seemed to be reaching in her coat pocket for something. Gray and Razor had a brief stare down. Razor then smirked. Surprisingly, he gestured to sidewalk ahead of them. "You can go."

Gray didn't like the sinister grin, but he didn't stop to question the offer to leave. He lightly clutched Lauren's arm and began to lead her away.

But then Razor made an *eh-eh* sound in his throat. "You can go," he said, "but she stays." He licked his lips, which raised the hairs on the back of Gray's neck.

Gray deliberated. There were four of them—not good odds. But he wouldn't be leaving Lauren. He stood his ground, and Razor got in his face. Gray's heart was hammering now.

That's when he heard the roar of the motorcycle and Razor Ortiz flew like a rag doll, landing ten feet away. The man on the bike whipped around. He held the throttle with one hand, a long two-by-four in the other. An urban knight.

Gray yelled at Lauren to run. One of Ortiz's crew rushed up to Gray. The guy got into some half-assed karate stance, but went down with only two jabs to the face. The biker's lance then knocked another man off his feet.

Gray felt a body blow, knocking him to the ground. A heavy-set guy was on top of Gray now, wheezing, sweat dripping from his fat face. But then the man screamed and put his hands to his eyes. Lauren stood there still spraying his face with pepper spray. Gray pushed the man off of him and jumped to his feet. Gray's eyes started to water, the mist of the spray lingering in the air.

The biker pulled up next to Gray and flipped up the visor on his helmet. "You kidding me? How many times this gonna happen to you?"

"I—"

Arturo looked at the four men who were still on the ground. "You best get out of here. Go!"

Gray and Lauren sprinted back to the safety of the gallery. They heard Arturo's bike in the distance.

"Who was that?" Lauren said, her breath in rasps. "You know those guys? Why are they after you?"

"Not me," Gray said.

"Then who?"

"It's a long story."

"I have time."

CHAPTER 24

Gray and Lauren took a cab to an all-night diner downtown and he told her the story. About how he, Sam, and Arturo grew up in the same apartment building. Sam, raised by a single mother who struggled with alcohol. Arturo, by a drug-dealing bully of a father and beaten-down mother. About how the three in eighth grade had been arrested for joyriding in a stolen car. Arturo had boosted the vehicle and supplied the six-pack of beer. Gray's dad hired a lawyer for them all, and the guy got them into a diversion program. Gray never forgot that lawyer. He was the first adult to not talk down to him. He wasn't a big guy, a skinny Jewish fellow with a beard, but he seemed like the most powerful man in the world when he got them off with a slap on the wrist. A summer of outpatient group therapy for youth in distress. The counselor made them all read S. E. Hinton's *The Outsiders*. Gray wasn't sure why back then. One of the only times he'd ever seen Arturo close to tears was the day the counselor asked each of them to name the character they most identified with. Arturo refused to participate. But Gray knew that Arturo saw himself in Johnny Cade, the greaser who was neglected and abused by his parents. And he knew that Arturo wanted to be strong and cool, like the character Dallas Winston.

> *"Dally had it figured out," Arturo said.*
> *"Figured out? I guess you didn't read to the end of the book?"*

"I read it," Arturo said. "His problem was that he went soft about Johnny."

"I don't think that's what the author meant to—"

"You gotta stay hard or the world'll fuck you up," Arturo insisted. "And, besides, that hot girl in the book liked Dally the best; girls like the bad boys."

That last part was fair enough.

After more coffee, Gray and Lauren walked the tree-lined path along the reflecting pool that led to the Lincoln Memorial. Lauren hadn't said much, just listened as he reminisced. She was a good listener. He'd noticed this about her at the court. She could assess a person, a room, a situation, and acclimate perfectly. A byproduct of a proper upbringing, elite private schools, he presumed.

"That summer Arturo's dad went after his mom. Arturo grabbed a baseball bat. It resulted in a fractured skull for the old man, and a trip to juvie for Arturo."

"Oh my God," Lauren said.

"By the time we were seniors in high school, Arturo was already the school and neighborhood's main drug dealer, and was working his way up the organization. It's funny, though, even when we went our separate ways my senior year, he always looked out for me and Sam. I'd come home from the library and he'd be hanging with his crew outside the complex, and he'd call out to me, 'What's up, Ponyboy?'"

"He called you 'Ponyboy,' like Ponyboy Curtis?" Lauren asked.

Gray nodded.

"But you two don't talk anymore?"

"No."

Lauren seemed to know not to ask more. They stood at the top of the steps of the Lincoln Memorial looking out at the reflecting pool, Washington Monument, and Capitol dome cascading in the distance.

"Arturo's just a criminal now," Gray said.

"A criminal who saved us," Lauren observed.

"Not the first time," Gray said.

CHAPTER 25

Gray stuffed the thick SAT prep books into his backpack, his last night class before the big test. It wasn't one of those fancy courses, Princeton Review or PrepMatters, that cost more than his family made in a month. It was a free class, put on once a week by a college student who was earning credit toward her social work degree.

Jane had the look and idealism you'd expect from a young woman who'd teach such a class. She had a plain face—she was plain in most respects—with her practical shoes and frayed college sweatshirt. She was walking proof of what Gray's mom always said about inner beauty shining through. Gray had a crush on her, if he was honest about it.

Jane was at the door saying good-bye to the Rojas sisters, two of the only five students who'd taken the course. Gray purposefully hung back.

"So, you think you're ready for the test?" Jane said, as she packed up her things.

"Thanks to you, yes."

"You're gonna do great," she said with that enthusiasm of hers.

"I thought I knew the content pretty well," Gray said, "but I would've never guessed there were so many tricks and strategies to just taking the test."

"You won't need any tricks." She twisted around as if to make sure the others were gone. "Hey, I don't want you to take this the wrong way—and I know you said you're applying to D.C. State—but, well, your practice scores,

they're impressive. Have you considered looking into the Ivy League?" She hesitated. "I mean, there are scholarships . . ."

Gray smiled, "I'll look into it." He spared her his sob story about needing to stay nearby to help out at the restaurant because of his dad's health.

"Hey, are you hungry?" Gray asked. "My family has a pizza place, and I thought, you know, as a thank you, we could—"

"Ohhhh, I'd normally love to," Jane interrupted. "But I can't tonight." She looked into his eyes. "My boyfriend's meeting me for dinner after class."

The dreaded "boyfriend" line. He hoped it was true and not just a sad dodge. The security guard who escorted Jane to her car mercifully appeared in the classroom's doorway.

"I'll tell you what." Jane pulled out a pen and scribbled something on a sheet of paper. "You call me when you get your SAT results. We'll go out then to celebrate. But I'm buying." Gray waved good-bye, knowing he would never see her again.

Outside, the wind blew hard, the cold air stinging his face as he made his way out the tall fence that surrounded the high school. The next two blocks were the most dangerous at night.

He walked quickly on the broken sidewalk, trying to stay in the shadows. The headlights of a car approached. He could hear the loud bass from the vehicle's sound system. He kneeled next to a parked car, pretending to tie his shoe, until the music trailed off in the distance. He kept walking, relieved that the night would go without incident. Until he heard a voice call out from the stoop of a dilapidated row house.

"What you got in the backpack?"

Gray turned to the stoop. There was the flare of a lighter and bellow of smoke. A kid stepped from the shadows. Angel Ortiz, the heir apparent to the Ortiz throne. The family had run this patch of gloom since before Gray was born. Angel had dropped out of school last year. He was decidedly no angel. Two figures, one holding a bottle wrapped in a brown paper bag, materialized from behind Angel.

Gray kept walking.

"I asked you a question, motherfucker." Angel skipped down the steps and onto the sidewalk.

"I don't have anything. Just some books," Gray said.

"Just some books," Angel repeated in a mocking, exaggerated Caucasian accent. His friends chuckled at that.

"Why you talk so funny? You trying to be some white college boy?"

Gray had heard this before. Gray's mom insisted on proper English, and even bartered with a speech therapist to clean her house in exchange for sessions with Gray and his sister. Beyond his diction, the kids at school somehow took offense at his scholastic endeavors. It had been a season of shoulder bumps and indignities in the halls of Obama High. But it was nothing Gray couldn't handle.

"I don't want any trouble," Gray said.

Angel laughed. "He don't want any trouble," again with the mocking voice. Angel's friends were on the sidewalk now. They wore hoodies and hard faces. Angel jabbed a finger in Gray's chest. "If you don't want no trouble, then why you over here?"

"Look, I don't—" Gray doubled over as Angel sucker punched him in the stomach. For most people, an unexpected blow like that would put them out of commission for two, maybe three minutes. Time for the body to reset, to replenish the oxygen stolen from the lungs. But Gray had spent every Sunday since he was ten at the boxing club with his father. He could take a hit. He'd long wondered if he'd ever have to use his father's training outside the ring. He realized that he'd have little choice tonight. And when you're on the ropes, his father always said, don't forget to still play offense.

Gray jolted upright, and threw a hard right in Angel's face, bringing him down. One of the others took a swing, but Gray bobbed, then returned with an uppercut to the jaw. He went down too. Gray turned to look for the third guy, but then felt a hard blow to the side of his face, the sound of shattering glass. He was on the ground now, his vision blurry. He touched his face and felt wetness. The others then started kicking him. He curled up in a ball, caging his head with his arms. He took a boot to the ribs. A heel slamming his head against the pavement. He was seeing flashes of light and dark, starburst. He started to fear that they were going to kill him.

Then, the beating suddenly stopped.

Through the haze, there were figures moving about.

When they came into focus, Gray saw Arturo. He had a metal wand—like the cops use—and was bringing it down on Angel and his goons. It reminded Gray of an orchestra conductor, or even a ballet dancer, the way Arturo gracefully moved about, the wand slicing the air until it landed with a sickening thud.

Things finally went still. He saw Arturo's hand. Gray grabbed for it and pulled himself up.

"Leave you alone for one fuckin' minute." Arturo examined Gray's face. *"Looks like we're gonna have to get you stitched up."* Arturo ripped off his shirt and handed it to Gray to put on the gash. He then put Gray's arm around his shoulder to help him walk.

"Impressive muscles and tattoos," Gray said. *"But you know I've got a girlfriend, right?"*

Arturo blurted a laugh. *"You wish."*

Angel Ortiz looked up from the ground. His face was bloodied. He then moved like he was trying to get to his feet.

Arturo let out an exasperated sigh. *"Some people just don't learn."* He gently removed Gray's arm from his shoulder. He then stomped Angel back to the ground.

Arturo looked at Angel's two friends. They averted their eyes, stayed down. Arturo then grabbed Angel by the back of his hoodie and pulled him to his feet. He called out to the others.

Their eyes lifted to Arturo, who held up semiconscious Angel by the collar.

"They got the message, man," Gray said.

Arturo said, *"I want you to tell your crew what happens if you mess with us."* He looked at the two boys on the ground, cocked his arm back, and hit Angel square in the face.

Gray saw Angel's eyes roll back in his head before he hit the curb. The sound was the worst part. The crack of skull hitting pavement. Then Angel Ortiz's last ragged breath.

CHAPTER 26

Emma Milstein clenched the wheel of her Toyota with her right hand, her cell phone with her left. She was stuck in morning traffic on the Beltway.

"Sounds like you wasted your night," Cartwright said into the phone.

"The whole thing is a waste of time. Arturo Alvarez has an airtight alibi for the Franklin fire and Dupont Underground killings, he was in prison. I know we need to talk to him, but his connection to the convenience store and the law clerk is thin." Next week would be Thanksgiving. And soon, December 5. And they had nothing. Acid crept up Milstein's throat.

"That's why they call it an investigation, I guess," Cartwright said. "Are you coming in to the office or heading straight to HQ?"

They had an appointment with the FBI general counsel's office to learn more about the convenience store owner's lawsuit against the Bureau. It might explain why the victim's father wouldn't talk to them. And hopefully provide some useful information so they could stop focusing on the bullshit leads, like Alvarez. "It depends on traffic. Don't wait for me if I'm not at the field office in time. I'll just go directly to headquarters."

Milstein heard a beep on the line. "I got another call coming in, I'll talk to you soon." She clicked off.

"It's Simmons," the junior agent said, all business.

Cartwright always joked that the young agent admired Milstein, and tried to mimic Milstein's demeanor. Milstein kind of liked it.

"Hey, what's up?"

"Scott asked me to get some information from Google relating to the Franklin fire."

"Right. They got back to you?"

"Yeah, they ran a report listing every time someone searched for the newspaper reporter's name."

"They get any hits?"

"After filtering out the junk, they found multiple hits for Adam Nowak and, in particular, searches looking for his home address."

Milstein felt a rush of adrenaline. A possible break. If the person who searched for the reporter's address was who broke in to steal his research, it could identify the perp.

"Can they tell us who?"

"Not a person, but a location." Agent Simmons paused a beat. "I'll e-mail you the details, but the searches were on a computer located at One First Street, Northeast."

"Do we know who owns the place?"

"Kind of," the agent said. "It's the Supreme Court."

CHAPTER 27

Gray sat behind his desk, tired from the late night, but electricity was still flowing through him from the encounter with Razor Ortiz and his evening with Lauren. He slugged down more coffee and tried to focus on his work. He was getting close to having a complete first draft of the *Jando* opinion about illegal search and seizure. It wasn't the sexy *Filstein* case on the president's drone program, but Gray treated *Jando* like it was the most important decision of the term. His own *Marbury v. Madison*. He also had to finish a speech the chief was giving later that evening at Georgetown Law.

Lauren appeared at the doorway to his office. She too looked tired, her hair pulled back, small crescents under her eyes. "Hey," she said. She gave a fleeting smile, dimples indenting her cheeks.

"Hey." He let it linger for a moment. Then he noticed she was carrying a bankers box. "What's in the box?"

"It's your lucky day," she said, dropping it on his desktop. "Office rotations. I drew the short straw and got the closet. You're now with Praveen. Mike's with Keir."

The day was starting off well. "So I can move? Right now?"

"Yeah, unless you want to stay, then I'd be happy to—"

"No, I'll go," Gray said, jumping to his feet. Finally, he'd be in close proximity to the chief. And he'd have some company, though Praveen wasn't much of a talker.

Gray picked up a stack of his work papers. "You mind if I come back for the rest later? I can grab the mail cart and get it all in one trip."

"No problem," Lauren said. "I have a question, though, about this office."

"Sure. Is it the smell? You get used to it."

"No, but thanks, now I'm fixated on it." Lauren wrinkled her nose. "My question is whether it's always so empty on this hall? I mean, does anyone ever come up here?"

"Not really. The chief came by once, but I don't think I've ever seen anyone on the hall after-hours."

"Well, maybe that's when you should come by to get your things." She held his glance for a long moment.

"Maybe I will," he said. "If you play your cards right."

As he walked to his new office, his cell phone rang. The caller ID showed no name, but he recognized the number from last night.

"Hello," Gray whispered as he stepped down the stairs to the main floor of the court.

"It's Agent Milstein."

"Look, I'm sorry Arturo took off. He wasn't running from you. It was—"

"We can talk about that later. For now, I wondered if you could do me a favor?"

Gray stopped in the Great Hall next to a bust of Chief Justice Rehnquist. "What do you need?" Some tourists were at the roped-off entrance to the courtroom chamber, more annoying selfies.

"I need you to find a computer for me."

"What do you mean? Find what computer?"

"A computer in the court. I have a terminal number, OFS087, and I need to know who it belongs to."

"How would I figure that out? I'm not a tech person. I don't run the computer system."

"I thought the computers might have some identification port or stamps on them. It would help a lot if you could check."

"Why don't you just ask the court's police? They could get the tech people to give you this information in five minutes." He was starting to think that Milstein wasn't supposed to be talking to him. "There's probably more than a thousand computers in the building. I don't know how I'll—"

"I have to go now. Please, Grayson. The ID is OFS087." She clicked off.

CHAPTER 28

Milstein and Cartwright walked the long hall of FBI headquarters. The famously ugly building had seen better days. It wasn't as prestigious to work out of the field office over on Fourth Street, just five blocks away, but at least you didn't have to worry about breathing in mold or the other toxins that floated in the air at HQ. The building was so bad that soon headquarters would be shuttered and thousands of FBI employees relocated to a new building in the suburbs. As usual, though, politics had the project delayed.

They found the general counsel's office and checked in for their appointment. As they sat in the plain reception area, Milstein filled in Cartwright on the information Agent Simmons had obtained from Google: someone had used a computer at the Supreme Court to search for Adam Nowak's home address. Milstein didn't mention that she'd asked the law clerk to hunt for the computer in the Supreme Court. They'd been ordered to steer clear of SCOTUS, so better that she left Cartwright out of it.

Cartwright nodded with approval, then said, "You feeling okay? You look a little peaked."

Milstein presumed it was the bags under her eyes and the wrinkled clothes. The temp apartment, and this fucking case, were getting to her. And that was nothing compared to the interagency politics. A Homeland team was investigating the Franklin fire, the

Supreme Court's squad was handling the attack on the chief, and she had Dupont Underground and the convenience store. Each guarding its turf, as Aaron Dowell made a play for a task force that would take over everything.

"I'm fine," she said. "Thanks for your concern." There was more sarcasm in that than she'd intended.

"Hey, I spoke with Peggy, and we wondered if you'd like to come to our place for Thanksgiving? The kids would love to see you. It's just gonna be us and some of Peggy's family and—"

Milstein stood up quickly when the woman came into the reception area, mostly so she could end the discussion. She loved Scott's family, but the sweet cliché of the Cartwrights wasn't going to make her feel any better.

"I'm Liz Evanson," the young woman said, sticking out her hand. She had dull brown hair and serious eyes, a no-nonsense way about her. Milstein immediately liked her. Evanson escorted them to a conference room. Next to a long table sat a dozen bankers boxes.

"This is what's left of the file," Evanson said, gesturing to the boxes. "The rest has been purged. You were lucky we had these since we keep hard copies for only about ten years, usually. No one uses paper files anymore." The young woman smirked, the superiority of a millennial.

"Are any of the lawyers who worked the case still here?" Cartwright asked.

Evanson shook her head. Turnover at HQ tended to track the election cycle.

"Can we get a copy of all this?"

"I hate to say it, but our policy is that nothing leaves the building," Evanson said. "You're welcome to use the room as long as you'd like, though."

Cartwright exhaled loudly as he surveyed the boxes. "We're not lawyers," Cartwright said, "so I'm not sure where to even start."

"Are you permitted to disclose what you're looking for?" The young lawyer had been around long enough to know that information often was need-to-know.

Cartwright smiled. "If we knew what we were looking for, I'd tell you. Hey, you're not related to Hank Evanson, are you?"

The woman nodded. "He's my uncle."

Cartwright clapped his hands together. "I could see it in the eyes. I saw him on TV a couple weeks ago protecting the pres." Cartwright looked at Milstein. "He's secret service."

Milstein nodded. "I kinda got that."

Cartwright said, "Tell him hello from me. It's been too long." "I'll do that."

Cartwright then cast his gaze over the bankers boxes again, shaking his head.

Evanson pulled out the index that was on top of the first box. "If I was trying to get up to speed, I'd start with box number eight. It's the settlement file. This case settled so if things haven't changed too much since then, there should be a settlement memo. Main Justice handles the actual litigation in civil cases filed against the Bureau, but our office is copied on important filings, and included on key decisions, especially settlements. There should be a memo explaining why we should spend Uncle Sam's money to settle the case."

Milstein lifted the box labeled "8" and set it on the table.

Cartwright took off his jacket and hung it on the back of the chair. He smiled at Evanson. "Looks like I need to cancel some plans."

Evanson hesitated, then said, "Tell you what. If you sign for them, and *promise* to keep them secure, I'll have a copy of the file made and sent to the field office. I'll try to get them to you next week before everyone takes off for Thanksgiving, but no promises."

Milstein gazed at Cartwright. He never disappointed.

"You'd do that? I don't want to get you in any trouble," Cartwright said.

"Don't worry about it."

"That's just great, Liz. Just like your uncle. You're good people."

Evanson chuckled, as if she knew she'd been played. "I'm just down the hall if you need anything."

Milstein rummaged through the box and soon found a memorandum with the subject line SETTLEMENT RECOMMENDATION— CONFIDENTIAL. She read the memo as Cartwright poked around in another box.

"No way," Milstein said.

"What?" Cartwright said, excited. He scooched next to her at the conference room table, trying to read the memo over her shoulder.

Milstein said, "This explains why Matsuka won't talk to the Bureau. This guy wasn't just beaten by the agent, he was nearly killed."

"Does it say why, what it was all about?" Cartwright asked.

"Yeah, a kidnapping case in the nineties." Milstein kept reading as she simultaneously paraphrased for Cartwright. "Two young girls, sisters, were abducted. Their teenage brother apparently tried to stop the perp and was knocked on the head, suffered a traumatic brain injury. The last place they were all seen was at Matsuka's convenience store."

"Why'd Matsuka get the beatdown? He wasn't the perp who took the kids, right?"

"A witness reported seeing the kids talking to a worker at the store, Matsuka's cousin, Ken Tanaka. Turned out that Tanaka had priors for molesting a kid. When they couldn't find Tanaka, I guess the agent in charge thought Matsuka was holding out. The agent beat the guy until he gave up the cousin's location. The memo says that the Bureau low-balled the settlement offer because the information the agent beat out of Matsuka helped find Ken Tanaka and they managed to save one of the girls. The other girl was dead by the time they got there."

"If I was on that jury," Cartwright said, "I wouldn't give Matsuka a penny. I don't care if it was his cousin—protecting a child molester warrants a beating."

"Why didn't it come up in our database searches?" Milstein asked.

"I'm not sure, but maybe because the team wasn't searching for anything on Tanaka, the child molester. Or because the files are so old and maybe not in electronic databases. And remember, the storekeeper changed his name—probably because of the shame about helping the perp hide—so computer searches for Matsuka wouldn't get any hits."

"Get this," Milstein said, still reading the memo. "The agent who beat Matsuka—his name is Kevin Dugan—put canned food in a bag and used it to club Matsuka. That's exactly what happened to Matsuka's daughter."

Excited, they spent the next few hours fishing through the boxes. Cartwright found a file that contained photocopies of newspaper stories about the case. "Here we go," he said.

"What?" Milstein said.

Cartwright handed Milstein the photocopy.

"Look who the judge was in the case against the child molester," Cartwright said.

Milstein felt goosebumps ripple up her arms. "I'll do you better than that. Look who wrote the story, and the defense lawyer who represented piece of shit Tanaka."

SUSPECT IN WHITLOCK CASE FREED ON TECHNICALITY
By Adam Nowak
Washington Post Staff Writer

Sunday, April 21, 1997

WASHINGTON, D.C.—A federal district court judge today threw out key evidence against Ken Tanaka in the kidnapping and murder of Kimberley Whitlock and related kidnapping and other charges concerning Kimberley's surviving siblings, John and Susan Whitlock. The children were abducted in the Hamilton Heights neighborhood on January 5 after witnesses saw them talking to Tanaka, who worked at his family's convenience store. District Court Judge Edgar Douglas held that "the rule of law compels this difficult decision," because the evidence that led to Tanaka's arrest was obtained in violation of his constitutional rights. Tanaka's public defender, Amanda Hill, could not be reached for comment.

Cartwright smiled. "No, I can one-up that. Look at the date the kids were abducted." He placed a finger on the newspaper story. "The fifth of the month."

CHAPTER 29

"You ready to go?" the chief justice asked.

Gray held the phone to his ear as he put on his suit jacket. "I am. Just printed the speech."

"Great, meet me at the car."

Georgetown University Law Center was only a short walk from the Supreme Court building, but the court's police insisted on escorting the justices to all public events. With rush-hour traffic, it took the motorcade of black Cadillacs twenty minutes to go less than a mile. The chief read the speech on the drive over.

"Well done, Grayson. Nice work," the chief said, folding up the speech and tucking it in his suit pocket.

The event turned out to be a bigger production than Gray had anticipated. The large auditorium was filled to capacity with students, academics, and a cast of VIPs. The chief and Gray were ushered around like temperamental rock stars, everyone anxious that they were properly accommodated. The chief was good-natured about it. He was gracious with his time and acquiesced to the repeated requests for photos.

At six o'clock, the dean strutted onto the stage. Gray stood in the wings and stared out at the crowd, which cheered loudly. The dean gave what could only be described as an over-the-top love-fest of an introduction. Gray almost blushed for the guy. He supposed that in this economy—with law school applications plummeting and grads coming out of school $200,000 in debt with few job prospects—being a law school dean was probably a tough business. Reeling in a Supreme Court justice was a major coup. The chief waited next to Gray, no sign of nerves. Not a care in the world.

The dean was starting to wrap it up. "Before we bring out the chief justice, we have a surprise for him tonight." The dean gave a conspiratorial smile.

The chief looked at Gray. His brow furrowed, as if Gray was in on it.

"No idea," Gray said.

The dean continued. "It is a rare honor for us to have *one* sitting member of the Supreme Court come speak at the Law Center. But when word got out that the chief justice would be here—and he would be receiving a lifetime achievement award—we got a call from a very special guest who graciously offered to present him with tonight's honor."

The room went quiet. Gray felt someone push by. Then he heard a familiar voice. "Step aside, Bones," the man said as he walked confidently onto the stage.

The dean continued, "Ladies and gentleman, with us to present the award is Justice Peter Wall." The room erupted. Springsteen making a surprise guest appearance at a New Jersey night club.

Wall turned and gave a smirk to the chief, who was smiling and shaking his head. Wall stood at the podium, playfully swatting down the applause. When the room settled, he began.

"Lifetime achievement award." Wall said it with a sigh. "When I heard that my oldest friend would be receiving this tonight, I have to admit, my first thought was, 'Are we really *that* old?'" A titter from the audience. "But, if there's anyone in this country who has *achieved*—and I mean that in the best sense of the word—it is Chief Justice Douglas." More applause filled the hall.

Wall paused a beat and looked out at the room with a contemplative stare. "I met Ed in high school and we became fast friends, and later roomed together in college. Those carefree days—the pleasures of dorm life of which I suspect a few of you know—were some of the best of my life." He let the students snicker at the implications of that.

"Back then, I never would have imagined that our paths would intersect so often in life. College, then law school—I couldn't shake this skinny guy who was always beating me out in everything we did." More laughter.

"But after law school, we parted ways for a time. I worked as a federal prosecutor, and he went to a large law firm. I thought *finally* I'll be able to get somewhere without being in this guy's shadow." Wall took a sip from a glass of water. "But then I got a call about an interview for my dream job: a position with the Office of the Solicitor General. Now, for those of you who aren't familiar with OSG, back then—as it is today, I suppose—it was the most sought-after law job in the country. The principal task of the office is to represent the federal government before the Supreme Court. It was a small office that rarely had openings. So I got to Washington in my new suit and fresh haircut and I was ushered up to the fifth floor of the Justice Department. I spent the morning meeting everyone and things, I thought, were going pretty well. They made a point of telling me that only one spot was available, but I tell you, I believed it was mine. So, then came lunchtime and two assistant SGs took me to out to an extravagant lunch: the cafeteria in the basement of Main Justice. And when I got down there I couldn't believe what I saw." He paused a moment. "It was Ed standing in line with his food tray with two of the other lawyers I'd met that morning: he was interviewing for the same job." Another burst of laughter from the audience.

"It got worse. In some kind of Machiavellian interview tactic, the lawyers from OSG didn't dine with us. They pointed to a two-seater in the back and had me and Ed eat together. I'm not sure if it was because they knew that we were old friends or if it was some test. Maybe they just didn't want to spend lunch with us. But there we were again." He let a moment pass, allowing the audience to picture the scene. "Why do I bring all this up? Besides highlighting that we are indeed *old*, you would think that the ambitious young version of myself would take a disliking to the person who always seemed one step ahead, beating me out of everything. But that was never the case. Even back then, you couldn't help but like and admire Ed. He was then, as he is today, a person of character, of charm, of wit. A person who made *you* a better person. And I feel as though I'm certainly a better person today because of him. So here we are, decades later, and it is my great honor to present this lifetime achievement award to my colleague, my brethren, my closest friend, the chief justice of the United States."

The crowd went nuts over Wall's remarks. The chief patted Gray on the back and walked in that slow and steady stride of his to the podium where he and Wall locked hands and then pulled to an embrace. There was something storied about it all. These two brilliant men went from school boys to the highest court in the land and remained the closest of friends. Gray thought about his childhood friends, Sam and Arturo.

The chief justice waited for what seemed like forever for the applause to die down. "I want to thank the dean and my dear friend Justice Wall for those kind remarks. Peter was too modest to finish the story about our lunch in the Justice Department building. *He* got the job, not me. As it turns out, though, they had another unexpected opening and we both were hired. I like to blame me losing out initially on the fact that I fell ill after lunch and I performed terribly in the afternoon interview with the solicitor general. I felt great all morning and then *wham*." The chief smacked his hand on the podium. "Right after lunch, it hit me, I had no idea whether it was the flu or what." The chief then gave a broad smile. "But, now that I think about it, during lunch I left Peter at the table to get some napkins, and when I returned my drink tasted funny . . ."

CHAPTER 30

Milstein and Cartwright had their first real break. Not a tenuous connection between a local crime boss and one of the victims, not a hunch about a Google search from a computer in the Supreme Court, but a real lead. Amanda Hill, the lawyer killed in Dupont Underground, had represented the man accused of abducting the Whitlock kids. Sakura Matsuka was the daughter of the man beaten by an agent investigating the kidnapping. And Chief Justice Douglas was the trial judge who had thrown out evidence that allowed the perpetrator to go free. The targets of the killer were all connected to the Whitlock case. And they were all killed on the fifth of the month, the same day the Whitlock kids were abducted.

"Peggy okay with you staying late?" Milstein asked. They were still at headquarters, eating Chinese takeout in the conference room.

"No." Cartwright smiled.

Milstein stabbed her chopsticks into the rice container. "So who would have a motive to kill people connected to the Whitlock case?"

"Ordinarily, I'd start with the perp, Ken Tanaka," Cartwright said, "but he's dead."

"Yep. Simmons just texted me more details. Two years after they threw out the evidence against him in the Whitlock case

Tanaka moved to Pennsylvania. Worked as an ice cream man, and molested two other kids. He was killed in prison by another inmate."

"Who said there's no justice?" Cartwright said.

Milstein considered who else would have the motive to kill Tanaka's defense lawyer, the judge who allowed him to go free, and the daughter of the man who tried to protect a child molester.

"How about the parents of the Whitlock kids?" Cartwright asked.

"Also dead."

"Is anyone associated with this clusterfuck of a case alive?"

"The kids didn't have a father in the picture. And their mother killed herself shortly after the perp went free."

"Those kids just couldn't catch a break."

"Speaking of the kids, how about them?" Milstein asked.

"We know whoever attacked the chief justice was a man," Cartwright said, writing on a legal pad. "The Whitlock boy would be in his thirties now. We can start there. We'll also try to track down his sister."

Milstein tapped on her phone, texting Simmons to make finding the Whitlock brother a priority. "Beyond the family," she said, "how about the agent who beat the storekeeper? I don't think it's a coincidence that Sakura Matsuka was beaten with a bag full of canned food from the store—the same way the agent beat her father."

Cartwright nodded. "I've already e-mailed records to pull Kevin Dugan's Bureau file."

"Why kill the convenience store owner's daughter, though? She was only a kid at the time all this happened. It was her old man who was protecting a child molester, not her."

Cartwright added, "And if it's John Whitlock or Kevin Dugan, why the games with the feather pens and the Supreme Court? I don't get it."

"What I don't get," Milstein said, "is why the chief justice didn't mention the Whitlock case to us."

"That's a good question. We should ask him," Cartwright said, pouring a full packet of soy sauce on his noodles.

"Aaron won't let us."

"You don't think he's keeping stuff from us, do you? Covering for the justices?"

"That's a good question too." Milstein pinched the bridge of her nose. "We've got only two weeks before the fifth of the month, Scott."

"We'll find him, Em. We've got to."

CHAPTER 31

It was nine at night, and Gray packed up his things to head for home. He wished Lauren hadn't left the office before he got back from Georgetown so he could make that visit to her office she'd mentioned, but she was gone. He thought about Agent Milstein's call, her request that he hunt around for a computer. He wasn't comfortable providing information from the court to an outsider, but he still hadn't shaken the photos of the little girl murdered in the filthy catacombs of Dupont Underground. Or the bloody, swollen face of the woman at the convenience store. He didn't know a thing about the court's computer system, but he examined his own computer and found a placard with an ID number: OFS102. Milstein wanted him to find OFS087. It stood to reason that the 100 series meant computers on the first floor, and 0 series the ground floor, though he was just guessing. Praveen was still pecking away on his keyboard, so Gray couldn't check Praveen's computer to confirm. If he was right, then Milstein's suspect was someone on the ground floor. That floor had hundreds of employees, including the clerk's office, the police office, the gift shop, and the cafeteria. It also housed the cube farm for the marshal's aides where Gray used to work. Since the marshal's aides distributed the feather pens before oral arguments, it made sense to start there. Gray left his office and headed downstairs. On the way, he ran into Mike in the hallway. He had a messenger bag slung over his shoulder.

"How was the speech?" Mike asked.

"It went over well. Justice Wall made a surprise appearance and introduced the chief."

"I heard. The Wonder Twins." Mike rolled his eyes. "You got off easy. I've got to prepare questions for the chief's Shakespeare trial." The Shakespeare Theatre Company held an annual mock trial based on Shakespeare's plays, and the chief and other justices often served as judges. "I can barely keep up with our real cases, now I get to read *Twelfth Night* in my free time. Why can't the justices just Netflix and chill like the rest of us?"

Gray laughed. "You getting out of here?"

"Meeting up with a girl I met on Tinder." Mike grinned. "I can see if she has a friend . . ."

"As inviting as meeting a stranger from the Internet sounds, I'll pass."

"You sure? It could be *interesting*." Mike pulled his hand out of his jacket pocket, raised his fist in the air, and released a string of condoms, letting them dangle.

Gray smiled in spite of himself. "Really, I can't." Looking at the condoms, he added, "And those are too small for me, anyway. I need Magnums." The guy was rubbing off on him.

"A'ight, then," he said. "I'll give you a full report in the morning." He started to walk away, but stopped. "You're not coming because of work, right?" He hesitated. "Not because of Lauren?"

Gray tried not to react. "Lauren? Why would—"

Mike held up a hand.

"Just be careful with that, okay?"

Mike telling someone to be careful. That was rich. But what did he mean?

Gray walked to the ground floor. The broad corridor was empty, and his footsteps echoed distantly. He thought about his days as a marshal's aide, how long ago it seemed. He stopped in front of the keypad at the door to the cube farm. He punched in the code from when he worked in the office: 1234. The four-digit code still worked. When you have an entire police station in the building, a certain casualness to security takes hold. He hesitated, but made his way into the office, which was lit only by the glow from the exit signs.

He scanned the rows of cubicles, and it took him back to those Sunday nightshifts when he was an aide. His sister was right: he hadn't been Sunday boxing with his father since he'd started as a clerk. He should try to go this week. He gazed about the open space, his eyes settling on Martin Melnick's office in the back. As good a place to start as any.

Stepping quietly, he moved to Martin's glass-walled office. Martin had left the desk lamp on. There were stacks of papers and twisted paperclips. Gray leaned over to inspect the computer tower, looking for the ID placard. Before he found it, he was startled by a voice.

"Slumming?"

Gray leapt up to find Martin standing there holding a McDonald's bag.

"Hey, Martin. Sorry, I've been trying to find my phone charger and thought maybe it was here."

"Under my desk?" Martin plopped down and pulled out his Quarter Pounder and fries. "I didn't take it if that's what you think."

"No, of course not. I used to plug my phone into a power strip over here, and kept meaning to come by to check if my charger was still there." He looked down and there was no power strip.

Martin took a mouthful of the burger and ketchup ran down his chin.

"Anyway, I guess it's not here. Hey, why're you here so late?" Gray said, changing the subject. "You're working too hard."

"Believe it or not, it's not only the clerks who work hard."

Gray realized that, to Martin, Gray had crossed over to the dark side.

"Have a good night." He could feel Martin's hard glare following him out. He'd be unable to search the remaining computers with Martin there.

When he made his way back to his office, Praveen had left for the night. It was rare for him to leave before ten o'clock. The guy was a machine. Gray eyed Praveen's workspace. Every clerk station had two separate computer systems, one for court business that was connected only to an intranet, where they stored the pool memos and other court documents. The other computer for Internet searches, e-mail, or anything external. Praveen's everything-else computer was logged in. Gray rolled his office chair to Praveen's workstation and leaned down to examine the computer tower tucked under the desk. He found the ID number.

OFS087

Gray jammed his hand in his pocket to pull out the scrap of paper where he'd written the ID number Milstein had given him. He wasn't seeing things. It was the same number.

CHAPTER 32

Why was Milstein looking for Praveen's computer? What did it mean? Gray glanced at the computer screen again. He shouldn't. But a quick peek wouldn't hurt anyone. Gray pulled down his co-clerk's Google search history. The guy wasn't one to mindlessly surf the Web, so all Gray expected to find were searches relating to the court's work. That was most of it. Hein Online, Google Scholar, Westlaw. But one entry jumped out at him. A Google map of a residential address in Arlington, Virginia. The time stamp showed that Praveen made the search fifteen minutes ago.

Gray heard someone in the hall so he quickly clicked out. The custodian came in and began emptying the trash bins. The clerks' work papers went in shred boxes, designated for destruction, not the ordinary trash cans. Those mostly contained empty take-out food containers and Red Bull cans. Gray waved at the woman, who wore ear buds, and she gave him a quick smile. He noticed something in Praveen's trash bin. A crumpled bag with the Capitol Hardware logo on it. That was unusual. The store was at Tenleytown, a long subway ride away. And Praveen didn't exactly seem like the home-improvement type.

When the custodian's back was to him, Gray lifted the bag from the can and looked inside. It was empty except for a receipt at the bottom. He'd gone this far, so why not? He fished out the receipt and waited for the woman to finish her work before examining it. He then flattened the small crinkled piece of paper on his desk. The itemized purchases took his breath away. Duct tape. Nylon cord. A pair of pliers. It read like a serial killer's grocery list. Gray was letting his imagination get the best of him. Then he thought of the Google map. If Praveen was about to do something insidious, shouldn't he try to stop it?

That question continued to bandy about his head as he sat in the car outside a house in Arlington, Virginia. It didn't look like a serial killer's lair. It was a Colonial on a quiet street. The house had a FOR SALE sign in its front yard. Praveen's Ford Fusion was parked discreetly down the street, which was unusual if only because of the empty spaces in front of the house. So the question now was what to do? If Praveen had bought the tools for butchery—yes, he kept reminding himself how ridiculous that sounded—should Gray just wait for it to happen? He should call Agent Milstein. Or 911. No, he'd look stupid. He was being foolish.

The place was dark, no porch light on. He was about to leave when he saw a flicker of light coming from one of the basement windows. Maybe he'd go have a quick look. A young Mexican American leering in windows in this neighborhood probably wasn't a great idea. He argued with himself for another minute, but soon was walking up the path. As he got closer to the front steps he could see flashing lights escaping through the slits in the blinds covering the basement window.

He ducked around to the side. Crouching on his heels, he peered into the window. A small vibration rattled in his chest, the bass drum from loud music. Or was that his heartbeat? The light continued to strobe, now changing colors. It was blue and moved to the beat of the music. He thought he could make out two masses. One of the forms was reaching toward the ceiling—dancing? But the arms weren't moving. Gray felt a jolt when the other figure seemed to be lashing at the person whose arms were raised. It was then that he understood. The figure was tied up, hanging from a support beam in the basement.

CHAPTER 33

"Nine-one-one, what is your emergency?"

"You need to get to Eighteen Taft Street in Arlington. Someone is being attacked," Gray said into the phone. He was pacing small circles in the patch of yard at the side of the house.

"Who's being attacked? Sir, could you please slow down."

"Eighteen Taft—just get here!" Gray clicked off. He'd tried calling Agent Milstein, but it went to voice mail. He'd left a message, so between that and 911, help would arrive soon.

He paced some more, listening for sirens. Was he really just going to wait outside? His pulse thumped at his temples. The little girl in Dupont Underground sprang to mind. Her delicate neck purple from bruises.

Gray swallowed hard, and ran up the brick portico to the front door. He saw one of those boxes realtors store keys in, not secured on the door handle, but lodged in the space between the screen and front door. The hinges squeaked as he opened the screen a gap. Gray looked around the neighborhood. The nearest house was at the mouth of the cul-de-sac. He turned the door's handle quietly, and it was unlocked.

The main floor was dark, but he didn't turn on the lights. The beat of the music was coming up from the basement, vibrating the hardwood and up his legs, which only elevated his anxiety.

He should leave. Why on earth would he take this risk? Was it that he subconsciously liked playing the hero?

Feeling his way to the kitchen, he rummaged the drawers until he found a large chef's knife. The music, some kind of scream metal, was seeping out from a door just outside the kitchen. The door to the basement.

Gray turned the door handle, his mind flashing to *Silence of the Lambs* and Clarice Starling stumbling around in the dark, music blaring, as the skin-taking killer stalked her through his night-vision goggles. He should sprint out the door and wait for the police. But he stepped, one foot at a time, down into the seizure-inducing strobe lights of the basement, knife clutched in his hand. His plan was simple: turn on the lights to disorient, then charge Praveen.

The screaming from the singer over the distorted guitars was unsettling, and Gray felt a prickling sensation all over his body now. He could make out the figures. The one whose hands were tied to the support beam overhead was moaning now, and the other figure was in front of the bound mass.

Gray found the light switch, and counted down in his head.

Three. Two. One. And he clicked on the light.

CHAPTER 34

If Gray hadn't been so goddamned scared, his hands shaking, his clothes damp with sweat, he might have seen the comedy in it. Praveen's expression was priceless. Eyes wide, naked except for a pair of black chaps with the crotch cut out, hands tied loosely on a beam above him. His partner, a muscular guy in his early twenties, in a similar getup. On his knees with whipped cream all over his face, presumably the same stuff covering Praveen's junk. A pair of pliers on the concrete floor nearby. There was also a glass pipe.

Any violence going on here was consensual. Praveen's hardware-shopping list suddenly took on a whole different light. The duct tape, to bind hands, the cord, to playfully lash one another, and the pliers—Gray didn't want to think about what those were for.

The three men stood there frozen for what seemed like an eternity. Then came the heavy boots thundering above them and stomping down the basement steps. Gray stood shell-shocked as an officer held a gun at him.

"Drop the weapon! Do it or I'll shoot!"

It was then Gray realized that he still clutched the kitchen knife. He let it fall to the ground and the steel clanked on the cement floor. Gray soon was on the ground, a knee rammed in his back, arms yanked behind him. He saw one of the officers roughly pull Praveen's arms free from the support beam, and both he and his paramour were on the ground now too.

"This is a mistake," Gray heard himself say.

After the police had the scene under control, Gray heard the officers snickering as they assessed the various sex toys and gear strewn about the room. Praveen said something, but Gray couldn't make it out.

"Tell it to the judge, ladies," one of the officers said.

Gray had long worried about how he'd mess things up for himself at the Supreme Court. He'd recommend a *cert* grant for a clearly unworthy case, he'd write a bench memo that failed to catch a key issue, he'd draft an opinion the chief found amateurish. But never—not once—had he entertained the thought that his downfall would come from being caught in a basement with another clerk, bondage gear, and drugs. A blaze of glory, it wasn't.

CHAPTER 35

Gray and Praveen sat in the back of the police cruiser. Gray tried apologizing to Praveen, but his co-clerk held a blank stare, lost in his own head. The clerks had never suspected Praveen was gay, much less that he engaged in Craigslist hookups. Frankly, they never thought of Praveen as anything but a serious little work machine.

Gray had tried to explain their way out of the arrests. He was a lawyer, he mistook the situation, there was no crime, they were consenting adults. But Gray overheard the cops talking. As it turned out, Praveen and his friend—who'd been shuttled away in another cop car—had broken into the house. The other guy's mother was a realtor, and he'd used her lockbox code to get into the property. It wasn't the first time. And the kicker: that glass pipe.

Gray gazed absently out the window of the cruiser, the street-lights streaming by, the cops up front separated by the mesh cage. He was reminded of the last time he'd been in the back of a patrol car.

"When do we get to talk to a lawyer?" Arturo asked.

Sam, who was crammed next to Gray and Arturo in the back-seat, was crying, shaking her head for Arturo to shush.

The cops ignored him. Arturo raised his voice. "I asked you a question."

The cop in the passenger seat up front twisted around. "Shut the fuck up!" The guy had seen-it-all eyes and seemed exasperated about having to take a group of middle schoolers to the station house for joyriding. The end of his shift probably.

"We got rights," Arturo said.

The cop chuckled. "Tell that to your new friends in the cell when they bend you over."

At that, Gray joined Sam with the tears.

But there was no cell or abusive cellmates. Just a waiting room with walls covered in anti-crime posters. A teenager in cuffs: DRUGS COST MORE THAN YOUR BRAIN CELLS. *A little girl alone on a swing:* ARE YOU GOING TO BE THERE WHEN SHE NEEDS A PUSH? END GANG LIFE.

And then Dad appeared at the door. He looked tired, angry. A man in a suit was with him, skinny with a beard. Dad's expression softened when he got a look at Sam.

"Let's go," he said, gesturing to the door.

"Dad, I'm sorry, we—"

Dad held up a hand, and Gray knew better than to keep talking. He and Sam kept the waterworks going as they sauntered out. Not Arturo; he strutted, as if he didn't have a care in the world.

When Arturo arrived at school the next day, he had two black eyes and a split lip.

One of the cops up front said something into the radio. Gray couldn't make it out, but the officer sounded angry. Gray knew the feeling. He cursed ever meeting Agent Milstein. She'd sucked him into all this. Asking for his help. Showing him crime scene photos. Feeding his imagination.

"There," one of the cops said, intruding on Gray's thoughts. The police cruiser rolled to a stop.

A wave of worry traveled through him. They weren't at the station house. A highway underpass. It was all graffiti and grime.

"Why are we stopping? What's going on?" Praveen asked, his tone laced with fear.

One of the cops got out of the car. He opened the rear door and roughly put a hand on top of Praveen's head as he hoisted him out. Gray watched as they escorted Praveen away. An interior light flashed from a Suburban tucked away near some brush by the underpass. There was a silhouette of a sedan parked next to the SUV.

The officers uncuffed Praveen and marched him to the Suburban. What the hell was going on? The back door of the Suburban opened, and a weary-looking Indian man climbed out. He said something to the officers, who nodded and then walked back to the patrol car. The Indian man barked something at Praveen, who looked at the ground. The man yelled something again, and Praveen lifted his head timidly. The man slapped Praveen hard across the face. Gray understood now. Praveen's father. When Praveen was arrested someone must have called his old man, the White House chief of staff. Strings were being pulled.

But without someone to save Gray, what would they do with him? That question was answered when the black sedan's door opened.

CHAPTER 36

"That was a stupid move, calling 911," Agent Milstein said. She started the engine and tore out from the underpass, the tires flinging rocks against the wheel wells. She made her way from the murky side streets to the interstate. "What were you thinking?"

"I don't know. You asked me to find the computer at the court. It was Praveen's. Then I guess my imagination got the best of me."

"Ya think?" Milstein said. She kept her eyes on the road. "If you thought he was up to something, you should have called me *before* you went to the house, not after. You should've waited. Not gone off like some bull in a china shop. If you would've called, I could've told you that we know Praveen isn't the perp." She jerked the wheel, racing around other cars.

"How was I supposed to know that? You haven't exactly been a fountain of information. I was just trying to help." Gray wondered if the feds had investigated everyone at the court. With more than four hundred employees, that seemed unlikely. They probably narrowed the field, focusing on men. The male clerks were a good place to start.

Milstein drove in silence for another few minutes. Finally, she said, "Look, I know this is stressful and we appreciate your help. I should've been—" She hesitated. "I should've been more forthcoming. I'm sorry, and I want you to know that I do appreciate that you've been trying to help."

Gray let out a breath. His heart rate was returning to normal. "It's okay. You're right, it was stupid."

"No, I actually should've never involved you."

There was a long silence. Gray stared out the window as Milstein finally pulled off the interstate. He looked at the agent. "If you tell me what you're looking for, I might be able to help."

"We've got a solid lead now. I think you should stick to being a law clerk."

"Seriously, I wanna help. But I can't if I don't know what I'm looking for."

Milstein seemed to be deliberating whether to say more. She let out a breath through her nose. "This will sound unusual, but is there anyone around the court who likes owls?"

"Owls? Like the bird?"

"Yeah, you know, anyone a bird watcher or collect figurines of owls or seem to have an interest?"

"Not that I can think of."

"How about the name 'Whitlock?' Have you heard anyone mention the name or a case from the nineties?"

Gray shook his head.

Milstein pulled up to Gray's place in Georgetown.

"How'd you know I moved? How'd you—"

Milstein gave him a look.

"Thanks for helping me tonight," Gray said.

"My pleasure," Milstein said dryly. "Go be a law clerk, Grayson."

Gray got out and watched the car fade into the night. He could've lost everything tonight. He decided he should follow Milstein's advice. Leave the investigation to the professionals. Focus on being a law clerk. This once-in-a-lifetime opportunity he'd been given. If there was a killer amongst them, the FBI would find him. He hoped.

CHAPTER 37

The next time Gray saw Praveen it was, well, awkward. Gray arrived at work around seven-thirty, but Praveen had been there for some time, already buried in a stack of briefs. Praveen lifted his head, said hello, but that was all they spoke of it. So for the next three hours they worked in silence, the only sound the clicking of computer keyboards. The buzz of the intercom broke the quiet. From the speaker, Olga said, "The chief wants to see you and Praveen—now."

The floor fell out from under him. Had the chief found out about the arrest? Praveen too looked like he'd been punched in the gut. Gray considered for a moment working out their story, but decided that they needed to just go take their medicine.

They made the death march to chambers. The chief was standing behind his desk, yelling into the phone. Keir was there, and looked at the floor when he saw them. Had that little punk found out and told on them? That son-of-a—

"You tell her I won't stand for it," the chief barked into the phone. "I won't. For the rest of her days in this building she can count on getting assigned every boring piece-of-shit opinion we get. A lifetime of dogs." The chief listened again, and his face reddened. "You just fucking tell her!" The chief slammed down the phone.

Gray had never seen him lose his cool before. The funny thing was that the episode had the opposite effect on Gray. Praveen also looked like a weight had been lifted. They were summoned to chambers not because of Praveen's *Fifty Shades of Grey* incident, but instead something about one of the cases.

The chief turned his attention to the clerks. "Cutler changed her vote on the *Filstein* case." Gray immediately understood the significance. It was the biggest case of the term. The president's drone policy. The vote initially was five-four with the chief in the majority. Gray recalled the clerk happy hour when Keir said Cutler was joining the chief's side, giving him the fifth vote. But she must've changed her mind, turning a win for the chief into a loss. If Cutler flipped, Keir's draft of the chief's majority opinion would become the *dissenting* opinion.

The chief's jaw set. He looked at the three clerks. "I need you to talk to Cutler's clerks. Find out what you can. Also, talk to Justice Marcus's clerks, see if there's any way we can bring Marcus over to our side. You tell his clerks I'll owe him." The chief paused. "Where the hell are Lauren and Mike? We need them on this too."

It was not uncommon for justices to use their clerks to backchannel. Academics referred to it as the "clerk network." Gray doubted anything would change the vote, but he was just happy that he wasn't explaining Praveen's escapade.

The chief was breathing heavily. He turned and slammed his fist on the desktop. "Cutler *will not* get the best of me."

CHAPTER 38

Milstein stood in line at a food truck parked in front of the field office. There was a line of a half-dozen trucks, most painted in primary colors with giant logos on their sides. Milstein's truck sold Lebanese street food, and her mouth watered thinking of the shawarma sandwich. She wasn't supposed to eat at any of the trucks. The head of the field office had banned FBI personnel from patronizing them since he viewed large vehicles so close to the building a safety risk. But the shawarma was worth Neal's wrath. Milstein's phone chimed and she glanced at the caller ID. She immediately stepped out of line.

"Special Agent Milstein," she said, in her usual annoyed phone voice.

"This is Doctor Ladner from Hayfield Correctional."

"Thank you for getting back to me so soon, doctor," she said, hoping he might catch the sarcasm since she'd left him an urgent message a couple days ago. Milstein walked on the red brick that lined the front of the field office to a secluded spot near some shrubs. "We need some information on one of your former patients, John Whitlock."

"Yes, I got your message. I remember John, though I can't discuss anything specific about our sessions. They may be prisoners, but I still owe them a duty of confidentiality."

"Understood. We're having trouble finding Whitlock and wanted to see if you had any insights as to where he might go? We were told that he didn't have any close friends on the inside, but that you were someone who got to know him."

"Is he in some kind of trouble?"

"I can't divulge the specifics, but we need to speak with him. It relates to what happened to him when he was a boy." Milstein decided against suggesting that Whitlock was a suspect himself. She sensed that the doctor was invested in Whitlock and might be more forthcoming if he thought he was helping his former patient.

"I don't know where John is. When he's off his medication, he often turns to the streets. We made good progress. But unfortunately, they don't get the support when they're on the outside."

"Does he have any family that would take him in? Any friends?"

"If I recall, John never knew his father, and his mother passed away when he was a boy." This Milstein already knew.

"How about other family?"

"Not that I'm aware of. He was placed in the system after his mother died. I believe his younger sister was adopted, but not John. If he had any other family, they likely couldn't deal with raising someone with a significant disability."

"You mean John's brain injury?"

"Exactly. You can imagine how hard it is to adopt a kid in his teens, much less one with baggage and a disability. The system bounced him around until he was eighteen, then released him into the wild with no skills. It was only a matter of time before he was homeless or locked up."

"Is Whitlock still angry about what happened? Is he the type to seek revenge?"

There was a long silence on the other end.

"You think John is seeking out revenge?" When Milstein didn't respond, the doctor said, "That doesn't sound like John at all."

"What do you mean?"

"For starters, John has significant impairments. Long-term planning, revenge, it isn't within his abilities."

"So you think it's impossible for him to plan out a crime?"

"Impossible? I don't know. But if the crime required any level of planning or organization, I'd say it's highly unlikely. But beyond that, John isn't a violent man. The best way to describe him is a sweet six-year-old in a grown man's body."

"You say he's not violent, but I thought he was in for assault and battery? He nearly beat a man to death in a bar fight. Doesn't sound like he's a total stranger to violence, doctor."

"Yes, but it was because he was defending a woman at that bar. If you look at his history, he's high functioning, but has impulse control problems because of his injury," the doctor said. "Every time he's been violent it was because he thought he was protecting someone. He was disciplined at his special needs school for violence against a schoolyard bully. He's had many run-ins over the years of this sort. His condition often makes his responses disproportionate. But he was always trying to defend, not harm."

"Nevertheless, doctor, he's been a violent man."

"Yes, driven by a need—a need he doesn't fully understand— to protect. I can't go into specifics of my sessions with him, but he has great guilt over what happened when he was a boy."

"We know about his sisters."

"So you can imagine what that might do to a young man, particularly one who suffers a disability related to the trauma. The guilt caused his mother to commit suicide. Imagine what it did to him. This was a home with no father. He was only a teenager, but he was the man of the house. He feels like he should have stopped the man who took his sisters."

"But doesn't that also suggest he might go after those he thinks were involved in what happened to his sisters? The people he thinks destroyed his family?"

"I just don't see it," the doctor cut in. "His disability makes him unable to hold even menial jobs. Every time he's released he ends up back on the street. He can do very well when he's on his meds, but his history shows he won't take them unless he's in a controlled environment. And revenge? Against who? The perpetrator is dead, John knew that much. So who? Even if there was someone else, how would he find them? I don't think John owns a computer, much less knows how to use one. John can function with direction, with supervision, but without it . . ."

"Is there anything you can tell me that could help us find him? Somewhere he might go? The kind of places he liked on the street?"

"Like I said, once they leave the facility, they're on their own."

"Is there anything else you could tell me that may help us?"

"I can send you his file here at Hayfield. It contains a photograph of him, the visitor register, copies of any letters he received. He's a loner, so I doubt any of it will be helpful, but I can have it scanned and e-mailed to you."

"That would be great."

"Have a good Thanksgiving, Agent Milstein."

Milstein ended the call, and walked back to the food truck. The doctor's description of Whitlock did not fit the profile of the perp. The Behavioral team thought the killer was highly educated, organized. The crimes themselves said that much. The Franklin fire was masterfully executed. The fire was started and locks placed on the outside doors without anyone seeing the perp. For the Dupont murders, the perp had sent Amanda Hill an untraceable computer message. And the convenience store had been doused with bleach. None of it sounded like a street person with the IQ of a young child. But if not Whitlock, then who?

CHAPTER 39

By midweek it was clear that Justice Cutler wasn't changing her mind on the *Filstein* case. That afternoon, Keir called a clerks' meeting to discuss last-ditch ideas on how they might turn Cutler around. When Gray walked into Keir and Mike's shared office, Mike was on the tattered couch tossing the football up in the air and catching it. Praveen and Keir sat at the two workstations.

Lauren arrived last. "I talked to Travis again, and Cutler isn't budging," she said.

"Are any of Cutler's other clerks still around?" Praveen asked.

"Just Cynthia," Lauren said. "The rest have left for Thanksgiving."

Keir clasped his head with a hand, massaging his temples. "This is a disaster. My flight leaves in two hours. This was gonna be my biggest case of the term."

"Yeah, that's what's important," Lauren said.

Keir shot her a look. "Fine, you all give up."

"We're not giving up," Mike said. "Lighten up, man. It's not the end of the world." Mike took a deep breath, let it out slowly. "Let's go talk to Cynthia. I'll come with you, since I don't want you scaring the shit out of her." Mike looked to the rest of them. "Maybe you guys can talk to Justice Marcus's clerks." Mike tossed the ball to Gray.

Keir stomped out of the room. Mike followed after him, mim-icking Keir's melodramatic gait. He flashed them a smile before marching out.

"That guy can never be serious, he's got no respect," Praveen said.

Gray gave Praveen a hard look, and Praveen's eyes hit the floor. Not the best time for Praveen to get on his high horse.

"Let's split up," Gray said. "We approach Justice Marcus's clerks one-on-one. They're more likely to speak freely that way. And maybe one of them disagrees with their boss and will be willing to try to convince Marcus to go our way."

Lauren nodded. "Praveen, you know Mark, right?"

"Yes, we were in the same section at Stanford."

"Okay, you take him. I'll take Noah. He's always looking at my ass, so maybe that will help. Gray you try the same strategy with Helen. She thinks you're cute."

"Is it the scar? The girls always like the scar," Gray said with a smirk.

Gray found Helen in the courtyard outside. She was sitting at one of the iron patio tables eating her lunch out of a Tupperware container. She had red hair and freckles, and a high voice that Gray suspected caused people to underestimate her. He'd heard she was brilliant.

"Pretty good weather for November, right?" Gray said. He sat down next to Helen.

Helen looked up from the brief she was reading. "A lot nicer than Cambridge in November." She took a bite of fruit from the container.

"You traveling for Thanksgiving?" Gray asked.

"I leave for home tonight. Trying to get some things wrapped up before I go." She looked down at the brief again, signaling that she didn't have time for chitchat.

"Where's home?"

Helen's eyes lifted again. She rested her fork in the container. She gave him a long, skeptical look. Then: "I can save you a lot of time with the small talk. He's not budging on *Filstein*."

"*Filstein?* What makes you think I'm here about *Filstein?*" He gave Helen a sly grin.

A faint smile crossed Helen's lips. She stared over at the lamppost in the courtyard for a long moment. "You ever notice all the turtles worked into the architecture around here?"

Gray followed her glance. There were turtle sculptures at the base of the lamppost. "No, I never noticed them before."

"There's actually all kinds of animals around the building. I never noticed them either, but Justice Marcus can't walk anywhere in the building without pointing them out. He says the turtle represents the slow, deliberate pace of the law. He thinks the court, like the turtle, should move slowly."

Gray understood where she was going with this. "So just because the drone policy has been around for a long time, that's a good reason not to change it?"

Helen shrugged. Then, she added, "Besides, after what the chief did in the Anton Troy case, it's not like Justice Marcus is in the mood to do him any favors."

Gray was taken aback. Justice Marcus always voted to stop executions. "What do you mean?" Gray asked. "The chief voted to stay Troy's execution. He and Marcus were on the same side on that one."

Helen emitted a faint noise of disbelief. "Maybe you don't know your boss as well as you think you do."

Gray wished Helen a happy Thanksgiving, then skulked out of the courtyard, his thoughts more on Anton Troy than the *Filstein* case. In the hallway, he noticed a small lion's head carved into a bronze gate. Then, on the trim framing the elevator doors, an owl. Helen wasn't kidding about all the animals. Gray recalled Agent Milstein's question: *Is there anyone around the court who likes owls?*

He stopped by Keir and Mike's office, but the lights were out and their computer screens dark. They must've given up. He then went to his office. Even Praveen was gone. Gray gathered up his things and decided to see if he could catch Lauren before she took off. Both her parents had passed away, but she said her aunt was visiting for the holiday. He walked up to the second floor and past the hallway filled with stacked chairs used for events in the East Conference Room. He tapped on Lauren's door.

Lauren poked her head out and looked down both ends of the hallway. She pulled him inside, then shut and locked the door.

She pressed her body against his. Their lips met. A Rachel-McAdams-and-Ryan-Gosling-in-the-rain kiss that nearly buckled Gray's knees. As Lauren unbuttoned his suit pants, she whispered in his ear: "Since I won't see you tomorrow, I wanted to give you something to be thankful for."

CHAPTER 40

Gray's mom answered the door on Thanksgiving wearing an apron over her favorite blouse. She hugged Gray, then took the wilting flowers he'd picked up at CVS. In the living room, Gray's father sat facing the old television. Emilio was on the floor sorting through some trading cards. He jumped up when he saw his uncle, and hugged Gray's waist.

"The stranger returns!" Miranda called out from the kitchen.

"Can I get you something to drink?" his mom said.

"Tell him to get off his ass and get his own drink," Miranda said. "And perhaps help us out in here. What is this, 1950?"

"Miranda, watch your language," his mom said.

Gray sauntered over and peeked in the oven at the turkey. He picked up the spoon for the mashed potatoes and was going to steal a taste, when his mother smacked the top of his hand lightly.

"Go relax with your father," she said.

Miranda rolled her eyes.

His father nodded hello, but kept his glance on the television. Gray sat on the floor next to Emilio.

"Excited for your big day coming up?" Gray said to his nephew.

"Mom said I can have my birthday party at Chuck E. Cheese!" Emilio gave a gap-toothed smile.

"Birthday? I meant your other big day. I heard you were getting married."

"Nooooo," Emilio giggled.

Gray glanced down at the playing cards. He recognized them. "I see Grandma found my old Pokémon cards? Do kids still collect these things?"

"Not really."

"But you like them?"

He looked up at Gray with his large brown eyes. In a whisper, he said, "I'd rather play the Pokémon game on Mom's phone, but she won't let me. But it makes Grandma happy to see me playing with the cards. Mom says it reminds her of when you were a little boy. It also means I don't have to help in the kitchen."

"Smart," Gray said. He picked up one of the cards, his thoughts meandering to the days when he, Arturo, and Sam would spend hours sitting on that very floor, the cards spread out in front of them. The carpet was different. Dad had replaced it himself, but otherwise the apartment was stuck in time. His home was always a sanctuary for Arturo and Sam. A safe place.

On cue, Sam arrived at the door. She held a bottle of wine and cheek-kissed everyone hello.

"Your mother couldn't make it?" Gray's mom asked.

"She's not feeling well," Sam said. They all knew what that meant.

An hour later, they held hands as Dad said grace, then stood and carved the turkey.

"Your sister said you brought a girl to Sam's show. Someone special?" His mom smiled.

"Her name is Lauren. She's my co-clerk." Gray took some turkey from the platter and passed it on. "I'll keep you posted if you need to start scouting wedding chapels."

His mom let out a sigh, shaking her head at the deflection.

Sam jumped in. "I don't know, he looked pretty taken with her. I haven't seen him that smitten since Jessica Silva in the seventh grade."

Miranda said, "He dodged a bullet with Jessica. I saw her at Safeway. She's got five kids and a giant ass."

"Miranda!" his mom said, laughing in spite of herself.

"How's the job going?" his father asked.

"It's going great, actually. I'm working on my first opinion."

"I thought the justices write the law?"

"They do, but the clerks do the first drafts of the opinions. And if the chief likes it, he'll use a lot of my draft. So my words will be in a Supreme Court case forever."

"That's wonderful, Grayson," his mom said.

"You know what you're gonna do when the clerkship ends?" his dad asked.

"The term ends in June, so I have some time to think about it, but I'll probably take a job at a big law firm."

"I thought you wanted to do public interest work?" His dad cut into his turkey roughly, his eyes not leaving Gray's.

"Yeah, someday. But the firms pay a $400,000 signing bonus."

His father guffawed. "Four hundred thousand dollars? For what, writing papers?"

"It's not just writing *papers*. Corporate clients want the best, and the Supreme Court clerks are considered the best."

Gray caught the look from Sam. But she always stayed out of the scuffles he had with Dad.

"There's more to life than money," his father added.

"I know that, Dad. But if I commit to three years at a firm, I get a four hundred–K signing bonus, then two hundred-a-year salary. A million in three years. I can pay off my student loans. And pay you back . . ."

"I'm in no rush."

Gray's mother reached for Dad's hand, signaling for him to stop.

"Can't you just be happy for me?"

"I am happy for you, it's just—"

"It's just what?"

His father picked at his food. He seemed to be pondering, deciding on the words. "When I was a boxer—"

Gray interrupted with an exasperated groan. He'd spent a lifetime indulging his father's ringside wisdom. He loudly plopped a scoop of mashed potatoes on his plate.

"Grayson Manuel Hernandez," his mother said. It was never good when she said his full name. No escaping it now, he'd be hearing Dad out.

"When I was a boxer," his father repeated, "the biggest fight I ever had was at this arena in Colonia Doctores. We was so poor then." Dad glanced at Gray's mom, who held a reflective smile. Gray's parents tended to romanticize their poverty. "So, I'm excited, anxious, this was gonna be my big break. And they take me to this fancy dressing room where I met the promoter. I go in there trying to act like it's all no big deal and I meet the guy, an American, who wore this expensive suit and this big gold watch." His father cupped his hand at his wrist, like he was holding something the size of a baseball. "So after everybody had been introduced he pulled me aside, asked if everyone was treating me okay. He told me he used to be a fighter. I'd never really been around anyone who'd made a lot of money fighting, and he was a nice man, so I decided to ask him for some advice. I told him I had a family and I was tired of working for nothing. I wanted a better life for you and your sister." His mother tightened her squeeze on Dad's hand. "You know what he told me?"

Gray bit the side of his lip, then raised his hands: *Do tell.*

"He told me to stop boxing. If I cared about my family, I should stop while I could. Before it was one hit too late." His father's tone intensified. "I told him boxing was my dream, the only thing I was good at. I just needed one big fight, one big payday. I thought he was crazy. And, he said something I've never forgotten. I didn't understand it then, but now that I'm older . . ." his voice trailed off.

Gray let the thought sit there. His dad didn't speak. He was gonna make Gray ask. *May as well get it over with.* "So, what was it? What'd he say?"

"He told me about a Chinese proverb, a warning. It goes, *May all your dreams come true.*"

Gray scoffed. Chinese wisdom from a Mexican who sold Italian food for a living. Gray said, "Can't you ever just—" He was interrupted by the ring of his phone. His mother frowned when he hurriedly pulled it from his pocket.

Gray held up a finger. It was a special ring assigned for only the chief justice.

Chief Justice Douglas began without pleasantries. "I unexpectedly have a friend in town who needs a place to stay. I hoped he could use the condo. Can you stay somewhere else tonight? Just for one night. Would you mind?" There was a loud noise in the background, the hum of a large engine.

Gray was surprised. He didn't realize that he was on standby and could be ousted from the condo on a moment's notice.

"No problem. I wouldn't mind at all."

"You're sure? He'll be in at ten tonight and out by eight tomorrow morning."

"It's really no problem. I have a lease on the old place until summer, so I can stay there."

"Excellent. It's just for tonight, then the place is all yours again. I'd explain, but I'm at the airfield, and I'm next in line for takeoff." The chief was a pilot who often took short trips in his private plane.

"Safe travels, chief."

"Thanks, Grayson. Happy Thanksgiving."

Gray returned the phone to his pocket. Everyone was looking at him. "What?" he said.

"Something wrong with the condo?" his dad asked.

"No, everything is fine." His dad hadn't liked that he was staying there rent free. *Nothing is free, son. No handouts,* another pearl of wisdom from Manny Hernandez. But the guy just didn't understand how the world worked. These people were different. Dad, whose only schooling had been in rural Mexico, for Christ's sake, didn't get it. And let's face it, the promoter was onto something. Mom once confided that it was the concussions that ended his father's boxing career. The injuries explained Dad's occasional memory lapses and flashes of anger. Gray felt bad about the mean thoughts. He recalled the devastation he'd felt when he'd learned his father's cancer had returned. The disease had stolen Gray's chance to go away to school since he needed to stay to help with the pizza shop. But his dad was better now.

"I don't think you should be—"

"Look," Gray cut him off. "Can we enjoy the meal, and you just leave the Supreme Court to me?"

The table went silent. The sound of knives and forks scraping on plates. Sam finally and charitably changed the subject. "Emilio, what do you want for your birthday?"

The table grew loud again as Emilio talked about video games and Marvel superheroes and his birthday party. After dinner, Dad gave Gray the cold shoulder, but he still handed Gray a beer.

As his parents said good-bye to Miranda and Emilio, Sam sidled up next to Gray. "Are you okay?"

"I'm fine, I just wasn't in the mood for him to get on me today. He doesn't get it."

"He just wants what's best for you. And you have been kind of a dick."

"You too?"

Sam shrugged.

Gray left around nine-thirty, hoping to get to the condo to grab some clothes and toiletries before the chief's guest arrived. Then it would be back to his cramped old place. He wondered if the roaches missed him. On the drive, he thought about his father. *There's more to life than money.* How would he know? He'd never had any money. Who was he to give advice? Gray wasn't some ten-year-old who hung on the man's every word anymore. In the pit of his stomach, though, Gray knew Sam was right. He'd acted like a jerk.

He pulled up to the building, and was jarred by the sight of the man walking into the lobby. Justice Wall. Was that who was staying at his place tonight? Wall was married, but had a reputation for having a wandering eye. At least according to the gossip mill—the secretarial pool—at the court. Maybe the chief was lending Wall the condo to meet some hot young thing.

Gray would have to live without his clothes. As he pulled out of the parking lot, another jolt shot through him.

Lauren slinking into the building.

CHAPTER 41

The Monday after Thanksgiving, Ben Freeman walked into the conference room in the FBI field office, Scott Cartwright at his side. Freeman was a tall African American man who wore an expensive suit and *really* expensive shoes. Milstein's ex had been a clotheshorse. He'd always gotten on her for not being more stylish. But she preferred comfort over fashion. Just as well. She'd learned that an agent, particularly an attractive female one, would be marginalized if she looked too fashionable.

Milstein stood and introduced herself. "Thanks for coming," she said. "I know the holidays are busy. I hope traffic wasn't too bad." Freeman worked as head of corporate security at Capital One's offices in northern Virginia. It was less than twenty miles away, but the journey could easily take more than an hour in traffic.

"Happy to do it. This building brings back old memories. And, frankly, my office is a ghost town this time of year. The executives disappear from Thanksgiving until the new year."

"You were stationed at the field office?" Cartwright asked.

"Just down the hall there," Freeman said, motioning with his chin. "You mind if I get some coffee?" Freeman stood and walked to the coffeemaker and studied the machine. "We didn't have these contraptions when I worked here, though. Whatever happened to a good old-fashioned coffee pot?"

Cartwright jumped up and helped Freeman work the machine, which made one cup at a time using small pods popped into the device.

"How long have you been in the private sector?" Cartwright asked.

"Going on fifteen years now." Freeman took a sip of coffee, then cut to it. "So, you wanted to talk about Kevin Dugan?"

Cartwright nodded. "We understand you worked the Whitlock kidnapping with him?"

Ben Freeman exhaled loudly. "You read the file?"

"What's left of it," Cartwright said. "Tough case."

"A shit show all around. It got the best of Dugan. He was a good man, but he had little girls of his own, and the pressure got to him. The thought of that monster doing God knows what to those poor girls on his watch, well, he couldn't take it."

"I understand you had to testify against Dugan?" Cartwright asked.

Freeman looked at the table. "Two times. First in the case against the perp, Ken Tanaka. I considered lying about what happened, but it wouldn't have mattered, it was all caught on the store's video cameras. But, I'll tell you, I was still shocked the judge threw out the evidence. They let a child-molesting killer out, then prosecuted Dugan."

"You had to testify in the criminal case against Dugan?"

"Thankfully, no. The prosecutors pled it out to probation, a slap on the wrist. No one wanted a decorated agent who saved a young girl to go to prison. If Dugan hadn't tortured the storekeeper, they wouldn't have found the perp in time. When we got there, Tanaka had already killed one of the girls, but we saved the other. Anyway, after Dugan entered the guilty plea, the storekeeper found some shady lawyer who sued Dugan and the Bureau for violating his civil rights. Only in America."

"And you testified in the civil case?"

Freeman nodded. "A deposition. It killed me to do it. By then, Dugan's wife had divorced him, moved away with the kids," Freeman said. "Meanwhile that child killer got out."

"Worse than that," Cartwright added. "Tanaka did it again. Molested two kids."

"Yeah. At least he got what was coming to him on the inside. Shanked his first week."

"Have you seen Kevin Dugan lately?" Milstein finally asked. She was growing impatient. Cartwright's interview style was designed to disarm, but they knew all this already and didn't have the time. December 5 was less than a week away.

"No. Haven't seen him in years. I'm not exactly on his Christmas card list. One of the guys on my team at the bank was friends with Dugan. He'd heard that Dugan was doing private-eye work, and that he was an alcoholic mess."

"His investigation company had an address in Fairfax County," Milstein said. "Turns out it was a drop box. He was living in a motel, but no sign of him—no credit cards, cell phone, anything, in the last year."

"Can I ask why you're looking for him?" Freeman said.

They weren't just looking for Dugan, it was an all-out manhunt.

Milstein said, "Tanaka's defense lawyer, Amanda Hill, was murdered. And you may have heard the chief justice of the Supreme Court was attacked?"

"I heard about the chief justice. I didn't remember who Tanaka's attorney was."

"Also, the storekeeper who Dugan assaulted, the guy's daughter was murdered in the convenience store," Milstein said. "Bludgeoned with a shopping bag filled with cans of food."

Freeman's eyes flashed. He then seemed to understand why he was there. "Someone's going after people connected to the case?"

"Or their families."

"I can't believe Dugan would—you didn't know him. He was a good man."

"A good man who lost everything, like you said," Milstein said.

Freeman shook his head. "Why now? It's been twenty years. It doesn't make sense."

Milstein agreed with that. It didn't make sense. But the Behavioral team said that it doesn't have to make sense. The trigger for a serial killer is a very personal thing. And it could stay dormant for years. Behavioral also said the profile of the victims often holds the key to solving serial crimes.

Freeman said, "What about the Whitlock family? They'd have just as much motive to do this as Dugan."

"There's not really a family left, but we're looking into it," Cartwright said. "The brother, John Whitlock, suffered a brain injury, and has spent time inside. The Behavioral team thinks revenge is a possible motive, but there is a level of planning here that suggests someone educated, perhaps with a law enforcement background given how little evidence is left at the crime scenes, so the brother doesn't seem to fit. But we're tracking him down. The little girl, Susie Whitlock, was adopted, and it's been a real pain in the ass cracking those records. We know the perp is a man, so we're focusing on the brother."

"And Kevin Dugan," Freeman said.

Milstein said, "So since someone killed the defense lawyer, judge, and the storekeeper's kid . . ."

"I'm a target too," Freeman said, finishing the thought. "The guy who ratted him out." There was some bitterness to it, as if he'd never recovered at the Bureau from the betrayal. Freeman composed himself. "You don't need to worry about me." He opened his suit jacket, revealing an empty shoulder holster. "I left it at the office since I knew I was coming here. But if Dugan or anybody else comes at me, they'll regret it."

Former agents always had the worst bravado. "It's just a good idea to keep on your guard," Milstein said. "And be particularly careful on the fifth of the month." She didn't explain why the date mattered, and Freeman didn't ask.

"Will do. I appreciate the heads up."

"A couple more questions, if you have time?"

"Of course."

"Did Dugan have any connection to the Supreme Court?"

"You mean other than that the judge who threw out the evidence against Tanaka is now a Supreme Court justice?"

"Yeah, any other connection to the building or personnel or some fixation on the court?"

"Not that I'm aware of."

"How about owls? Did he like owls or geese or have an interest in feathers?"

Freeman crumpled his brow. "I assume there's a good reason you're asking, but no, not that I can think of. Dugan is a family man. Meat and potatoes kind of guy." Freeman glanced at Cartwright a beat, then back to Milstein. "He was solid . . . until all this happened, anyway."

"Until all this," Milstein repeated.

They escorted Freeman to the elevator banks and shook hands. As they walked back to Milstein's office Cartwright said, "Handsome guy. I asked around about him. Wife passed away. He's made some serious money." Cartwright hoisted his brows up and down.

Milstein narrowed her eyes.

"Just sayin'."

She wanted to be annoyed with Cartwright's levity, but it was how he dealt with stress. Freeman offered no new information. They were no closer to finding the perp. And they had less than a week.

Milstein saw Neal Wyatt walking resolutely toward them. He didn't look happy.

"I was just coming to see you both. I have news. And you're not gonna like it."

The dreaded T-word. Task force.

CHAPTER 42

Gray turned into the shopping center, which was on an ugly stretch of road in Rockville, Maryland. The center was fast-food overkill, with a McDonald's, Wendy's, Taco Bell, and Pizza Hut. He saw the familiar giant rat's face over a red CHUCK E. CHEESE'S sign and searched for a parking space. He opted for a spot at the lot's outer perimeter to avoid having to park next to anyone. He lived in fear of a door ding. The burden of having an expensive car. One owned by his boss. He'd gotten caught in traffic and was running late. Why Miranda planned a party at 5:00 p.m. midweek was beyond him. He pulled the large gift from the passenger seat and headed inside.

As expected, the place was sensory overload, with the din of children playing, blaring music, and video games. The woman at the check-in station directed him to the room assigned for Emilio's party. He threaded through the chaos, finally seeing some familiar faces near the door to a party room. Inside, Miranda was stabbing candles into a sheet cake. She glanced up at him. "I was worried you were still pouting and weren't gonna show."

Gray rolled his eyes.

Neighbors, employees from the pizza shop, and longtime friends sang "Happy Birthday," and Emilio struggled to blow out all eight candles. Gray looked over at Dad. He beamed with pride. His father caught Gray's eye and gave a small nod. Not the warmest greeting, but Gray supposed he deserved that given his performance on Thanksgiving. He'd been bound up, tense, ever since. Angry with himself for lashing out at his parents. Angry about Lauren. They weren't dating, so it wasn't necessarily fair of him. But they'd shared some moments, and he thought she'd felt it too. More so, he couldn't respect her seeing a sitting justice, particularly one who was married. He needed to let it all go, if only for his nephew. He made his way over to the birthday boy. "Nice job blowing out the candles. What'd you wish for, little man?"

"Can't tell," Emilio said. "Won't come true if I do."

Gray's mom handed him plates of cake to distribute to the guests. Gray moved them along the assembly line as Miranda and Sam poured juice for the kids.

"I think the wish was for a new Gamemaster 8200," Gray said. It was the latest, obnoxiously priced, gaming system.

Miranda jumped in. "No, my little boy wouldn't wish for video games." She squeezed Emilio's pudgy cheeks. "He knows his mama wouldn't want that in our house. Video games rot the brain."

"I guess he shouldn't look in that box over there," Gray said, giving his sister a defiant smile.

Miranda glowered at him. The look hadn't changed since they were kids and big sis was bossing him around.

Emilio had a delayed reaction, but took a big bite of cake then jumped from his chair and ran to the box.

"Well, open it already," Gray said.

Miranda stood next to Gray as Emilio ripped at the wrapping paper. "You don't open the gifts in front of the guests," she said, annoyed. "It's different than when we were kids."

"Where's the fun in that?"

"And, you shouldn't have. It's too expensive. It's—" Miranda looked toward the door and quickly made her way through the kids to greet the other guest who'd arrived late.

Lauren stood at the entryway, holding a gift bag that had silver tissue spilling out of it. Miranda greeted her with a hug.

Gray felt his jaw tighten. He'd been avoiding her around the court. They were all so busy preparing for the December oral arguments, he wasn't sure she'd noticed. Since seeing her slither into the condo after Justice Wall, Gray had decided that he wasn't going to waste more time on Lauren Hart. From now on, they were colleagues, co-clerks. Period.

"Hey," Lauren said.

"Hey," he said, his tone cold, uninterested.

She was about to say something when Emilio ran up to her. He stuck out his hand. "I'm Emilio."

"I know! I've heard so much about you. I was so happy when your mom invited me to your party." She smiled, her teeth gleaming.

"My mom says Uncle Grayson wants you to be his girlfriend."

Gray nearly choked on the lemonade he was drinking.

"Kids," Miranda said, putting a hand on Emilio's shoulder, a mother's move signaling that a squeeze was coming.

Lauren gracefully moved on. She crouched down to Emilio's height. "I hear someone likes video games." Emilio smiled as Lauren handed him the gift. Lauren simultaneously mouthed *sorry* to Miranda.

Gray must have told Lauren about the video system he'd bought Emilio, though he didn't remember mentioning it. But *she* remembered. She was interested in his family. It was getting harder to stay mad at her.

And for the next hour, Lauren charmed all of the guests. Gray's father succumbed first, but Manny was always a sucker for a pretty face. Mom was harder, but she invited Lauren to help clean up, the ultimate sign of approval. Mom even came over to Gray and whispered in his ear, "She's lovely."

Gray was starting to think he was being silly. There had to be an explanation for why she and Justice Wall were at his condo. Across the loud game room, he saw her talking to one of the parents as kids galloped around, high on sugar and the lack of supervision. He was about to walk over when he saw Lauren answer a call on her phone.

She looked nervous and slipped away from the group, making sure no one was in earshot. When she was done with the call, she went over to Miranda and they hugged good-bye. She caught his eye from the distance and waved to him. She then disappeared out of the place.

Gray made his way over to the large window that looked out onto the parking lot. He saw Lauren slip into the back of a black town car. Lauren had a car, so why would she take an expensive car service? Did someone call her and pick her up? If so, who? He had a sickening feeling that he knew the answer.

"What's wrong?" Miranda said, walking over to him. "You're not mad she left early? That would be pretty rich given that you never have time for anyone."

"Save it, Miranda."

His sister studied him, realizing she should back off. "Well, I liked her."

"So did I," Gray said. "So did I."

CHAPTER 43

The next morning, Gray found Keir, Mike, and Praveen in his office. When he walked in, Keir said, "Finally." Keir wore a wrinkled white shirt and had a five o'clock shadow, scruffier than Gray
had ever seen him. Keir held up four straws in his hand.

"What's up? And what's with the straws?" Gray asked.

"Justice Cutler isn't going to budge on *Filstein*. And neither is
Justice Marcus," Keir said. The chief could fight all he wanted, but
the Rule of Five carried the day on everything at the marble palace. "Short straw has to tell the chief."

"Why only four straws, what about Lauren?" Praveen asked.

"She didn't answer her phone. Probably late again," Keir said
with distaste. "And she drew the short straw last time with the office moves."

Mike drew the first straw. He did some type of juju chant while
he did it, followed by *"Yes!"* when he pulled a long straw.

Praveen frowned and tugged at a straw, and he too got a
long one.

"Just you and me, Hernandez," Keir said. He gave Gray a
steely gaze. It was stupid since the chief surely already knew the outcome of *Filstein* from his discussions with the other justices. But after
his rant, none of them wanted to be the bearer of the official word.

Kill the messenger and all that. Gray took in a breath and pulled. The short straw. He sank into one of the office chairs.

"Story of your life," Keir said, strutting away.

By now, Gray had become accustomed to Keir's jabs, the seal references, and other douchey comments over the term, so he wasn't sure why this one got to him. It was no better, no worse than standard Keir. Maybe it was because Gray had recently spent time in the back of a patrol car, maybe it was Lauren. But he'd had enough. "What'd you say?"

Keir looked at Gray, surprised at the edge in Gray's voice. He seemed to debate whether to retreat. But Keir wasn't the type who'd cower when there was an audience.

"You heard me," Keir said.

Gray stood up quickly, aggressively. "Why don't you come over here and say that to my face instead of mumbling it under your breath? Or maybe you need your daddy to do it for you."

Mike jumped from his seat. "Whoa, guys, relax."

Keir's jaw tightened at the daddy's boy comment. Gray had spent many hours psychoanalyzing why Keir was such an ass. Lauren thought it was the years of living in the shadow of Keir, Sr., a legendary judge on the court of appeals. The judge was hard on Keir, and most people assumed that Keir got his clerkship, and everything else, because his dad was legal elite. It probably wasn't true. But it was sure hard to feel sympathy for the guy. Gray knew it was just the right nerve to pinch.

But Keir hit back. "Look, if this is about Lauren, I've got no problem with you having my leftovers."

The remark sent Gray barreling at Keir, ramming him into the office wall. Keir swung wildly, and missed when Gray instinctively ducked. He remembered a few things his old man had taught him. Keir then came at him with some type of prep-school wrestling move and brought Gray down to the floor. He soon had Gray in a pretzeled-up hold, but Gray broke free and pushed his elbow back and connected with Keir's nose, which elicited a howl. Gray felt hands on his arms, as Mike and Praveen tried to pull the two apart. Then a voice cut through the melee.

"Enough!"

Gray looked up and saw Chief Justice Douglas, red faced, cheeks trembling. They were literally shaking. Mike and Praveen released Gray's arms. Both Gray and Keir were on the floor, looking up at their boss, the chief justice of the United States.

"Get up," the chief commanded.

Gray jumped to his feet. Keir was slower to rise. His nose was bleeding, dripping all over his shirt and the floor.

The four clerks stood side by side, the chief pacing the line like an angry drill sergeant. In a forced calm, the chief said, "I don't know what this is all about, but it goes without saying that bar fights belong in bars. And *here*—" The chief justice paused for a long moment. "—violence will *not* be tolerated."

The chief took in another deep breath, calming himself. There was another long stretch of silence. Finally: "I know you've been under a lot of stress, you're sleep deprived, and I've been working you pretty hard. And I also know I lost it myself about Justice Cutler." A pause. "But if you *ever* do something like this again . . ." He let his stare complete the sentence.

"You," he said pointing to Keir. "Go get cleaned up. And then get back to work." His head then turned to Praveen and Mike. "You two, scat." He waved them out.

That left only one person.

"Grayson, come with me." The chief stormed out of the office and to his chambers. Gray followed after him. Standing before the chief's desk, Gray thought about apologizing, but then he remembered one of the chief's rules: *No apologies*. The chief fell into his broad leather chair, and studied Gray.

"It took you long enough," the chief said at last.

Gray didn't understand.

"That little prick has been riding you since Day One. And it took you until *now*—the December sitting—to do something about it."

This was not going how he'd expected. He was at a loss for words.

"Besides the Supreme Court trivia, you like movies, right?" the chief said.

"Yes."

"You know in movies where the guy on his first day in prison beats up the first inmate who messes with him? You know, to send a message to the rest of the animals?"

Gray nodded.

"It's no different in Washington." The chief kept his eyes fixed on Gray's. "If you don't learn anything else from me about this town—about life—I want you to remember how good it felt to bloody his face. And the next time, I hope you remember that taking guff may seem like the mature thing to do, and that you're above it all. But the only thing people understand in this world is power. And you show power through force. And you use force the *first* time someone disrespects you, not two months later. Do you understand?"

Gray nodded. A new lesson in the education of Grayson Hernandez: *No mercy.*

"I said, do you understand?" the chief repeated, his tone harsh.

"Yes, chief."

"Good. Now get out of my office."

CHAPTER 44

Later that afternoon, Lauren popped by Gray and Praveen's office. She had a concerned look on her face. Praveen glanced up at her, but then continued typing.

"Are you okay?" she said to Gray. "I heard about you and Keir."

"That's funny," Gray said, "I heard about *you* and Keir."

Praveen stopped typing. He stood and said, "I'm going to get some coffee." A clumsy escape. Praveen obviously didn't want to bear witness to relationship drama. But their co-clerk stopped at the door when he heard the buzz of the intercom.

Praveen picked up the receiver and listened. "No, Lauren's here, I'll tell her. We'll be right there." He hung up the line. "The chief wants to meet about the *Wakefield Estates* case."

Five minutes later, the five clerks sat around the chief's desk, the usual formation. These gatherings, where the clerks got to work through tough legal questions with the chief, were one of Gray's favorite things about the job.

The chief addressed them all. "First off, now that everyone's cooled off, I think it's important to mention that for this to work"—the chief waved a hand around in the air—"we have to be a team." His gaze cut to Keir, then Gray. "Am I understood?"

Keir unexpectedly stood and extended his hand. Gray took it.

"Okay, we've been due for some good news, and I have some," the chief said. "Justice Cutler has come back to us on *Filstein*."

"Yes!" Keir's spirits seemed immediately lifted.

The chief gave a satisfied smile. "We're going to have to accommodate some changes to the opinion, but she's back on board. Keir, we can talk later. For now, let's talk about *Wakefield Estates*."

Gray was impressed at how the chief switched gears. He supposed that Douglas was used to vote-changing in important cases. The chief also never let them forget that the court *always* issued all of its decisions by June. Always. *Filstein* was just one of seventy-two cases. As Gray sat with his brilliant, if annoying, co-clerks, he reminded himself of the rare opportunity he'd been given. To work on the most important cases of the day. Gray would no longer get caught up in relationship or workplace drama. No longer get sucked into FBI investigations. He was done.

"So, as I understand it," the chief said, "the government not only paid residents above fair market value for their homes, but also gave relocation expenses and no-interest loans for new houses?" The *Wakefield* litigation involved eminent domain, the government's ability to take private property for public use so long as it paid a fair price. A local government in Massachusetts was trying to clean up a blighted area, a crime-filled community known as Wakefield Estates.

"That's right, no one disputes that the government paid more than fair value," Lauren said.

"So what's the beef?"

"The community was predominantly minorities," Praveen said. "They wouldn't come in and do this to a white neighborhood."

"But that would prevent local governments from *ever* cleaning up blighted areas where minorities live," Keir said. "Most of the crime in the community occurred in Wakefield Estates, and most of the residents themselves had been begging the local government to do something about it."

"But the local government here is in bed with a major developer," Lauren said. "It's time to revisit what 'public use' means for eminent domain. It's supposed to mean using the land for the public, not building condos for rich people. But the lower courts have been misreading the Supreme Court's cases, and allowing unsavory relationships between government and companies."

Mike, whose dad was a land developer, said, "I think that's easy to say when you grew up on an *actual* estate. Have you ever even driven through a blighted area?"

Lauren said nothing.

The chief justice smiled. "I'm glad I'm not the only one struggling with this." His gaze settled on Gray. "I'd be interested in your views, Grayson."

They all expected Gray, he presumed, to side with the African Americans whose homes would be torn down and replaced by shiny new condos. Funny how even educated people assumed that all minorities think alike. He considered staying out of the fray, playing it safe, but he decided to plead truth. "I think the kids in Wakefield know nothing of the world. The only people with money are the drug dealers. I bet every single kid there knows someone who's been murdered. There's no opportunities for them." Gray thought about the public housing building across the street from the apartment complex where he grew up. It was where Arturo first got pulled into crime.

The other clerks kept their eyes on the floor, uncomfortable. "So I think Wakefield Estates is a kind of prison," Gray said. "And when someone offers to pay you to get out of a prison, you take the money and you run."

There was an awkward silence.

"Well, okay then," the chief said. "I don't think this is one that the briefs and record will answer. I have an idea for this month's First Saturday event. We're going to have to ditch Justice Wall's team. And you'll need to pack a bag . . ."

On Saturday, December 5, Gray found himself in a Cessna traveling to Massachusetts. The first airplane ride of his life—not that he told anyone that—and he and his co-clerks were jammed in a plane that was not much bigger than an SUV. He kept thinking of all the rock stars who died in planes like this. The flight was bumpy, and he gripped the arm of the seat. Keir took a nap.

The chief was a longtime pilot and often flew to his second

home on Martha's Vineyard. The chief spent most court recesses on the island, and for the December recess, the clerks would join him. They'd work out of the chief's place until Christmas. But first, they were stopping in Massachusetts to tour Wakefield Estates.

They landed with a hard bump on a small airstrip in an industrial area, met by six officers from the court's police force. Three black Suburbans were waiting for them. The chief and clerks climbed into the middle vehicle of the motorcade.

Instead of a walking tour of Wakefield Estates on their own, they observed from a bulletproof SUV. It wasn't like a scene from *Grand Theft Auto*. It was mostly a lot of stares, and young black men ducking into alleys between dilapidated houses. Gray had seen his share of poverty, but he was surprised at the state of the community. A few homes had been cared for. But most were ravaged, windows covered in plywood, tires and debris in the yards. Overgrown lots where bony stray dogs roamed. A man in rags pushing a shopping cart. Gray was convinced more than ever that the solution for the residents was to take the money and run. Even Praveen and Lauren, who were against the government taking the property, looked less certain now.

The chief stared out the window, his face full of despair. "You forget how lucky we all are, what a bubble we live in." He looked at Grayson. "I've been thinking about what you said, and you're right. If you can get out of poverty and have a better life, you should. And you should never look back. Let's get the hell out of here."

CHAPTER 45

"You okay, Em?" Cartwright asked.

Milstein didn't look up from her office computer. "I'm fine. Would you stop asking me that?" She continued to type, tapping out instructions to the team. It was December 5, and they had no bead on Kevin Dugan or John Whitlock. Nothing. A small army of agents had been working around the clock.

"They interview Dugan's ex-wife again?" Milstein asked.

"Yeah, and the kids. Dugan had fallen out of their lives and into the bottle years ago. They have no idea where he is. But the ex still doesn't think he'd turn violent."

"How about the Supreme Court interview reports?"

"I read them myself. Aaron's team met with every justice. And they're scrutinizing every staff member who fits the profile. He ordered a twenty-four-hour security detail for all of the justices today. The chief justice is out of town and they sent a travel team for him as well."

Milstein continued to type. She was amped up on caffeine and adrenaline. She felt Cartwright staring at her, and finally looked up from her screen. He had a concerned look on his face.

"Stop looking at me like that."

"I know you're stressed out that it's December fifth, but we're doing everything we can." He gave a half smile. "The junior agents are starting to call you Carrie Mathison."

Great, they thought she was acting like the bipolar agent from *Homeland*. She sighed loudly and ran a hand through her hair. It felt greasy and unwashed, which it was. "I just can't believe we still have nothing. What if he murders another kid? Another woman?" Milstein's voice broke. She collected herself. She'd never shed a tear in the office, and wasn't going to start now. She looked at Cartwright. "If he strikes again, they're for sure gonna give the investigation over to the task force and Aaron Dowell."

Cartwright came over and put a hand on her shoulder. "This isn't all on you. And the writing's already on the wall about the task force. If the killer doesn't strike, they'll say we were wrong. If he does strike, they'll say we failed to stop it. This has nothing to do with you or me. It's politics."

By 2:00 a.m. there'd been no homicides reported in D.C. or the surrounding area. Cartwright came back to Milstein's office and put two tumblers on her desk. He filled each with two fingers of whiskey.

"Congratulations," Cartwright said. "We made it."

Milstein nodded. "You saw the e-mail from the Director of National Intelligence?"

Cartwright nodded. "Aaron's getting his task force."

The DNI's e-mail said that Milstein and Cartwright were still on the team. But that surely meant they would soon be marginalized. The e-mail also said that "the task force will spend virtually all resources focused on finding former Special Agent Kevin Dugan." Exactly what Milstein would expect from an uncreative thinker like Aaron Dowell.

Milstein smelled the whiskey and shuddered. She steeled herself, then downed the glass. "Fuck Aaron Dowell."

CHAPTER 46

After the depressing tour of Wakefield Estates, Gray and his co-clerks filed back into the chief's plane and headed to "the Vine-yard," as the clerks called it. Gray didn't know what to expect of this stomping ground of presidents, CEOs, and the idle rich. In the end, it didn't matter. The clerks spent those first days sequestered in makeshift offices in the chief's second home.

Despite the close quarters, Gray kept his distance from Lauren. She played all-business on the plane and at the chief's place, but he could tell his purposeful indifference was getting under her skin, which was fine with him.

They worked on finalizing the decisions scheduled for release the first week of January. There was Gray's *Jando* search-and-seizure case, and Mike's dissent in the school speech case. And there was Lauren's tax case. As the smartest of the group, Lauren was penal-ized with the most challenging cases involving technical areas of the law. Keir worked exclusively on *Filstein*. Historically, the court released blockbuster cases like *Filstein* the last week of the term in June. But the chief wanted the decision locked down as soon as pos-sible. He didn't want to give Justice Cutler time to change her mind and switch sides again.

Gray excused himself to the restroom. He was about to shut

the door of the bathroom in the back of the main floor when Lauren slipped inside behind him. She shut the door and faced him.

"What are you doing?" Gray whispered. He did *not* want to be caught in the restroom with Lauren in the chief's home. Clerk relationships weren't strictly forbidden, but they weren't encouraged either. And bathroom hookups at a justice's house were a definite no-no.

"I've been trying to talk with you, but we're never alone." She turned on the tap to conceal their voices. "Is there something the matter? You've been so cold to me. If this is about Keir, it was a long time ago, it meant nothing, I—"

"It's not about Keir," Gray said.

"Then what? What is it?"

"Nothing," he said.

She stared at him for a long time.

"Just disappointed, I suppose." Gray let that hang there.

"What's that supposed to mean?"

Gray turned off the water and unlocked the door, but she stood in his path. She gazed at him with those eyes.

"How'd you like my condo?" he said.

She looked at him like she didn't understand.

"In Georgetown. I believe you were someone's guest there on Thanksgiving."

She held his stare. "You've got the wrong idea. You don't understand—"

There were voices in the hallway. They froze, listening for whether someone was waiting outside to use the restroom. After a long moment, Gray opened the door a crack. No one was there. "Let's talk about this later," he said. Lauren started to speak, but Gray shook his head. "Later."

Later didn't come until the end of the trip. As promised, at four o'clock on Christmas Eve the chief released them. He was hosting some friends from the island for dinner, and the clerks were welcome to stay. Keir, Mike, and Praveen left right away, rushing to catch the last ferry off the island. Gray didn't understand the urgency. They were five hundred miles from D.C. and it was unlikely they'd make any flights out tonight. But perhaps the real reason he didn't rush off was Lauren's text asking him to stay.

"Chief, I was thinking of showing Gray around the island," Lauren said. "Want to come?"

"I've got some work to do and I need to get ready for my guests, so you both go ahead. Feel free to use the Jeep. The keys are on the hook in the kitchen."

Lauren took charge as usual, driving Gray to her favorite spot on the island. Gray shouldn't have been surprised that Lauren had been to the Vineyard before. Never "off season," she said, noting that many of the businesses were closed in the winter and that her family had "summered" there. He never got used to *summer* and *winter* as verbs.

At the western end of the island, Gray gazed at the cliffs and the old brick lighthouse ahead. The sun was coming down and it cast yellow highlights across the vast field.

"In the summer, this area is packed with tourists," Lauren said. She told him that the island had only 15,000 year-round residents, which increased to 115,000 during the summer. She parked the Jeep, grabbed a rucksack she'd packed, and led him through the tall reeds. There was a chill in the air, but it was unseasonably warm for December.

"It's not what you think," she said marching through the reeds. "I wasn't at your place for—"

"You know what?" Gray interrupted. "Let's not. It's Christmas Eve."

"No, you have the wrong idea." She stopped walking. "I was there to see *you*."

Gray had spent a good amount of time thinking about Lauren at his condo, picturing her in the arms of Justice Wall. He'd also worked through the various innocent reasons she could've been at his place. But he'd missed the most obvious explanation: she was there to see Gray.

"But I thought your aunt was in town for Thanksgiving?"

"She flaked on me. So I went over to the homeless shelter and volunteered to serve dinner. Then I thought you might want some company."

"Why didn't you just say so?"

"I didn't know you saw me there." She hesitated. "I would've mentioned coming by your place, but that night I saw something I probably shouldn't have."

"What do you mean?" Gray said, intrigued.

"When I knocked, Justice Wall came to the door." Lauren had a glint in her eyes. "I saw a woman in the apartment."

"That's not exactly fresh news. Everybody knows Wall has—"

"It wasn't just *any* woman. It was Dora Baxter."

"The solicitor general?" The SG was the government's top lawyer before the Supreme Court. An affair was bad enough, but the relationship created possible conflicts of interest for Justice Wall and Baxter. Also, the administration was grooming Baxter to be the next nominee when the court had a vacancy. It was a scandal in the making.

"You're sure?"

"I wouldn't forget her. Remember I told you what a bitch she was to me at my interview for the assistant SG spot?"

"Was she there for work?"

Lauren's eyes widened. "I don't think so."

"All this drama. It's like the Real Housewives of One First Street."

A breeze blew across the field and Lauren wrapped her arms around him as they continued walking. "Are your parents angry you're missing Christmas Eve?" she asked.

"You have no idea."

Lauren stopped at a secluded spot. She pulled a blanket from the rucksack. And then a bottle of wine. She arched a brow.

"Where'd you get that?" Gray asked.

"Let's just say the chief won't miss a bottle from his vast collection." She then unzipped Gray's jacket and put her cold hands inside his shirt. His anger at her dissipated as she pulled him on top of the blanket where they were surrounded by tall blowing reeds. She unbuttoned his jeans, aggressive, hungry for him. After slipping out of her leggings, she straddled him, eyes closed as she put his hands to her breasts.

There was an excitement, outside where they might be caught, an electricity he'd never felt before with anyone. Afterward, lying on his back staring into the sky, he thought about how his life had changed so quickly. A high-powered job, penthouse condo, luxury sports car, and a beautiful woman. But then his father's voice intruded on his thoughts:

May all your dreams come true.

CHAPTER 47

It didn't feel like Christmas morning. No snow, no Salvation Army bell-ringer outside D.C.'s Union Station, just weary-looking travelers. Three giant wreaths, lit up in white sparkling lights, hung under the station's three triumphal arches, but they seemed out of place in the sixty-degree weather. It was a December for the record books, with multiple humid, foggy days, and temperatures reaching the seventies.

Ben Freeman was excited to see Jay. Since Jay had left for NYU, life was too quiet. The house lonely. Truth be told, he missed waking up his cranky kid for high school, which started *way* too early to be healthy for any teenager. He missed the fights about curfew, Jay's obsession with his smartphone. There were some tough years after Sharon died: the acting out, the constant fighting, the distance between them. But his Jay had come back to him.

Ben was parked at the pick-up line, and watched as a group of travelers exited the station and lined up for a cab. Hopefully passengers from Jay's train. Then he saw his son. He looked good with his bald head, light sweater over broad shoulders. With him, a pretty blonde with a cheerful smile, leggings tucked in her boots. Jay had said her father was an investment banker, hopefully not like the assholes Ben knew from work. Tough-talking alphas who wouldn't last a week at Quantico. Jay's girlfriend laughed at something he said. Ben took note that no one gave the interracial couple a second look. Times had changed since he and Sharon had gotten married.

Ben rolled down the window and called out to them. But a car with an Uber sticker in the window pulled up to the curb, obstructing his view. When the car pulled away, Jay and his girlfriend were gone. Did he forget Ben was picking them up? He tried to suppress the annoyance. It was so Jay to forget.

Ben was boxed in now and couldn't catch up to the Uber. He fished out his phone and dialed his son's mobile. After a few rings Jay picked up.

"Hey, Dad! Merry Christmas! We just arrived. Should be there in about thirty minutes."

"Hey, buddy, Merry Christmas to you too." He didn't let the annoyance sneak into his tone, not wanting to spoil his son's good cheer. "Are you forgetting something?"

"Ah, I don't think so, what?"

"That your old man said he'd pick you up at the station?" He chuckled to let Jay know he wasn't mad. "I'm sitting outside Union Station. I just saw you get in the Uber."

Jay said, "But your assistant e-mailed me, said you were sending an Uber?"

"I didn't ask her to—" A wave of terror ripped through him. "Jay, you need to get out of the car."

But his son didn't respond. Jay was talking to the driver. "Why are you pulling over? What are you—" There was the sound of a struggle, Jay howling in agony followed by a woman's scream.

"Jay . . . *Jay!*" Ben yelled into the phone desperately.

Then an unfamiliar voice on the line: "Mr. Freeman?"

"Who is this?" Ben screamed into the phone.

"If you want to see your son alive ever again, you need to do exactly as I tell you."

CHAPTER 48

On the last day of the year, Gray and his co-clerks were back at the Supreme Court, putting the final touches on the January decisions. He felt rejuvenated from the trip to the Vineyard. Gray's mind drifted briefly to that spot in the blowing reeds, and he was looking forward to seeing Lauren tonight for New Year's Eve. One of Justice Anderson's clerks was having a party, so the plan was to finish up around seven, get cleaned up, then head over. Hopefully they could spend some time alone after the ball dropped. But then the phone rang and they were summoned to the chief's chambers.

"I can't tell you how sorry I am about this." The chief justice wore a tuxedo, apparently on his way to a party. He'd stopped by the office to break the news to them in person: he needed them to work late. "Justice Cutler insisted that I get her the revised draft of *Filstein* by tomorrow morning."

"On New Year's Day?" Mike asked, dumbfounded.

The chief nodded sympathetically. Cutler was on a power trip, toying with the chief. He'd swayed her back to his side on *Filstein*, but Cutler could always flip. She was the crucial swing vote the chief needed. Gray and his co-clerks stood there, trying not to look annoyed about the last-minute request.

"No problem, chief," Keir said. "I've looked at Justice Cutler's memo, and I think I can handle this by myself. There's no need for everyone else to stay."

Gray was surprised that Keir was taking the bullet, but then he realized that it wasn't about saving his co-clerks' night. Keir simply didn't want to share the glory of working on *Filstein*.

"That's very thoughtful of you, Keir," the chief justice said. "But this is a lot of work, and I think we'll benefit from the team's help. I think Cutler's wavering again, so I'm concerned."

Keir gave a reluctant nod.

"You understand all of her points?" the chief asked.

"We've got it covered," Keir said without looking at the others. "She just wants to make sure the decision can't be used to interfere with any other executive orders, that it covers only the drone policy."

The chief nodded, yanking at the sleeves of his tux. "That, and she wants to gum up the opinion with citations to her own prior decisions. I swear, the ego on that woman."

Cutler was abusing the process. After the justices voted on a case, the chief got to assign who wrote the majority opinion. He assigned *Filstein* to himself. As was customary, he sent around a proposed opinion to the justices. Cutler had sent back her "join memo," the way a justice indicates she plans to formally sign-on to another justice's draft opinion. Often the justice simply joins unconditionally. Cutler's join memo, however, had several strings attached. Cutler wanted the chief to include a new section in the opinion, and provided a list of several of her prior decisions that she "suggested" the chief work into the majority decision.

"She's demanded the draft first thing in the morning," the chief said, "so I'll try to review it when I get home tonight, which could be late. If you haven't already e-mailed it to me, I'll let you know when I'm home and online."

Gray and the others gave defeated nods. So much for New Year's Eve. They wouldn't dare send the draft opinion to the chief until he was home. He'd expect them to continue to polish the draft until the last possible minute.

"Thank you again," he said.

The five turned to leave his chambers, but the chief called out to them. "I almost forgot." He walked from behind his desk and handed Gray a business-sized envelope. "Please deliver this to Wall's chambers. Slip it under his door if he's already gone."

Gray felt Keir's glare, annoyed that Gray was given responsibility for the famous "envelope" and its mysterious contents. Gray normally would have marched immediately over to Wall's chambers and made the delivery, but Keir called a meeting. Keir was still the lead on *Filstein*, so tonight Gray and the others were his minions.

In the reception area of chambers Keir said, "All right. I'm going to work on trying to limit the decision without totally gutting the thing. Praveen and Mike, can you draft the insert Cutler wants about executive power?"

"No problem," Praveen said. Mike was tapping on his phone, likely canceling on whatever girl he'd lined up for the evening.

Keir turned to Gray and Lauren. "Why don't you two figure out how we're going to work in Justice Cutler's opinions. I've never even heard of half of these stupid cases she wants thrown in. The chief never cites Cutler's decisions—I think he'd rather cite *Korematsu* than one of Cutler's cases—but he said to accommodate her." In *Korematsu v. United States*, the court upheld the internment of Japanese Americans during World War II. It was widely considered one of the worst Supreme Court cases in history.

"Gray and I can split them up," Lauren said.

Keir handed Lauren a list of citations. Although Keir and Gray had reached a truce, Keir still preferred to deal with Gray through intermediaries. Gray and Lauren went to his office to pull the cases from Westlaw. As they waited for the printer to spit them out, Gray sat back in his chair and stared at the envelope. It was rumored to contain all the votes from the term, including the one in the Anton Troy case. He thought back to his talk with Justice Marcus's clerk, Helen, just before Thanksgiving.

After what the chief did in the Anton Troy case, it's not like Justice Marcus is in the mood to do him any favors.

Did the chief really vote against saving Troy? The envelope could hold the answer. He plucked absently at the privacy sticker sealing the envelope. Gray then held up the envelope to the light.

"What are you doing?" Lauren whispered.

"I told you what Helen said about the Anton Troy vote," Gray said.

Lauren shook her head. "She was just trying to justify Justice Marcus not changing his vote on *Filstein*. There's no way the chief voted to execute Troy." She walked over to him. "I heard a clerk once peeked inside and was fired on the spot."

She was right. Gray tossed the envelope on the desk.

"Smart move. I was worried I was going to have to tackle you to the floor to stop you."

"Really? Maybe I should tear into it then," he grabbed for the envelope, laughing, but knocked over his mug. Coffee spilled all over the desk.

Lauren raced to save the envelope, but it was too late. She picked it up by its corner and let the brown liquid drip on the desktop. Gray pulled out some napkins he kept in a drawer from the many lunches at his desk and blotted the envelope, soaking up the coffee. They found a fan in a storage closet to air it out.

"You don't think Wall is waiting on it, do you?" Gray asked.

Lauren grimaced.

Amid the loud hum of the box fan, they read Justice Cutler's cases, trying to identify harmless places they could stick them in the draft *Filstein* opinion. It was hard to concentrate with the noise, and the distraction of worrying about Wall calling for the envelope that was propped against the fan.

Near midnight, the envelope was finally dry to the touch. "I'm going to run this over now, so we can watch the ball drop," Gray said. Lauren had already pulled up the revelry of Times Square on her iPad.

Gray rushed to Wall's chambers. The envelope had a large brown stain on it now, but maybe the contents had been spared. Or maybe Justice Wall would assume the chief had spilled the coffee.

The reception area was dark but for a cut of light coming from the small opening of Wall's office door. Gray could hear Wall speaking with someone. He was surprised he was in the office this late on New Year's Eve. Gray was going to knock when he heard a woman's voice.

"Who do they belong to?" She was upset, angry.

"I don't know, I suppose my wife could've left them."

"Your *wife* left her underwear in your office couch? You think I'm a fucking idiot?"

Gray backed away from the door.

"Calm down," Wall said.

"I'm risking everything seeing you, my career."

"And I'm not?" Wall said.

"*You* have life tenure," the woman said. "Maybe I should ask your *wife* if the panties are hers."

"So now you're threatening me?"

"Maybe it's not a threat."

A shadow cast over the light from the crack in the door. Gray stood motionless, holding his breath. Justice Wall peered through the opening, but Gray wasn't sure if the justice had seen him. Wall's door slammed shut.

Gray stood in the dark. He'd definitely deliver the envelope later. He made his way back to his office. The countdown for the new year was bellowing from Lauren's iPad.

Ten . . . nine . . . eight . . . seven . . .

Lauren walked up to him and took his hands in hers. "I'm glad I met you, Grayson Hernandez."

. . . six . . . five . . . four . . .

"I'm glad I met you too."

. . . three . . . two . . .

One!

On the iPad, the crowd erupted, couples kissed, and confetti floated in the sky. Lauren softly kissed Gray, then whispered in his ear, which sent a tingle down his spine.

"Happy New Year, my love."

CHAPTER 49

Milstein woke on New Year's Day with a splitting headache. She wished it had been the result of a wild night out. But she'd celebrated the end of a shitty year with a shitty night watching TV and waiting three hours for her delivery pizza to arrive. During those three hours, she'd downed a full bottle of Kendall Jackson and some stale crackers.

The new year meant that the task force officially took over the case. Even before the new year, though, Aaron Dowell had directed the investigation. As expected, Milstein and Cartwright had been relegated to secondary tasks. And everyone was focused singularly on finding former agent Kevin Dugan. To be fair, he fit the profile of the perp: white, male, educated, a motive for revenge. And he'd shown a propensity to violence when he'd beaten the storekeeper all those years ago. There didn't appear to be a sexual component to the crimes, so that meant there was likely an ideological or personal motive. Dugan wasn't some jihadist, but he had an extremely personal reason for the killings: to punish those who had taken everything from him. Why was he so hard to find? That itself elevated suspicion.

But other "whys" flooded Milstein's thoughts. Why the Supreme Court quill pens? Why was the killer leaving them at the

crime scenes? Why was he toying with them with silly messages—
random words at the scenes, cutting one of the victim's hair—like
it was *Silence of the Lambs*? And why kill the reporter at the Franklin
Theater? It appeared he was running a story about the decades-
old abduction of the Whitlock kids, but why now? And why kill him
for it and steal his research files? The only thing they knew was that
someone had used a computer at the Supreme Court to research
the reporter's home address shortly before the Franklin attack.
Maybe it was a coincidence. But show Milstein an agent who believed in coincidences, and she'd show you someone who shouldn't
be an agent.

Milstein thought about showering, but decided she'd spend the
day in sweats. She wondered what her ex, Chase, was doing right
now. Probably with his family in New York. Or on some exotic trip
with his new girlfriend. Milstein eyed the bankers boxes in the
shallow light of her living room. The FBI's assistant general counsel,
Milstein thought her name was Evanson, had them sent to the field
office. The litigation file from the storekeeper's civil lawsuit against
the Bureau. Milstein had lugged a few of the boxes home. Her glam-
orous assignment from the task force was to write a report summarizing the entire litigation file. Only one box to go. She might as
well finish. She carried the box to the couch and opened the lid. It
included transcripts—Kevin Dugan's civil deposition by the looks
of it. Three volumes. They must have questioned him for days.
There also were some old VHS tapes. The lawsuit was in the nineties, so they'd videotaped the deposition. Milstein didn't have a
VCR—did they even sell them anymore?—so she'd have to read the
transcripts. Or maybe the Bureau had an old machine in storage.

Her cell phone rang. Cartwright's beefy mug came up on her
screen. No doubt calling to invite her over. But she wasn't in the
mood for football or family today. So much for her New Year's res-
olution to be more social. She swiped the call to voice mail. Holidays were the worst. She thought for a moment to when she was a
kid, before the divorce, her dad and mom dressed up, their modest
Long Island home smelling of cookies.

Her phone rang again. *For fuck's sake, Cartwright. Give it a rest.* She answered the line. She expected his usual upbeat *Happy New Year!* But instead Cartwright said, "He did it again."

Milstein felt her stomach drop.

"Ben Freeman. And Freeman's son and a young woman, they think it was the son's girlfriend."

"Murdered?" She thought of the handsome former agent. So sure he could handle himself against any attacker.

"Not just murdered, Em."

"What do you mean?"

"It's—" Cartwright seemed to be catching his breath. "Can you come now?"

"Sure. Where?"

"I'll text you the address. Ben Freeman's house in McLean. And, Em . . ."

"Yeah?"

"If you haven't eaten breakfast yet, you should wait."

CHAPTER 50

Gray took New Year's Day off, but was back at his desk on Saturday, January 2. It was quiet around the court, and Gray managed to finish his bench memos for the upcoming arguments and even got ahead on the *cert* pool memos. He also gave his *Jando* opinion a final sign-off. The Reporter of Decisions, a persnickety man charged with making sure the opinions had no grammar errors and complied with the court's style guidelines, had e-mailed Gray proposed revisions.

Lauren appeared at his door. "You see it yet?"

"See what?"

"Pull up the *Washington Post* site."

Gray did so and his eyes locked on the headline: DUPONT UNDERGROUND AND FORMER FBI AGENT'S MURDER CONNECTED TO SUPREME COURT.

"They think the Dupont Underground murders and a former FBI agent's murder are related, *and* somehow connected to the court," Lauren said.

Gray clicked on the link. The story was short on details, but according to an unidentified source, evidence connected the Dupont killings to the recent murder of a former agent and his son and another woman at the agent's home.

Gray shuddered over the description of the crime. Sources

said that the agent's son and son's girlfriend had been dismembered. They'd been dead for nearly a week before they were found on New Year's Day. Gray scrolled down the site. The story included photos from the Dupont Underground murders. The killer had spray-painted something in the tunnels near where the bodies were found:

owl

Three is Enough

"I wonder what that's all about," Lauren said.

"It explains why the agent was looking for anyone around here who liked owls," Gray said.

"What agent?" Lauren asked.

Gray hesitated. Milstein had always been so stern with him about not disclosing anything. But this was Lauren. "After the garage attack, an FBI agent contacted me. It's a long story." He wasn't quite up to telling her or anyone about his paranoid suspicions or about the embarrassing Praveen debacle. Milstein had told him to just be a law clerk, and that's what he was determined to do.

"They don't think this is related to the attack on you and the chief, do they? Is that the Supreme Court connection?"

"No . . . well, maybe, but I think they've been focusing on a kidnapping case from the nineties."

Lauren looked at him. "I didn't know I was dating a wannabe G-man."

Gray smiled. "I didn't know we were dating."

"Three is enough?" Lauren said, studying the photo of the graffiti sprayed at the Dupont Underground scene. "Why is that so familiar?" Then, she said, "It reminds me of *Buck v. Bell*." Gray knew the decision, which was considered another one of the worst Supreme Court cases in history. Justice Oliver Wendell Holmes had upheld a state's right to sterilize a mentally disabled woman. Referring to her and her mother and daughter, he wrote, "Three generations of imbeciles is enough."

"That's weird," Lauren said, pointing to the photo of Dupont victim Amanda Hill.

"What?"

"I could swear I saw the chief and that woman out on the plaza this summer. I remember because they seemed to be having an argument."

"Hmm, that is weird." Gray looked back at the photo on the screen, the messy spray paint on a grimy wall:

owl

The closest he ever came to an owl clue at the court was noticing the animal symbols all over the Supreme Court building. Turtles, lions, owls. Ever since Justice Marcus's clerk told Gray about them, he'd started noticing animals everywhere. Owls among the motifs on the frames outside the elevators, in the ornamental metopes in the Great Hall, and even one on the frieze in the courtroom.

"You think it says 'owl'?" Lauren asked. "The *L* looks weird to me."

Gray examined the spray-painted word more closely.

owl

She was right. The *L* seemed off. Like it might be an *H*. Could it be *O-W-H*? What could that mean if it wasn't the word *owl*? He thought about it more. *Three is enough.* O-W-H. Oliver Wendell Holmes.

Then it hit him.

"Give me the phone. I need to call the FBI."

CHAPTER 51

Gray called Milstein several times, but it always went to voice mail. If the former FBI agent's murder really was connected to Dupont Underground, she was likely busy. He tried her one more time before he left for the First Saturday event. He'd hoped that the chief and Justice Wall would cancel since Saturday was so early in the the year, but no luck. This one, thank God, was less physical than zip lining and there would be no scary trip in a small plane. They were attending a "mixology" class at a place called Ripple in Cleveland Park, a drink-making course taught by a well-known D.C. bartender. It still surprised him the weird things rich people did with their money.

Ripple was in a long, narrow space, filled with attractive young Washingtonians. The private room in the back was set up like a classroom with tables facing the bartender, a bald, unshaven guy with sleeve tattoos, who instructed them on how to make the drinks. It wasn't ten minutes into the gathering when the chief and Justice Wall turned the whole thing into a competition. A blind taste test to see which team made the best drink. The event ended with everyone tipsy, except Praveen, who sipped soda water.

With inhibitions down, the clerks asked the justices a lot of questions. What's it like to be a member of the court? Were they going to the State of the Union next week given the president's criticism of the court at last year's speech? What's the best part of the job? The worst? And then the questions turned personal.

"You both met in high school?" Lauren asked Justice Wall, though she knew the answer to the question.

Wall, thick-tongued, said, "Boarding school. We met on the cricket team, right, Bones?"

The chief justice nodded.

"Is it only Justice Wall or did everyone call you 'Bones'?" Lauren asked the chief.

But it was Wall who responded. "I came up with it. He was skinny as a rail; couldn't hide behind a stripper pole if he needed to. Though there were one or two times we tried."

The chief seemed to grow uncomfortable. Gray couldn't tell if it was the ribbing or because Wall was letting his guard down too much.

"All right, enough about two dumb prep-school boys," the chief said.

"Is that when the competitions started?" Lauren pressed.

The room went suddenly quiet. The competition between the men was obvious, but also unspoken.

"Since the beginning," Wall said, "Bones and I had to one-up each other. He was number one, I was number two in our high school class. He got into Yale first too. But *I* stole his girlfriend in college. And *I* got the job at the SG's office." Wall was less playful than he was during his remarks at Georgetown. "But, alas, he got the center seat."

The talk turned more serious when Wall's clerk Audrey asked about the media reports that the Dupont Underground murders and the killing of the former FBI agent and his family were connected to the Supreme Court. The question seemed harmless enough, but it appeared to sober up the chief.

"As I'm sure you can understand, the investigation is confidential. But, truthfully, I'm in the dark as much as you. We need to trust that our police squad is looking out for us. What I do know—what I can assure you—is that none of you are in any danger."

The chief then thanked everyone for coming, signaling that the question-and-answer session was over. "Next month," he said, "we'll try paintball."

Gray could only image the carnage of Douglas and Wall in camo, paint pellets flying.

The group started gathering their coats and bags. Gray noticed the chief justice watching the way Lauren straightened Gray's shirt collar, so he decided to put some distance between them. He made a point of leaving first and alone. The plan was to meet at Lauren's place in Logan Circle.

Gray stood on Connecticut Avenue, looking for a cab. His iPhone was dead, so he couldn't get an Uber. Across the street was the Uptown Theater, one of the oldest movie houses in the District. When he was a kid, taking the subway to the Uptown was a special treat. It had a giant single screen and grand balcony. The theater had seen better days, however. The bulbs on the *p* in UP-TOWN had burned out, and the building looked tired. With only one screen, it was hard to compete with a megaplex less than a mile away.

As he looked over at Ripple to see if the others were making their way out, he heard a woman give an exaggerated clear of the throat in the parking lot nearby. He turned to look when she did it again. Agent Milstein. She was leaning against a dark sedan. She made eye contact with him, then disappeared into the car.

Gray scanned the area. None of the clerks had left Ripple yet, so he walked over quickly and climbed into the sedan.

"How'd you know I was here?" Gray asked.

Milstein cocked her head to the side.

"Right," Gray said, "you're the FBI."

A hint of amusement crossed Milstein's lips. "If only it was so easy to find someone," she said. "Your voice mail—you said you were going to Ripple." She rolled her neck. "Your call sounded urgent?"

"I think I found something."

Milstein sighed. "Found what?"

"You've been looking in the wrong place."

She gave a rattle of the head, like she was getting annoyed he was keeping her in suspense.

"The killer didn't paint the word *owl* on the wall at Dupont." Gray pulled up a link to the *Post* story on his phone and zoomed in on the photo he'd bookmarked:

owh

"The *L* isn't an *L*. I think it's an *H*. The killer carved O-W-H."

"And that's supposed to mean something?"

"Oliver Wendell Holmes. O-W-H."

Milstein released a loud breath.

"Oliver Wendell Holmes was one of the most revered Supreme Court justices," Gray said. He was feeling less confident in his great detective work.

"I know that, Gray. But even if you're right that the letter is an *H*, it could mean anything. Thousands of people probably have the same initials."

"But did thousands of people use the phrase 'Three is enough' in a judicial opinion?"

Milstein's eyes narrowed. He had her attention. "Go on."

"Holmes was known as one of the court's great writers. He was kind of the king of catchy one-liners, like 'clear and present danger' and the idea that free speech doesn't mean you can 'shout fire in a crowded theater.' But he's also known for authoring one of the most offensive lines in Supreme Court history." He explained Holmes's "three generations of imbeciles is enough."

"Wait, wait, wait," Milstein said, holding up her hands. "Holmes said you shouldn't 'shout fire in a crowded theater'?"

Gray gave a slow nod, realizing that he'd inadvertently given her some other useful information.

"At the Franklin Theater," Milstein said. "Some of the survivors reported that before anyone saw the smoke or blaze, someone started shouting that there was a fire, causing a panic, a stampede."

His heartbeat quickened with the thrill of giving her a real lead. The killer may have based two crimes—Dupont Underground and the Franklin fire—on decisions by Oliver Wendell Holmes.

Milstein seemed lost in thought. She then pulled out a folder. "There's something I want you to see."

CHAPTER 52

Milstein found Cartwright in the field office gym, huffing on the elliptical machine, like he did every Monday morning. The baggy shirt covering his large frame was wet with sweat. For such an active person, he seemed incredibly out of shape. All Peggy's big meals, and the beer he loved so much.

She told him about the meeting with Grayson.

"It's interesting," Cartwright said, "but we're supposed to be focusing on Kevin Dugan, not the Supreme Court. Aaron's confident that Dugan's the perp and they feel like they're closing in on him." His arms moved back and forth on the machine.

Milstein rolled her eyes. "The task force has two dozen agents looking for Dugan. They're so focused on Kevin Dugan, they're ignoring the connection to the Supreme Court. The killer spray-painted a line from a Supreme Court case at Dupont, and staged the Franklin fire based on another case. We know someone at the Supreme Court was looking for the reporter's address. And the feather pens. Does that sound like a Kevin Dugan revenge plot? Dugan was a broken man, not a sadistic killer. And the Whitlock case had nothing to do with the Supreme Court."

"No, there *is* a connection to the Supreme Court," Cartwright said. "Chief Justice Douglas is the guy who ruled that Kevin Dugan's beatdown of the storekeeper required a child molester go free. It also ruined Dugan. Helped in the civil case against him. And it explains why there's no physical evidence. Dugan knows what we look for, he was a career agent. And let's not forget, Dugan has disappeared. You don't drop off the grid unless you're planning something. I hate to say it, Em, but you seem like you're missing the forest for the trees."

"You know I hate stupid expressions."

"We need to focus on the Whitlock case. Finding Dugan."

"I'm doing that."

"Yeah? What's the status with John Whitlock's prison records? Have you checked the visitor logs? Called the halfway house he stayed at? Called homeless shelters?"

"Don't be a dick," she said. "And let me ask you: have you or the task force checked the morgues for John Does? Have you considered that the last anyone saw of Dugan he was destitute, an alcoholic mess who more likely died choking on his own vomit than committing the crime of the century? Have you asked yourself how he got the feather quill pens and why?"

Cartwright slowed his pace on the machine. "Good thought on the morgues," he said. This is why it was so hard to get mad at him. He could disarm conflict so casually.

Milstein said, "I've got Simmons calling around checking on the John Does."

"Keep making her work so hard, and she'll stop idolizing you," Cartwright said. He stepped down from the exercise machine and wiped his brow with a small towel. "Look, I'm fine focusing on the Supreme Court angle, but let's not lose sight of the ball here."

"I'm not. The murderer, he's trying to say something with these crimes. We just need to figure it out."

"You've been over and over that horror show, and you've found nothing."

Milstein hesitated, then said, "That's why I let Hernandez see more crime scene photos."

Cartwright frowned. "Em, I told you last time that was a bad idea."

"He saw something in the Dupont scene no one else did. Maybe he'll see something with the others. I'm desperate, Scott. You know what tomorrow is, don't you?"

Cartwright nodded. "The fifth of the month."

CHAPTER 53

"You said you'd tell me about the crime scene photos," Lauren said in a quiet voice.

They were sitting in the private clerks' room in the court's cafeteria. Two of Justice Anderson's clerks were eating lunch nearby.

Gray picked at his limp salad. He looked over to Anderson's clerks. "Can you tell your boss, please, for the love of God, can we just get some pizza or hamburgers in this place? The health food changes are killing me." As the most junior member of the court, Justice Anderson was head of the cafeteria committee, and recently overhauled the menu to make it more healthy. Anderson was also the note taker and door opener for the justices during their secret deliberations. The high court's hazing rituals for the newest justice.

Anderson's clerks laughed.

Lauren wasn't smiling.

"You really wanna hear about all this?" Gray said. "The photos are horrible." He put down his fork; the wilty salad was bad enough, now he had the bloody victims in his head.

Lauren looked at him. "Why'd she show you the pictures?"

"I'm not sure. She said they were closing in on the killer. She said people above her think they have the case solved, but she's not so sure. We were the only ones who understood the messages left at the Dupont killings, and who helped link the Franklin fire to an Oliver Wendell Holmes decision. Milstein thinks the other scenes might have similar clues."

"So they're gonna arrest someone soon?"

"I think so. Someone connected to the Whitlock case, but Milstein still thinks they're missing something."

Lauren ate a spoonful of her yogurt. "Did you see anything in the photos? Make any other connections?"

"Not yet. The woman at the convenience store, she'd been beaten with a bag full of canned food. It's hard to look at the pictures for more than a couple seconds at a time."

Lauren scrunched her face.

"Did you tell the agent about the chief justice visiting with Amanda Hill?"

"I didn't get a chance to. She was in a rush. But we know the chief isn't a suspect—he was attacked. And he was with us on Christmas when they think Ben Freeman was abducted."

"I know the chief isn't involved. But what if Amanda Hill was at the court about something else and just visiting him? It could give them something to go on. I still think you should've told her."

"Relax, Nancy Drew. I'll give her a call." He was kicking himself for getting dragged back into the FBI mess. He decided to change the subject. "You said you've gotta take off early today?"

"Yeah, doctor's appointment."

"Everything okay?" he asked.

"Of course. They make me see a shrink to get my Adderall prescription for my ADHD. Such a waste of time."

He'd seen a number of pill bottles in the medicine cabinet at her place. He didn't snoop, but it made more sense now. He didn't know she had ADHD. She was type-A, so it didn't seem to fit. She was always surprising him.

"Emilio's got ADHD, and Miranda says the same thing. I guess they make you jump through hoops because the meds are technically a controlled substance."

"Anyway, the doctor's office is in Logan Circle, so I'll probably just work from home rather than lug all the way back here."

"I'll call you if anything comes up. We've got everything covered for the chief, so no worries."

"Tell that to Keir." She finished her yogurt and placed the empty container on the tray. "Can I see the crime scene photos?"

Gray fished out his phone. He scanned the cafeteria before pulling up the images. Anderson's clerks were cleaning up their trays to leave. "Milstein only let me take a couple pictures of the crime scene shots. You sure you want to see them? You'll never be able to erase them from your memory."

Lauren nodded.

The first photo was of Ben Freeman's house. The killer had lined up Freeman's son and his girlfriend on the ground. He dismembered them, but staged the bodies so they were symmetrical. They looked like two people lying next to one another, but their heads and limbs were separated from their torsos. Lauren seemed like she was suppressing a gag. Gray quickly swiped to another photo, this one the convenience store. It wasn't of Sakura Matsuka's bloody corpse, but something the killer wrote at the store in Matsuka's blood: KORA MATSU.

"The victim's name was Sakura Matsuka, and the agent said that no one called her 'Kora' so they're trying to figure out what it means. They think the killer may have been interrupted, since he wrote only the first five letters of her last name, which is Matsuka, not Matsu."

Lauren's eyes twinkled with excitement. "Are you daft?"

Gray looked at her, confused.

"Are you kidding me? 'Kora Matsu.' Think about it, Gray. *Korematsu.*"

Gray recalled something Keir had said on New Year's Eve when they were working on the *Filstein* opinion.

The chief never cites Cutler's decisions. I think he'd rather cite Korematsu *than one of Cutler's cases.*

It was *Korematsu v. United States,* the notorious case where the court upheld Japanese American internment.

"I'm an idiot," Gray said. It was so obvious now. "Kora Matsu" wasn't a reference to the victim's name, it was to a Supreme Court case.

"I agree, you're an idiot," Lauren said, a hint of playfulness. She then turned serious. "You need to call that agent and tell her. Do you still have her number?"

"Yeah, I have her personal cell in my phone. And she gave me her card."

"Do you think it will get the other agents to focus on the Supreme Court?"

Gray shrugged. "Milstein said they've got tunnel vision on the Whitlock suspect."

"They should be focusing on the court, not wasting their time on that."

"I'll call her," Gray said. "Anyone ever tell you you're sexy when you're ordering people around?"

"Call her. Now!"

CHAPTER 54

Milstein received both a call and a text from Grayson. The messages said he had some additional information. Milstein would get back with him later. Cartwright was right, she needed to focus on Kevin Dugan, and close loose ends on the Whitlock case before chasing more leads on the Supreme Court front. Tomorrow was the fifth. The perp had broken the pattern for December, killing Ben Freeman on Christmas rather than the fifth of December. But, unlike everyone else on the task force, she was still assuming the fifth meant something to the killer.

She started by reviewing Agent Simmons's report on John Whitlock's prison visitor logs to see if they held any clues to help locate Whitlock. In two years, Whitlock had only one visitor. The log listed only "L. Smith." Simmons tried to track the person down, but Smith was the most common surname in North America. Hayfield Correctional didn't make copies of visitors' IDs, but they did record all visits. Milstein sent an e-mail to the prison's law enforcement liaison and requested the footage. Who knows how long it would take the corrections bureaucrat to send it.

Next, she needed to finish reviewing the Kevin Dugan lawsuit file, including watching the recording of Dugan's deposition. She'd had the tech guys track down an old VCR and set it up in her office. For the next few hours, as office lights went out and the halls grew quiet, Milstein watched the first of two tapes, fast-forwarding the long segments of irrelevant questions. By the end of the tape, the plaintiff's lawyer had questioned Kevin Dugan for nearly a full day yet had only gotten through Dugan's personal and professional background. No wonder civil cases lasted so damned long. Milstein chewed on a chocolate bar as she shoved the rectangular second tape into the clunky old machine. Ten minutes in, and the lawyer was finally getting to the relevant stuff. What Dugan discovered when he found Ken Tanaka with the Whitlock sisters. The video was framed on only Dugan, who hunched over a conference room table. The plaintiff's lawyer asked questions off screen, and Dugan's lawyer would occasionally bark an objection.

"And you arrived at the storage unit?"

"Yes."

"And what did you find?"

"She was sitting there, the younger one."

"Susie?"

"Yes."

"When you say sitting there, you mean—"

"I mean she was sitting on a stained mattress on the floor of the unit. Her hair was chopped up. And she was in shock. Her little stockings were torn." His voice broke. *"There was dried blood on her thigh."*

"Did she say anything?"

"No. She didn't cry. She was catatonic."

"And what about her sister, Kimberley?"

"I didn't see her at first, and then . . ." his voice caught again.

"You wanna take a break?"

"No, let's get this over with."

"You said you didn't see Kimberley at first."

"Yeah, so I started looking about the unit. It was small, filled with junk. Then I saw the large duffel bag."

There was a long silence. Even the lawyer didn't seem to want to ask. *"And what was in the bag?"*

"I unzipped it and she was in there. I saw her tiny head. Then

her neck, it was bruised. Then I realized that it wasn't attached to
her body, that he'd dismembered her."

"And then what did—"

Milstein's phone rang and she fumbled for the remote to pause
the video.

"Hey, Scott, what's up?"

"I hate it when you're right," he said.

"What?"

"Check your e-mail."

Milstein tapped on her keyboard and saw the e-mail from
Aaron Dowell.

They'd found Kevin Dugan. And he was dead.

CHAPTER 55

When his office phone rang at 11:30 p.m., Gray snatched up the receiver.

"I found something," Lauren said.

"Hey, where've you been? You never texted me after your doctor's appointment. I called and sent you texts and have been a little worried and—"

"Did you not hear me? I said I found something."

"Found what? What are you talking about?"

"About the murders. I mean, I found something important. We need to set up a meeting with the FBI agent."

"She hasn't gotten back to me yet. What is it?"

"Can you come over?"

"Now?" Gray said. "Yeah, sure. Are you gonna keep me in suspense?"

"I'll explain everything when you get here. Also, can you bring me one of my work files?"

"Sure. Where is it, your office?"

"No, I left it in my locker in the court's gym."

"I can't go in the women's locker room."

"It's late. It's not like anyone will be in there."

Gray took down the locker number and combination.

"It's a file, it has *Filstein* written on the cover," Lauren said.

"Got it, I'll go get it and be over in about a half hour. I hope this is some type of seduction game and when I get there you're gonna be naked on the—" The line clicked off.

Lauren normally would have liked the banter, but she seemed stressed out. Gray understood; he knew how playing detective could suck you in. It had landed him cuffed on the ground in a basement filled with sex toys.

After retrieving her work file from the ladies' locker room—and it was true, ladies' restrooms and facilities really are nicer—he tucked the file in his sports bag, one of those nylon drawstring back-packs. It was late and he wasn't planning on working any more tonight, so he left his papers in his office.

Gray drove on autopilot, his mind shuffling through the events of late. He was hopeful that Lauren really had found something, though he was annoyed he'd been pulled back into it all. He'd already spent too many hours speculating pointlessly about the crimes. Wondering if someone in the building could be involved. And yet his thoughts still skipped back to *who*? His co-clerks? Milstein seemed to have crossed them off the list. Martin, his supervisor from the marshal's office? But the man who attacked the chief in the garage was tall, strong. Fast. Nothing like Martin. One of the clerks from other chambers? Someone angry about one of the court's rulings? A nut? He thought about the homeless guy, Vincent. He was an imposing figure. But with his scraggly beard and soiled clothes, Vincent wouldn't have made it past the front security checkpoints. Besides, the feds must've already checked out the court fanatics.

At just past midnight, Gray pulled into a space in front of Lauren's row house apartment. The porch light was off. He didn't have a key, but she'd hear the doorbell. He grabbed the backpack and walked to the door. He rang the bell and waited. When she didn't answer, he turned the knob. It was unlocked. She must have seen his car. He stepped inside and called her name.

Her cat came meowing past him and he clicked on the light. The cat must have stepped in something since there appeared to be prints on the hardwood. He then got a sickening feeling. The prints were crimson.

He reached down and put a finger in the liquid. His chest heaved and his face grew hot.

"*Lauren!*"

No answer.

He ran down the narrow hallway to her bedroom. He slapped on the light. The last thing he remembered before the crushing blow on his head was a man in a ski mask.

CHAPTER 56

Gray remembered waking up on the floor. Looking for Lauren, but finding only a pool of blood. He must have called Agent Milstein because he remembered being in the back of a sedan and was now at the FBI field office. He didn't know what time it was, but he was tired, jittery, his hands wouldn't stop shaking. He'd refused to go to the hospital.

The room wasn't like in the movies—no grimy table, no one-way mirror. The facility was clean. Professional. Like he was a middle manager awaiting colleagues for a sales meeting in a room filled with pressed-wood furniture. He wore an oversized T-shirt and sweats they'd given him. They'd taken his clothes and run some type of test on his hands, standard forensics, he presumed. His backpack was on the table. Its drawstrings were open, and someone must have looked inside. Or maybe Gray had opened it. He wasn't thinking clearly. Everything was a haze.

Several agents had rotated in and out of the room. They each asked variations of the same questions. *When was the last time you saw Lauren? Why were you at her house so late? What exactly is your relationship with her? You know anyone who would have a reason to hurt her? You two having any problems?*

He understood they had to ask, but all he knew, the only thing he could focus on, was the pool of blood.

The door swung open and there stood Agent Milstein and a stocky guy. He thought he had been the driver that night he first met Milstein after the Anton Troy execution. Milstein's partner? Both sat down across from Gray.

Milstein looked at him. "You okay?"

What a stupid question. "Why are you wasting time here? You need to be out looking for her!" He choked back a sob.

Milstein didn't flinch, but her partner shifted uncomfortably in his chair. "There are dozens of agents looking for her, Grayson. An entire task force. But you may have information that helps us find her, even if you don't know you do."

"Was it him?" Gray asked.

Milstein hesitated. "We don't know. But you said he took her after midnight, so it's January 5, which seems to be an important date to the killer."

"She told me she'd found something," Gray said. "She asked me to come over after work to talk about it."

"Do you know what it was? What she'd found?"

"No. But earlier today, we made another connection between one of the murders and a Supreme Court case. That's why I called you." Gray told her about the killer's reference to *Korematsu v. United States* at the convenience store murder. "I thought you said that you were close to finding the guy?" Gray said.

Milstein and her partner exchanged a glance. Milstein said, "We've had some setbacks." She wouldn't say what.

They spent another hour or so asking Gray questions. It was going nowhere, so he asked if he could leave. He was exhausted, his head throbbed from where the man in the ski mask had hit him.

"I'll get someone to drive you," Milstein said.

"Please find her," Gray said.

CHAPTER 57

Gray couldn't be alone right now. He had the agent drop him off at Sam's place. It was just past four in the morning, and Sam answered the door groggy and annoyed, but her expression softened when she got a look at him. And he told her everything.

"It sounds like they've cleared everyone you work with. Does the court have any stalkers or creeps bugging the justices? Crazies pissed about the court's decisions?"

"Just anyone who cares about health care, abortion, campaign finance, gay rights, gun control, among others."

They talked until dawn. Gray was too upset, and Sam too loyal, to sleep, but at some point he dozed off. He awoke to the patter of rain. Sam had thrown a blanket over him.

"Morning," Sam said. She sat at the kitchen counter in the open loft. She was sipping coffee, and asked if he wanted a cup.

"That would be great." He stretched out his arms, glancing out the large rain-spattered windows into the gray sky.

Sam carried over a mug, and nudged her chin toward the television. The sound was muted, but a correspondent stood in front of the Supreme Court building, the marble stairs and portico cropped behind him. The screen then flashed to an image of Lauren. He felt a blow to the chest at the sight of her. Even in her court ID photo that they used, she had an imposing beauty.

He shouldn't have been surprised at the media frenzy. No law clerk from the Supreme Court had ever been the victim of foul play. And Lauren was a young, beautiful woman, the type of "pretty white girl" who fed media cycles, so it was going to get ugly. Especially since they had no body. Could she be alive? The media attention also meant that it was inevitable word would leak connecting a single perpetrator to Dupont Underground, the Franklin fire, the chief's attack, the convenience store, the former FBI agent, and now Lauren.

"They mention my name?" Gray asked.

"I don't think so."

Should he go to work? He fished out his phone to see if there'd been any word from the court about how to proceed. The battery was dead. The iPhone was one of the greatest inventions of his generation, so why couldn't his goddamned battery hold a charge? He decided that he'd probably be expected to come into the office.

"I should go home and get cleaned up." He still had on the oversized shirt and sweats the agents had given him. He was tired, grief draining the energy from him.

"You want me to come with you?" Sam had a concerned look on her face. "I'm not sure you should be alone."

He stood and gave her a long hug. "I'll be okay. I should go."

CHAPTER 58

Dora Baxter bent down and tied her running shoe, foot propped on one of the wet steps of the Lincoln Memorial. She pulled the laces tight, stretching her calf. She was tired, but only a little more to go. Her morning jog from her office at Main Justice to the foot of giant Abe Lincoln and then across the Mall to the Supreme Court building—exactly 4.8 miles—was getting harder every day. She wasn't getting any younger. If her mother didn't remind her of that, her aching joints would. Her mom didn't understand. Success in this town, particularly for a woman, required focus and discipline. You had to be twice as good as them to get half as much.

The day the Senate confirmed her nomination as solicitor general her mother said it was time to think about her personal life—meet someone, have some kids, have a life. What Mom didn't understand was that this *was* her life, and she liked it just fine, thank you very much. Besides, none of her married friends seemed all that happy. And the ones with kids, oy—all they seemed to be able to talk about was their spawn. They'd lost themselves. Even secretly seeing that sycophant Peter Wall, the latest in a long line of mistakes, had been better than turning out like her mother. Living someone else's dream.

She ran along the gravel path that bordered the reflecting pool, which was rippling from rain that had started up again. The breeze and drizzle felt good on her face as she made her way down the route lined with trees and overweight squirrels—the damn tourists couldn't resist feeding the fearless rodents. Thankfully, the rain had deterred most of the tourists this morning with only a hearty few up early wandering in their disposable rain ponchos.

She jogged around the World War II Memorial and then up the incline, her thoughts meandering. It had been a bizarre week. The media was buzzing that the Dupont Underground murders had a connection to the Supreme Court, though none of her sources knew what it was all about. But just that morning she'd gotten a security briefing e-mail stating that a Supreme Court law clerk was missing. Not to be insensitive, but Dora's main concern was the effect the drama would have on her cases still pending at the high court. The president himself had called her about the *Filstein* case. The outcome of the case could mean the difference between Dora being nominated for the next seat on the Supreme Court or simply left to move on to private practice at the end of the president's term. She needed the case decided. She needed to win. If she knew the high court—and she damn well did—the justices wouldn't let anything derail their case schedule.

She stopped at the crosswalk, jogging in place. Cars whipped down the winding lane heading into the heart of downtown, tires hissing from the rain. She was so tired. *Push yourself, Dora.* They were her father's words that always whispered in her ear—from the days on the soccer field, the high school debate team, studying for the SATs. Dad always pushed himself, which probably contributed to his fatal heart attack when Dora was a high school senior. Probably the reason she pushed herself, some notion that he was watching.

When the traffic signal changed, she jogged into the crosswalk.

She didn't feel the initial impact, just the disoriented feeling of flight. Then she was on the street. She tried to get up; her brain made the command, but her body wouldn't oblige. She was frozen on the blacktop. It was getting harder to breathe, and she heard her heartbeat in her ears. Her eyes shifted to the car that had stopped on the street. She realized that she'd been hit. The driver's door swung open and he stepped out of the car. Dora tried to lift her arm, but it didn't move.

You're not going to die. Push yourself, Dora.

The driver just stood there watching her on the ground from the distance. It was then that Dora noticed that the driver was wearing a ski mask. The driver hurried back into the silver sports car. The last thing Dora ever saw was the rear of the car speeding at her in reverse.

CHAPTER 59

Gray was relieved when the cab pulled up to the condo building and there were no reporters camped out. The whole morning had a surreal quality. Was this all a bad dream? He paid the cabbie and hurried up to his place. The landline was ringing, and Gray grabbed the receiver.

"Grayson," his dad said, "we were worried. We saw the news. Why weren't you answering your cell phone? Are you okay?"

"I'm sorry. I was with the FBI all night and then I slept at Sam's. My phone died, but I should have called." He pulled the iPhone from his backpack and connected it to the charger on the counter.

"It's all right. We're just glad you're okay." Then, in a gentler tone, "I'm so sorry about your friend."

Gray swallowed at that one. Despair washed over him. "They're gonna find her."

His father didn't respond.

"I need to get to the office," Gray said. "Tell Mom I'm okay. I'll call you later once I know more."

"I love you, son."

"I love you too."

In his bedroom, he ripped off the clothing the FBI had given him. He then took a hot shower, breathing in the steam. He tried not to cry, but soon his emotions overcame him. Lauren. After a long while, he turned off the water and tried to pull himself to-gether. He stepped out of the stall and wiped the fog from the mir-ror with his hand. He looked exhausted, his eyes sunken. He dried his hair with the towel, his head still tender from where he'd been hit.

He walked barefoot to the bedroom, leaving a trail of wet prints. It was then he noticed something out of the ordinary. In the corner of the room. Two small suitcases. They weren't his, and he was sure they weren't there the last time he was in his place. He lifted one of the bags and placed it on the bed. He unzipped the top and looked inside. Women's clothes. He pulled out some of the garments. *"Ouch."* He cut his finger on something sharp inside. A drop of blood hit the hardwood floor. His mind jumped to Lauren's floor. He needed to beat back the images. He hurried to the bath-room and ran his finger under hot water.

His iPhone pinged. Then the landline rang. He ran to the kitchen counter and scanned the text on his phone. It was from Sam:

TV says police think you are involved; looking for you. WTF???

Then he saw something unsettling in the kitchen sink. Hair. Long, black hair, as if a woman had gotten a haircut in his kitchen. Someone had been in the condo. What the hell was going on? He read Sam's text again.

Pain radiated in his chest. He heard a siren and rushed to the window. Several black sedans screeched to a stop in front of the building. That's when it hit him. The hair. He pictured the woman killed at the convenience store. Her hair cut into a jagged mess.

He should stay. He had nothing to hide. But then he ran to the bedroom and looked at the suitcases again. The bag in the corner had a luggage tag. He read the name, and the air was pulled from his lungs. Jay Freeman. The FBI agent's son.

Gray realized that someone was trying to make it look like he was involved with the murders. He hurriedly put on jeans, a T-shirt, and jacket. A voice in his head kept telling him to stay. The law would protect him. He was innocent. But then Gray thought of Anton Troy and how the law didn't protect Troy from a state intent

on executing him. And what was happening to Gray wasn't the result of an incompetent justice system. It was an orchestrated plan.

Gray grabbed some money he kept in a jar in the kitchen and
shoved the bills and his iPhone in the backpack. Inside, he saw Lauren's work file with FILSTEIN written on its cover in Lauren's me-
ticulous handwriting. He had another stab of sadness. She's such a
hard worker. Even in the midst of chasing down a lead about the
murders, she was going to work late on the *Filstein* case. But why
would she be working on *Filstein*? That was Keir's case. Gray pulled
out the file and opened it. It wasn't papers relating to *Filstein*. It
was a business-sized envelope. To anyone else it would have looked
like an ordinary office envelope. But Gray knew it was far from ordinary. It had a large brown stain.

Gray didn't know why Lauren had taken the chief justice's
famous envelope. But he was going to find out.

CHAPTER 60

Gray sprinted down the emergency stairwell. At the foot of the stairs were two doors, one that led to the garage, the other outside. He heard the screech of tires coming from the garage, and he watched through the small window on the door. Two sedans pulled behind the empty parking spot reserved for the chief's Audi. He'd left the car at Lauren's place last night. Men in blue Windbreakers, obviously federal agents, jumped out of the sedans and started sweeping the area.

He should go talk to them. But he wanted to examine what was inside the envelope. See what Lauren had uncovered. It could provide the answers to everything. His phone chimed in the backpack, but he ignored it. He ran out the door into the rain.

"Hey!" a voice called out to him.

Gray turned and saw another agent. He was squinting as the rain blew in his face, and he had a hand on his holster. Gray spied a bike rack next to the door. He started pulling on bikes, each catching on chains or U-locks. He kept tugging, not looking up, but he could hear the footfalls. The agent was yelling something at him now. Gray yanked at another bike, then another. And then a miracle, a mountain bike pulled free. He jumped on the bike and raced on a footpath that led down to the waterfront. He didn't look back, but the agent got so close that he could hear heavy breaths and the sound of the agent's strides.

Gray pedaled furiously, his adrenaline pumping, his body wet with rain and panic sweat. He stopped under the Key Bridge, far enough away that the agent had given up the chase. His phone pinged again. If he was really going to run, they could use it to track him. But was he *really* going to run? He started to question again if he'd lost his shit. But he could still plausibly say he wasn't evading capture, that he didn't know that the guy was an agent. That he was in shock. And, you know what? That wouldn't necessarily be a lie. He pulled the phone from the bag, and chucked it as far as he could into the Potomac. He then headed for the bike trail, recalling the chief telling him that it went on for more than ten miles.

He just needed a little time. Time to get out of the rain, time to think, time to review Lauren's file. He rode for a half hour, the rain lashing his face along the narrow trail lined with woodland. At one of the exit points on the trail, he saw a procession of cars, cherries flashing on their dashes, race past. He decided to get off the trail in case they were planning to box him in. From there, he took the back streets to his old neighborhood. He wanted to talk to his father.

When he reached Hamilton Heights, he peered around the corner to see if there was any activity outside the pizza shop. He saw nothing. Gray pedaled over and leaned the bike against a lamp-post outside the shop. The rain was coming down again, the wind pushing his wet clothes against his skin, though he wasn't sure if he was shivering from the cold or shock. The breeze carried the smell of rotten something to Gray's nostrils from the trash bags lined at the curb.

Gray peered inside the rain-spattered front window of the restaurant. Dad was there, mopping the floor. He took his time, work-ing a grid. Gray had witnessed the scene a thousand times before, but he'd never seen the dignity in it. He was about to go inside when he heard the roar of several vehicles pulling in front of the shop. They'd been waiting for him.

CHAPTER 61

Gray ran to the alley next to the shop, jumped a fence, and cut through an overgrown lot. He knew these streets from his boyhood, so he had the advantage. He darted behind a line of row houses and ducked next to some trash bins. A rat, a giant creature, seemed to notice him, but didn't move from working on a garbage bag that had spilled open. After a few minutes, Gray skulked down the lane, running along a chain-link fence that separated the small back patios and gardens. The homes were a mishmash, some well maintained and landscaped, others weed-filled messes. Gray's heart jumped when a dog lunged at him from behind a fence. He kept running until he hit another alleyway.

He still had the backpack. He wanted so desperately to review its contents—what was in the envelope—but first he needed to get out of there. But where to go? He obviously couldn't go back to the chief's condo or his old place. Sam's loft wasn't safe either. And he couldn't bring this mess into his sister and nephew's lives.

He debated turning himself in, but he just needed more time. He heard voices and jerked around. Two men, badges dangling on chains around their necks, rushed toward him.

"You there! Stop!"

He didn't look back, just ran as fast as he could. He made it to the steps leading up to Monroe Park.

The park was empty except for a group of what looked like middle-schoolers huddled at the rotting gazebo. When he approached, they put on a tough front, but he saw fear in their eyes. They had a bottle wrapped in a brown bag, and Gray assumed they were skipping school. They didn't look like hardened gang members. Several skateboards were propped against the gazebo, and one of the boys was resting his foot on a board.

Gray looked back at the entrance to the park. The agents hadn't made their way up. He had a feeling that they weren't storming in because they were building a perimeter. Trapping him.

He turned to the boys. "How would you guys like to earn a hundred bucks?"

The boys darted looks at one another, skeptical. "Doing what?" one of the boys said. He was the oldest, the leader.

"Lend me one of your boards. And ride with me out of here." Gray pulled out the money from his backpack.

The boys looked at one another again. After a moment, the leader said, "That's it, we ride with you outta the park, nothing else?"

"Nothing else. An easy hundred."

The older boy looked at his friends who were nodding. "Make it two hundred."

Gray couldn't help but smile. He handed the kid the wad of bills. "This is all I've got. But I want that hat too." He pointed to one of the boys, a stocky kid who wore one of those snapbacks.

And so there Gray was, jetting down the steep incline of Monroe Street, hunched over in the middle of a group of school kids. Eluding federal agents—via skateboard. He could see agents at the entrance of the park, talking into radios, two cars parked at the curb. None of the agents gave the young skateboarders a second look.

The rain had turned to mist, and they sped down the hill, splashing through puddles, the rhythmic *clunk-clunk, clunk-clunk* of the wheels going over gaps in the sidewalk. Gray crouched low in the middle of the group. They crossed the street and skidded to a stop. Gray looked up the hill. No one had followed. He'd made it. But he still had the same problem: where to go? He removed the hat and handed the oldest kid the board. The other boys were smiling, giving high fives. They waited for their friend, whose board Gray had borrowed, to come jogging down the hill. The kid gave a thumbs-up.

"You can take a board if you want." The older boy gestured to the beat-up skateboard Gray had borrowed for his escape. Gray smiled at the ridiculousness of it all.

"Thanks. But I'll be okay." He tossed the kid the hat.

"At least take this," the kid slapped two twenties in Gray's hand. "Think you'll need it more than us."

Gray gave an appreciative nod.

"Where you gonna go?" another boy asked.

Gray needed somewhere safe. Somewhere he could review Lauren's file. Somewhere police wouldn't track him. At that moment, he realized where.

"Not far," he said.

CHAPTER 62

Gray made his way into the bowels of Madison Towers public housing complex. The projects were forbidden territory when he was a kid, and he now understood why. The halls smelled of piss and vomit. Patches of mold spotted the walls, and figures, drug-addled hall dwellers, lurked in the shadows. He rushed through the maze and outside onto a center courtyard. The rain had stopped, but the sky remained dark, large brown puddles flooding the yard.

At the entrance to a second building stood two imposing men. Oversized baseball shirts, bald heads, tattoos.

The giants looked down at him, arms folded, their expressions half menacing, half amused.

"I need to see your boss." Gray looked up at the security camera mounted above the door.

"I don't see you in the appointment book," one of the men said, grunting a laugh, proud of himself.

"Look, I don't have time to fuck around, I don't—" Gray stopped at the sight of the gun. The guy held it sideways, pointed at Gray's chest. "He'll want to see me." It took more convincing, but the other giant finally put a cell phone to his ear and turned away. The camera mounted above the door then rotated, stopping when the lens was directed at Gray. The man with the phone then nodded, clicked off, and gestured for the other guy to lower the gun. He then led Gray up two flights of stairs. The stairwells made the hallways seem lavish. Gray held his breath until they ducked into a service elevator.

The guy pulled out a key card and stuck it in the slot. Not something you'd expect in a run-down housing complex. Gray watched the numbers above the door light up until they reached the top floor. But the elevator didn't stop. That was weird. Then he realized that the elevator was rigged—it was the illusion of only eleven floors, but there were twelve. The doors slid open, and there was more muscle stationed at the door of an apartment. The men stepped aside, and Gray walked in. For a moment he wondered if he was seeing things. The place looked like a Manhattan penthouse, not Section 8 housing. It had high ceilings, an open floor plan. Music blared from an elaborate sound system. Mounted on the wall, a massive television. The screen showed a newscaster talking into the camera, then a photograph of Gray.

On a large sofa, next to two women, sat the boss. The crime lord Gray had come to see. Gray's eyes couldn't help but lock on the gun and white powder on the coffee table. The man took a swig from a bottle of beer. He looked at the television, which still had Gray on the screen.

"Ponyboy, I wondered when you'd show up."

CHAPTER 63

Arturo gave Gray one of the spare bedrooms at the end of a long corridor. The apartment took up the entire floor of the building. It was a remarkable operation Arturo had going on up there: drugs, gambling, loans. Rooms for Arturo's inner circle and guests. And with the network of lookouts and escape routes, Arturo assured Gray that he would be safe.

"Why all the security?" Gray asked. "Cops?"

Arturo chuckled. "D.C. Metro guys make twenty-eight K a year, they're an easy problem to fix." He waited a beat, and explained the security precautions with a single word: "Ortiz." The name still sent a chill up Gray's back. The sound of Angel Ortiz's skull cracking on pavement.

Gray had replayed the incident over and over in his head. He didn't think Arturo had intended to kill Angel. But then Angel's two friends, the witnesses, turned up dead. Shot execution-style in an alley near the high school. Gray didn't know if Arturo was behind it, cleaning up loose ends, and he'd never asked. But the demise of Angel Ortiz and Company was the end of their friendship. It was also the start of a war between Arturo's set and the Ortiz clan, including Ortiz's younger brother, Ramon "Razor" Ortiz. Gray thought back to Razor's sinister smile that night with Lauren. Arturo to the rescue again. Gray wondered momentarily whether Razor could be behind Lauren's abduction. But that didn't make sense. It was someone connected to the Supreme Court. And Razor wasn't one for subtlety, so the mysterious messages left at the crime scenes didn't fit.

Gray pulled Lauren's *Filstein* file from his backpack. It was damp from the rain. He removed the envelope and pulled out the papers. Why had she taken the envelope? The first sheaf was stapled, though the corners were ripped, like the sheets had been ripped from a larger batch. On each page, a message.

The first: THE GREAT DISSENTER

The next page: THE WORST SCOTUS DECISION EVER

The next: THE 37TH LAW CLERK

The last: FILSTEIN SWING VOTE. WEDNESDAY. A RACE. FIRST THERE WINS. LEAVE 1FS @ 7PM.

The file also contained Westlaw printouts of old newspaper stories about Justice Wall's confirmation hearing.

Gray thought back to the first time the chief had given him envelope duty after he'd run down Justice Cutler in the hallway. How proud he was. Why would the envelope contain cryptic messages? Was this really the envelope the chief justice used to communicate with the justices, or did it just look like it? Maybe it wasn't real. No, the envelope and the papers had a similar brown stain. He recalled New Year's Eve when he'd playfully pulled Lauren into his lap, spilling his coffee. He felt another piercing pain in his chest. He needed to focus. Then he saw something scribbled inside the folder that held the envelope. In Lauren's handwriting: A GAME?

CHAPTER 64

"You're on the TV again, yo," Arturo said, poking his head into Gray's room. Gray pointed the remote at the set mounted on the bedroom wall and clicked it on. The room had a built-in headboard, sleek dresser, glass-topped desk. Arturo even brought in a laptop and portable printer. Gray marveled again at the balls it took to set up the top floor of a public housing complex like a pricey condo.

On the screen, the chief justice was standing in front of a bevy of microphones in the East Conference Room of the Supreme Court. The ornate, portrait-filled room was jammed with reporters. The chief must have been livid about the need to face the press like a lowly politician. Douglas wouldn't answer questions shouted at him. He just read from a prepared statement that said the justices were devastated about Lauren's abduction and the court was working with authorities to help find her. As for Gray, the chief said Gray was hired as a clerk after an incident that they now were investigating as possibly orchestrated. The suggestion being that Gray had somehow been involved in the attack on the chief justice in the garage.

"That the guy you said was so good to you?" Arturo asked.

"Yeah."

"Don't seem so good now."

"Ya think?" Gray said, not taking his eyes off the screen.

"And the girl," Arturo said, "she's your lady?"

Gray felt his throat catch. But he needed to stay focused, stay strong. "Yes," he said, his voice hoarse.

Arturo gave a small bow of the head. After a long moment, Arturo looked at the collage Gray had pinned on the wall. Gray had tacked up each page from the envelope under which he'd pinned handwritten notes.

"Looks like some *CSI* shit goin' on in here." Arturo took a swig of his beer. "Don't let Olivia see the holes in the walls, she just had the rooms painted. Interior design school."

"She your girlfriend?"

A reluctant nod. Then: "So, you figuring this shit out?"

"Actually," Gray said, "I think I have."

Gray gestured to the first sheet of paper. Arturo read it aloud, " 'The Great Dissenter.' "

"That's the key to it all," Gray said. He pointed to the GREAT DISSENTER page from the envelope. " 'The Great Dissenter' was a nickname for Oliver Wendell Holmes, who was a Supreme Court justice."

Gray explained to Arturo that the killer in Dupont Underground had spray-painted *O.W.H.* and a phrase associated with one of Holmes's cases on the wall. Gray then pointed to newspaper stories about the Franklin fire.

"I remember that," Arturo said. "Some motherfucker set the theater on fire and put padlocks on the outside of the doors."

Gray nodded. "Holmes is famous for an expression about the limits of free speech. He said, 'you can't shout fire in a crowded theater.' Some of the survivors of the Franklin fire reported that someone had started screaming, creating a panic even before the blaze was very big."

Arturo creased his brow. "You think this Holmes guy is involved in Dupont and the fire?"

Gray gave a dry laugh. "It's not Holmes who did it. He's been dead for years. The murders were just inspired by his work. By the lines in his decisions. The theater fire was before the family was murdered in Dupont. One was the answer to the other, one-upping each other." When Arturo didn't seem to be catching on, Gray added, "A game." The words Lauren had written on the file.

Arturo shook his head. "What kind of crazy mother—"

"It gets worse," Gray said, gesturing to the wall. He put a finger on the second sheet from the envelope: THE WORST SCOTUS DECISION EVER. Under it, a sheet of paper with KORA MATSU written on it. Under that, Gray had drawn a stick-figure depiction of the crime scene at Ben Freeman's house. Two bodies, side by side, dismembered.

"The convenience store victim's name was Sakura Matsuka, but the killer wrote something at the scene in her blood: 'Kora Matsu.' Everyone thought it was a reference to her last name. But it wasn't." Under the page from the envelope was an article Gray had pulled from the Internet entitled, "Worst Supreme Court Cases in History." Gray pointed to the first decision on the list: *Korematsu v. United States.*

"There's an infamous Supreme Court case where the justices upheld the right of the government to order Japanese Americans into internment camps during World War II." Lauren had figured that one out.

Arturo took another swig of beer, taking in what Gray was saying.

"The Supreme Court case is named *Korematsu.*" Gray paused. "*Korematsu.* Kora Matsu." Gray wondered if they'd chosen the victim based solely on her name. Or maybe it was the other way around, the idea for the challenge was inspired by her name.

"No. Fucking. Way." Arturo took another long sip of beer.

"There's more," Gray said. He placed a finger on the stick-figure drawing of Ben Freeman's son and girlfriend who'd been abducted at Union Station. He pointed again to the story listing the worst Supreme Court cases in history. "There was a case called *Plessy versus Ferguson.*"

"Don't tell me that couple was named Plessy and Ferguson?" Arturo said, his tone tinged with disbelief.

"No, but *Plessy* was the case that upheld racial segregation in public places, allowing the states to segregate schools. It was later overruled by *Brown versus Board of Education*."

Arturo gave him an *I have no idea what you're talking about* shake of the head.

"The holding in *Plessy* was that segregation was okay so long as the facilities provided to each race were equal—it was called the 'separate but equal doctrine.'" Gray paused. "It'd be okay to segregate schools if the schools for whites and blacks were equal."

"Schools are still segregated," Arturo said.

"Fair enough," Gray said, thinking of the two white kids who'd attended Obama High. "But not by law." Gray pointed at the stick figures. "The FBI showed me a photo of the former agent who was killed, along with his son and son's girlfriend. They were an interracial couple. Lined up side by side, dismembered. Separate. And the body parts were perfectly aligned. Equal. Separate but equal."

Arturo nearly choked on his beer at that one. "This is some gross shit. Who is it? Who did this shit?"

Gray's gaze moved to the television screen. The news was replaying Chief Justice Douglas's remarks at the press conference.

"No way," Arturo said.

Gray nodded.

"This is one sick motherfucker."

"Not *one* sick motherfucker," Gray said. "Two."

CHAPTER 65

"What do you mean, two?" Arturo asked, still examining Gray's crime scene wall.

"The chief's boyhood friend, Justice Wall. They're competitive as hell. And these papers"—Gray gestured to the coffee-stained pages from the envelope—"they came from the envelope the chief and Wall use to communicate with each other inside the court."

Arturo let out a loud breath. "Hold on. You think they were competing to come up with the most creative way to kill based on Supreme Court cases and shit?"

"Yeah. And it explains the alibis. The feds had no leads because everyone who could've been involved had an alibi for at least one of the murders. Wall was out of town for the Franklin fire, but the chief was here. The chief was out for Dupont, but Wall was in town. The chief was at the court the night the convenience store clerk was killed, but Wall never came in. The chief was on Martha's Vineyard on Christmas when Ben Freeman and the couple were killed, but not Wall. No one considered it was two people who could be in two different places."

Arturo's expression was skeptical. "This don't feel right."

"And maybe it was more than a game." Gray pointed to the newspaper story about Justice Wall's confirmation hearing. "This was in Lauren's file. The reporter who was killed in the Franklin fire wrote a scathing story about Wall during his confirmation hearing. And Lauren said this summer she saw the chief justice having an argument with Amanda Hill, the woman killed in Dupont Underground. Maybe they were doing each other's dirty deeds. The chief killed the reporter, Wall killed Hill."

"Did the justices have beefs with the other victims?"

"I don't know."

"So you think they're crazy psychos *and* calculating killers offing their enemies? Those two things don't go together. It don't make sense."

Gray agreed it sounded crazy, but he was onto something. He was sure of it. "There are famous examples of killers working together like this. Haven't you heard of Leopold and Loeb? Never mind. Maybe they've been doing it for a long time. Maybe they just never got caught."

Arturo's face crinkled. "You the smart one, Ponyboy, but I known me some killers, and this don't seem right."

"If it's not them, who?"

Arturo shook his head. "I don't know. But it don't matter. I'll help with whatever you need." Arturo added, "You have to know, though, nobody's gonna believe this shit, not without some proof."

Gray sat on the bed and exhaled loudly. Arturo was right. No one would believe it. Hell, he was doubting it himself.

Arturo then placed a finger on the third sheet from the envelope. "What about this one? 'The thirty-seventh law clerk.' That motherfucker better watch his back. Who is it?"

Gray stared back at him. "That one's easy," he said. "It's me."

CHAPTER 66

"No one followed you?"

"Nope," Sam said. She pushed into the bedroom of Arturo's apartment. She wore a rain jacket and baseball cap. She pulled off the cap and shook out her hair, which flowed past her shoulders. She looked about the room, shaking her head. Arturo was out "making his rounds," whatever that meant.

"You shouldn't have come," Gray said. "I don't want you mixed up in this."

Sam ignored him. "Can you believe this place? I need to have him decorate my loft."

"How'd you know I'd be here?"

"You had nowhere else to go."

She was right about that.

"The agents talk to you yet? I doubt my parents would tell them about you, so I don't know how else they'd—"

"They came by," she interrupted. "Some of your *friends* at the court"—she did air quotes as she said this—"told them about me."

"What'd the agents say?"

"It was a lot of implied threats about harboring a fugitive. That I didn't really know you. That you were basically a sadistic killer. You know, the usual . . ."

He wasn't clear if she was making light for his sake or her own. But it was helping him collect himself. To think more clearly.

Gray showed her the crime scene wall he'd set up in the bedroom. Her mouth was agape as he walked her through his theory.

"But the chief was attacked in the garage," Sam said. "He couldn't have—"

"Staged," Gray interrupted.

"You think it was Justice Wall in the ski mask?"

Gray nodded.

"I don't under—"

"They set the whole thing up so I'd be the hero."

"Why would they do that? What would be the point of it?"

"The feds had been looking into people at the court after the Dupont murders because the killer left behind a quill pen. Maybe Douglas and Wall realized they'd taken the game too far and wanted a fall guy if they needed one. Maybe they knew the press would find a connection between the killings, maybe they knew there'd be intense scrutiny. They needed the investigation closed before agents started looking closer at them."

"So pick the poor kid in the messenger's office?"

Gray nodded. That first day in the conference room, the job interview, the chief said he'd been to the pizza shop. Not the kind of place the chief would otherwise frequent. Unless he was looking into the background of their potential scapegoat. Gray reflected on the seduction of it all. The flattery, the condo that would give them a way to plant evidence, the loaner car that they could monitor or use to take them to their crimes.

Sam's face turned hard. "So why don't we call this agent you've been talking to?"

The thought had already crossed his mind. But any call to Milstein could potentially be traced to Arturo's place.

The bedroom door burst open and in walked Arturo. "The famous artist is here," he said. He opened his arms and gave Sam a hug. She blushed. "You guys hungry?" he asked. "My guys brought some dinner. I told them you liked Mr. Fong's."

They all converged in the living room. Arturo's crew fluttered around like caterers, putting out the Chinese food. During dinner, they kicked around Gray's options, and he kept coming back to the same place. Calling Agent Milstein. Arturo said he had an untraceable burner phone. "Keep the call under a minute. That's how long it takes to track a location," Arturo said.

"How do you know that?" Sam asked.

"Didn't you ever watch *The Wire*?" Arturo said with a grin, handing Gray the phone.

Gray decided it was worth the risk. He retrieved Milstein's business card from his wallet and tapped in the number.

"Milstein," the voice answered.

"It's Gray Hernandez."

There was a long pause. "Grayson, I'm glad you called. Where are you? What the hell are you doing running?"

Gray didn't answer. He eyed the stopwatch on Arturo's iPhone to make sure he was keeping it under a minute. He explained how the murders were connected to famous Supreme Court decisions. The competition between Douglas and Wall. By the time he was done, he had only twenty seconds left.

Milstein didn't react. "You should come in. It's the only way I can—"

"You need to be looking at the chief justice and Justice Wall. It's all a game."

Ten seconds left.

"Gray, it's not them. You need to trust me on this."

"Please," Gray said. "I know how it sounds, but you need to—"

Arturo snatched the phone from his hand and disconnected the line.

"She thought I was crazy," Gray said.

"She'll hopefully look into it anyway," Sam said. "You said she's—"

"Holy shit," Arturo interrupted. He stared at the television, which was muted. On the news ticker at the bottom of the screen: WORST WEEK IN SUPREME COURT'S HISTORY . . . LAW CLERK MISSING . . . GOVERNMENT'S TOP LAWYER IN HIGH COURT KILLED . . . LAW CLERK A SUSPECT . . .

"The world gone cray-cray up there at the Supreme Court," Arturo said.

Gray shushed everyone and turned up the volume. A cable news anchor stood in front of the Supreme Court building. "Adding to the bizarreness of it all, Dora Baxter, the solicitor general, the federal government's representative in the Supreme Court, died en route to the hospital after a fatal hit-and-run while on her morning jog. Witnesses say the driver ran down the prominent lawyer. But the initial impact was not what killed her. The assailant did the unthinkable, and reversed the car and ran over Baxter as she lay injured in the street . . ."

"No. Fuck no!" Gray shouted at the television.

Sam and Arturo looked at one another, unsure why Gray was so upset until the correspondent continued. "My sources tell me that federal agents are looking for a vehicle owned by Chief Justice Douglas—a car he apparently loaned to his law clerk Grayson Hernandez to drive during the term. Authorities are trying to locate Mr. Hernandez, whose whereabouts, I'm told by sources close to the investigation, are unknown."

They hadn't only planted evidence at the chief's condo. They took the car from Lauren's house and made it look like Gray had run down the solicitor general. Gray thought back to Lauren seeing Justice Wall and Dora Baxter at Gray's condo. Then to New Year's Eve, Wall and a woman arguing in his chambers.

"Maybe I should ask your wife if the panties are hers."
"So now you're threatening me?"
"Maybe it's not a threat."

Sam put her hand on his shoulder. "We're gonna get through this."

"The thirty-seventh law clerk," Gray whispered to himself. The words on one of the sheets in the envelope.

"What?" Sam said.

"Dora Baxter, during her confirmation hearings, was asked about the fact that the SG often is called 'the tenth justice.' Baxter joked that she'd heard that the more accurate description of the job was like being the thirty-seventh law clerk," Gray said. "Me and the SG, the thirty-seventh law clerks. Even now, they're still playing the game."

He decided right then that he was going to make them pay. To beat them at their own sick game.

CHAPTER 67

Gray and Sam holed up in the bedroom since they found it hard to concentrate amid the thumping music and partying in the rest of the place.

"You think they're ever going to stop out there?" Sam said.

Gray shrugged.

They had spent much of the night kicking around how to proceed. Should he call Milstein again? Should he call the press? He was so angry at himself for getting sucked into the chief and the court and all of it. It had been a cruel illusion—a setup—from the beginning. Arturo and Sam were having a hard time believing it, but it was true. Each crime was the answer to the other. The chief killed the reporter at the Franklin Theater, shouting fire in a crowded theater, starting the first challenge, "the great dissenter." Wall responded with another Oliver Wendell Holmes decision with the Dupont Underground murders and "three is enough." Wall then threw down the next challenge, "the worst SCOTUS decision ever," and the chief answered with the convenience store worker and *Korematsu*. Wall's response, the separate-but-equal decision and FBI agent Ben Freeman's son and girlfriend. Then "the thirty-seventh law clerk," Dora Baxter and Gray.

"What about the last challenge?" Sam asked.

She pointed to the wall. The last page in the envelope: FILSTEIN

SWING VOTE. WEDNESDAY. A RACE. FIRST THERE WINS. LEAVE 1FS @ 7PM.

"I'm glad you asked. That's what gave me the idea."

With the music seeping through the walls and Sam sitting across from him on the bed, he told her his plan.

"They're planning to go after Justice Cutler. I think the game is that they will kill her and try to blame it on me."

Sam gave him a skeptical glance.

"She's the swing vote on a case called *Filstein*. The chief and Wall both need her vote, but she keeps changing her mind. If she's dead, the case will be four-four and the lower court's ruling will stand. That would be a win for the chief and Wall. The challenge is 'Wednesday, a race, first there wins,'" Gray said. "Tomorrow is Wednesday. The challenge is a race to get to Cutler. They both have to leave the court—'1 FS' means One First Street—at seven o'clock, and the first one to get to Cutler and take care of her wins. We'll beat them there. Catch them in the act. Film it. A trap."

"But if only one of the justices made the challenge, how will the other know since Lauren took the envelope? Or what if they know she took it?"

"That's why we need to get the envelope back to the court tomorrow."

"You want us to break into the Supreme Court?" Sam said.

"It's not like we need to break in. The building is open to the public. And you forget, I was a messenger boy—I can get us backstage to the nonpublic areas. It's not as secure as you think. There's a police station in the building, but that's what makes everyone so lax about security. They think once you're in the building, all is safe and secure. And I know the back halls and security codes." Gray looked at Sam. "Once you're in the building, it will be just a matter of putting the envelope back in Justice Wall's in-box."

"Once *I'm* in?" Sam said.

Gray gave her a pleading look.

Sam lay back on the bed, gazing absently at two framed black-and-whites hanging on the bedroom wall. Gray followed her glance.

"Those were the first pieces I ever sold," Sam said. "It gave me the confidence to keep going, that I could make a living at it. That a stranger had come in and paid the overpriced amount the gallery demanded I sell them for on consignment just so I could have an ugly little corner of the shop."

"A stranger?" Gray said. "You didn't know it was Arturo?" Gray lay next to her.

"I made it because of a selfless act of a friend who sought absolutely nothing in return, not even a thank you." She turned and they faced one another on the bed. "I'm not sure you're right about the justices. But you tell me what I need to do, and I'll do it."

It was then that it struck him. In all of his longing to be accepted in the world of affluence, of legal elite, to never look back, it was Sam and his family, and even Arturo, who were there for him. Who believed him, who risked everything to help him.

He was never an outsider. He had just been looking in the wrong place.

CHAPTER 68

Gray awoke to shouting coming from outside the bedroom. It took a moment to shake off the grog—to remember where he was—but he leapt up from the bed. Sam instinctively jumped up as well, a confused look on her face. They'd both fallen asleep on top of the made bed.

One of Arturo's crew poked his head in the door. "We need to go," he said. He was calm, but they could hear a flurry of activity in the apartment. Gray hurriedly pulled down the papers he'd pinned to the wall, focusing on the ones from the envelope. He carefully placed them back in the coffee-stained envelope and then into Lauren's folder. He tucked the folder at the small of his back.

In the living room, Arturo's entourage resembled a pit crew at NASCAR, each person performing a designated task. The giant bald guys who guarded the entrance to the projects were collecting all weapons and loading them into heavy green canvas bags; the skimpily dressed women gathered all drugs; and the two hard-looking thugs who never seemed too far from Arturo's side, his personal bodyguard and consigliere, were inventorying bundles of cash.

Arturo was nowhere in sight. He wouldn't have left them, would he? Protect the president of the organization was a first priority,

Gray supposed. A teenage boy, he looked about sixteen, appeared in the doorway.

"The cops has found the way up here," the boy said. He gestured for Gray and Sam to follow, which they did. Others in the apartment shuffled behind, carrying the duffels and canvas bags. The boy led them down the long hallway to a stairwell. Single file they made their way down two flights. The boy led them to another apartment. This one had been vacant for some time by the looks of it. The walls were unfinished Sheetrock and the floors covered in a film of dust and grime. In the corner of the main room a hole was cut into the floor. The teenage kid gestured to it. Gray and Sam looked down into the chasm. It was a chute, the kind construction crews use to move debris out of a building. Essentially, a giant slide that went down several stories.

The boy skipped into the hole, and disappeared into the darkness.

Gray and Sam exchanged a look. Sam then sat at the edge of the opening. "See you down there," she said. It was almost a question.

She released her grasp as the chute swallowed her up. Gray waited a long moment to give her time to clear the area before he dropped in.

Gray skidded down the chute, which was made of plastic. He tried to slow his descent, burning his hands and making squeaking noises with his shoes, as he spiraled down.

He heard someone following after him from above, so he eased up on the side of the chute. The last thing he wanted was one of the bald giants landing on him. He could see a light at his feet. It grew in diameter as he sped down the final stretch of tube. Finally, he landed in a pile of foam and mattresses. He was in a dim basement. The teenage kid reached for Gray and they locked forearms, pulling Gray out of the landing area just before the others started plunging from the chute.

Gray was shaken up, but nothing was broken. The kid led them to an exterior basement door. He opened it a crack and treaded quietly up the stairwell, like a Vietnam tunnel dweller from the movies. At the top, the kid pulled out a hand mirror, scanning the area. He then whistled outside, and gestured for the group to come quickly. Gray and Sam climbed the damp stairs as fast as they could without getting a foot full of broken glass or needle poke. There was a rumble of motorcycles.

At the top of the stairwell, men on two bikes were waiting for them under the purple morning sky. There was a strong breeze, and it was finally starting to feel like January in D.C. The bikers gestured for them to hurry, and they climbed on. Gray clutched the biker's middle as they sped off. Sam's bike went a different direction. Gray looked back and the rest of the crew were climbing into a white van.

Then came the sirens.

Gray closed his eyes as the bike zigged and zagged, jumping curbs and making sharp turns as the sirens grew distant. At last they ripped into the narrow drive of a boarded-up house and to an overgrown mess of a backyard. The biker let Gray off and then sped away, never showing his face. Sam was already there in the urban jungle. Neither of them spoke.

Arturo appeared out of the broken screen door of the ramshackle house. He held a smile and waved them inside. "Just like the movies you love so much," he said with a grin.

Gray followed Arturo into the house, Sam at his heels.

The place was decidedly not like the apartment in Madison Towers. No expensive over-the-top renovation hidden by a dilapidated exterior here. It was exactly as one would expect. Dank and dark. Filled with the smell of chemicals and human filth. Masses sprawled about the gutted interior.

"Don't worry," Arturo said, reading their thoughts. "We won't be here long. We just need to stay until things cool off. Feds must've tracked you to my place, the phone, maybe."

Gray didn't mention that Agent Milstein once had Arturo in her sights. That Gray had given Milstein the tip to look for Arturo at Sam's art show.

Sam remained quiet. Eventually, she said, "I need to use the restroom."

Arturo grimaced. "I'm not sure you'll want to use one here."

"I'll be fine," she said.

"Let me walk with you, at least," Arturo said.

"I got it," Sam said and stomped away.

Gray walked to the window, opened a crack in the sheet that hung as the curtain, and peered outside. "Quite a sophisticated operation you have going, complete with an escape plan and safe house. You know, there's a whole straight world out there that could make great use of your talents."

Arturo smiled. "No fun in that."

"I guess your girlfriend didn't have time to decorate this place, huh?" Gray said.

Arturo gave a dry laugh. "This ain't one of mine," he said.

"No?"

"All my places are too hot right now. I got protection from the cops on the beat, but your shit is bringing in the *Federales,* so they gonna be all up in my spots."

"Who's place is this then?"

"Only Ortiz would run such a shit hole." Arturo gave a rakish grin.

"Razor?"

Arturo nodded.

"You guys reached a truce?"

Arturo let out a big laugh. "You been gone a long time, but not that long. Nah, I just thought, *Where's the last place anybody would look for me or mine?*"

It made sense. But it also was brazen as hell.

"I'm sorry I've created so many problems for you," Gray said. "I had no right to ask for anything, much less taking these kind of risks. I haven't exactly been a good friend."

Arturo looked at Gray for a long moment, like he was debating whether to say something. There had to be some resentment, some anger, that Gray had ended their friendship. Gray hoped Arturo would get it out on the table. After a long silence, Arturo said, "You remember Christmas Eve in fourth grade?"

Gray thought about it. He shook his head.

"I came over after he gave me a beating. I guess that happened a lot, so probably no surprise you don't remember. But you gave me a gift."

"Now I remember," Gray said. "The Pokémon card."

Both men smiled.

"It was a Charizard, first edition," Gray said.

"You didn't know it," Arturo said, "but I was coming over to say good-bye."

"Good-bye? Where were you going?"

Arturo cocked his head to the side. Gray then understood.

"But that card," Arturo continued, "I knew that it cost a lot. You worked so hard for your money. At your dad's shop. Mowing lawns in Northwest. You didn't take the easy way, like me. But you spent the money on me. I realized that someone *did* care about me. Someone *would* miss me."

"You were right about that."

"I promised myself two things that night." Arturo swallowed. "One, that I'd never turn out like *him*. And two, that I'd always be there if you needed me. I'm happy I got to keep at least one of the promises and help you."

Gray thought he saw a sheen in Arturo's eyes. Old emotions crowded Gray's chest. "You're not like your father."

Arturo looked away.

"You're not—"

They both startled at the sound of the scream from upstairs. Sam. They bolted simultaneously toward the stairwell. Gray took the stairs two at a time, Arturo close behind. At the top was a landing and long shadowy hallway. A blur of figures, the sounds of a struggle. The scene came into focus, two men attacking Sam. One was behind her, arms locked around her, the other approaching from the front.

Sam used the man trapping her from behind as a brace and raised both legs, kicking the other man, who was coming at her in a staggering grope. She slammed both feet into his face, which sent him flying backward and he landed in front of Gray, hands covering his bloody face. Sam then planted her feet and charged in reverse, ramming the other man's back against the wall. By the time Gray and Arturo had reached her, she had things under control.

Gray opened the bathroom door, which let in some light. It was then that he saw the fury in Arturo's face. Arturo grabbed the guy closest to the bathroom, the one who'd held Sam from behind, as he started to run off. Arturo clutched the man's stringy hair, and rammed his face into an exposed stud on the wall. He did it over and over until the man dropped to a pile on the floor. The other guy was still on the ground holding his bloodied face. When he saw what happened to his friend, he started scampering away, trying to get to his feet. Arturo's heavy boot came down on the guy's back between the shoulder blades. Arturo started to stomp the man. Gray stood there, frozen. By the time Gray snapped out of it, Sam was already at Arturo's side, pulling him away, screaming for him to stop. Arturo kicked the man, who rolled down the stairs. Arturo stepped slowly after him.

At the bottom of the stairs the man was twisted up, not moving. Someone bolted out the front door, the light eliciting moans from the drug zombies sprawled inside.

"Shit," Arturo said. "He's gonna go get Ortiz's crew. They'd love to find me here. We gotta go." He put a cell phone to his ear.

In the plush rooms of Arturo's apartment with all the partying and playful banter, even here talking about a Pokémon card, it was easy to forget what their old friend had become. But Gray realized that we're all our fathers' sons. Whatever Arturo had become, it didn't matter. Gray's plan wouldn't work without him.

CHAPTER 69

Milstein and Cartwright stepped off the grimy elevator. They were met at the door of Arturo Alvarez's apartment by two young agents manning the entrance.

"They called in the big dogs," one of the agents bellowed, putting out a fist that Cartwright reluctantly bumped with his own. "Missed you at the game last week," the young agent said.

"Yeah, been busy as shit. I'll try to make next week's game. Wouldn't want you youngsters to forget how it's done."

The agent laughed and held open the door. Milstein was thrown by the elegance of the interior.

"Scotty," an agent from the task force called out to him. Cartwright went over and shook his hand. Was there anyone Cartwright didn't know in this town?

Milstein sauntered over to them and the agent gave her a nod.

"I need to ask for this guy's decorator," Cartwright said with a chuckle.

"I know. Guy mistook the projects for the Ritz-Carlton, right?"

Cartwright shook his head in admiration. "Aaron around?"

The agent pointed his chin down the hall to the back of the apartment. "Not in the best of moods, so watch yourself."

"I always do, buddy."

Milstein followed as Cartwright walked toward the voices in a bedroom at the end of the hall.

The stylishly decorated bedroom had nearly a dozen agents milling around. Task forces always resulted in too many bodies mucking up a scene.

A tech was sealing up a laptop in an evidence bag, and a photographer was taking shots of some papers that had been pinned to the wall. Supreme Court Police Chief Aaron Dowell was studying the collage, shaking his head. Dowell flicked them a weary glance but didn't say hello.

Cartwright sidled up to Dowell. "You got a bead on them yet?" Cartwright asked.

"No. They had an escape route planned. Pretty sophisticated for drug dealers."

Cartwright didn't respond. Wisely so. Milstein knew Dowell would be embarrassed that his team let an entire crew slip through its fingers.

Dowell turned his scowl to Milstein. He gestured to the wall. It was primitive, but a pretty good replica of what agents used to connect dots in an investigation. Sometimes it was the only way to see the bigger picture. Dowell pointed at a stick-figure drawing of two dismembered bodies. Ben Freeman's murdered son and girlfriend. "Your friend Hernandez is pretty proud of his handiwork."

Milstein just stared at the wall.

Dowell blew out an exasperated breath. "If the kid wasn't so keen on calling only you, I'd have you off this case." He made a noise of disgust and stormed out. The other agents, with the exception of the tech, followed after him.

Milstein examined the gaps in the crime scene wall. Gray had taken some of the pages with him. Why? Milstein turned to Cartwright. "If Grayson is a killer, why would he go to the trouble to do all this?"

"You said he's smart," Cartwright said. "Maybe that's exactly the question he wants us to be asking."

"Not you too?" The task force had gone from tunnel vision, focused on Kevin Dugan as the prime suspect, until he inconveniently turned up dead, to an equal level of certainty about Grayson. Milstein's instincts had been correct. Dugan was a John Doe found in the Anacostia River. His body was too decomposed to identify, but it looked like a suicide. He'd been dead a year. Milstein decided not to throw it in Cartwright's face.

Cartwright said, "Look, someone inside the Supreme Court building was involved, you've said that from the start. Someone smart, sophisticated."

"Grayson has an airtight alibi for Christmas. He couldn't have taken the couple from Union Station."

"You said it yourself—this was a game. Usually games have two players. And *games* typically start with childhood friends. Gray had help from one of his."

"Arturo Alvarez is a street criminal. Turf and drug murders don't fit Behavioral's profile. And he and Grayson don't have any connection to the Whitlock case."

"Ha," Cartwright said. "*You* were the one who initially wanted to talk to Alvarez. And the crystal ball squad has been wrong before. Maybe Hernandez just read about the Whitlock girls and it stuck—he decided to use them as a decoy for whatever game he's playing. He tries to feed you the justices as the perps, but we know that ain't right. It's another diversion. And several witnesses saw Hernandez's car run down the solicitor general. I'm sorry, Em, but have you considered that maybe it isn't just task forces that get tunnel vision?"

A long silence fell between them. Milstein didn't want to admit it, but maybe Cartwright was right. But, then again, maybe he wasn't.

CHAPTER 70

Arturo's crew retrieved them from the drug den. Gray and Sam bounced around in the back of the Dodge van, sitting on a bench that ran the full length of the vehicle. Arturo stood, holding a handle affixed to the side.

"Sam told me you have a plan?" Arturo said.

Gray nodded. "We're gonna return the envelope to the justices. Let them think the game is still on. They may not know Lauren took it, so we'll put it back, and when they go to complete the final challenge, we'll be waiting."

"What final challenge?" Arturo asked.

"The envelope's last two pages. One was 'the thirty-seventh law clerk.' They killed Dora Baxter and I was next, so that challenge was in play. But there was one more challenge on the last page." Gray showed Arturo the page from the envelope.

FILSTEIN SWING VOTE. WEDNESDAY. A RACE. FIRST THERE WINS. LEAVE 1FS @ 7PM.

He explained what it meant: Douglas and Wall would race to kill the "swing vote" on the *Filstein* case, Justice Cutler. Maybe Cutler had told them she was switching sides again. Or maybe they'd just had enough of her. In any case, when Wall and the chief arrived at Cutler's house, Gray, Arturo, and Sam would be there to stop the attack.

Arturo and Sam exchanged a glance.

"We'll beat them to Cutler's house. Catch them playing the game."

"Oh, that's all," Arturo said. He was quiet for a long moment, then said, "We're gonna have to trust you on this one, Pony."

Gray said, "We'll need some supplies. First, I need some iPhones."

"How many?" Arturo asked.

"Ten."

Arturo didn't flinch. He made a call, and said it was done. Gray doubted that Arturo's connection was making a run to the Apple store. More likely the phones had been ripped from the hands of commuters on the Metro.

Next, they needed disguises. They stopped at a Jos. A. Bank downtown where Arturo strutted in, picked out a 42 regular suit, and had it fitted on the spot. Gray waited in the van, but could imagine the salesman's face as Arturo paid in hundred-dollar bills. Sam, meanwhile, hit the Ann Taylor nearby. Even in the midgrade apparel, the transformation of each of them was dramatic. Arturo, save the scorpion tattoo sneaking out of his collar, looked almost respectable. Sam was stiff in her outfit, but she was pretty as always. They then stopped at a CVS and Sam jumped out of the van and purchased the rest of the supplies: poster board, markers, garbage bags, duct tape, and makeup.

"You sure you wanna do this today?" Arturo asked. "Shouldn't we plan this out more? Seems kinda rushed." Spoken like a man who'd performed a few heists in his day.

"We've got to do it today, or it won't work. The challenge starts tonight at seven o'clock. And if we don't get the envelope back soon, they'll know something's up."

"All right," Arturo said. "What else you need?"

"I need one of those air horns, the kind they use at football games."

Arturo creased his brow, but nodded.

"And we need six of your men to meet us near the Supreme

Court. You need to be clear that none of them should bring a weapon or have any drugs or anything on them. And none should have any outstanding warrants."

Arturo gave a grin. "I'm not sure I can find six . . ."

By midday, they were buried in the crowd at the front of the Supreme Court. Normally, the masses cleared out around noon after the arguments. But today the plaza and sidewalk running along First Street were packed with tourists, reporters, and protesters. The media frenzy over Lauren's abduction and fugitive Grayson Hernandez. Gray watched as Arturo and Sam made their way to the side entrance of the court. Sam had used the makeup both for her face and to conceal Arturo's tattoos on his neck and hands. They'd filled the garbage bags with trash they'd pulled from a Dumpster, and the bags were now props for Gray, who was dressed as a street person. He'd smeared grease from the van's undercarriage on his face and shirt, and held a sign scrawled with incoherent nonsense. He'd also matted his hair with some dirt. Sadly, one of the best ways to be invisible in the District was to look homeless.

The building had always been surprisingly open, and news about Lauren had not changed anything. Visitors needed no appointment and didn't even sign in, they just went through dated metal detectors. A man and a woman in suits would breeze through. They were almost as invisible as the homeless.

Getting into the building was easy; getting back to chambers would be the challenge. The plan was to use one of the iPhones as a live video feed through FaceTime so Gray could guide their path. They'd cut a hole in Sam's handbag just small enough for the phone's lens and secured the device with duct tape so that it wouldn't move, a poor man's hidden camera that Gray could watch from another phone at his end on the plaza.

Gray watched the camera feed jostle about as Sam and Arturo emptied their pockets and put Sam's handbag through the X-ray machine.

At the end of the conveyor belt, Sam scooped up her bag and positioned it so the iPhone was properly angled, as they'd practiced in the van.

They were in.

Sam called Gray on another one of the iPhones.

Gray answered his second phone, still watching the other phone with the FaceTime feed. The ground floor of the court housed the gift shop and cafeteria as well as display cases with court memorabilia, so there were plenty of tourists wandering about.

Sam's voice: "You can see okay?"

"All clear," Gray said. He watched on the screen as Arturo took the elevator to the garage as Sam hung back. Gray smiled when Arturo exited the elevator five minutes later and gave a nod.

"He got the phones in their cars," Sam said. The plan required them to hide iPhones in the chief and Justice Wall's cars.

"He got by the officer?"

Arturo leaned down and put his face near the lens in Sam's purse and gave a large grin.

"Okay," Gray said into the phone. "Now at the statue in front of you"—the bronze statue of John Marshall was visible on his iPhone screen—"you need to take a right. From there, you'll see a staircase. Go up one floor."

As they made their way to the main floor, Gray lifted his gaze from the phone and stared up at the front of the court. The words etched above the portico—EQUAL JUSTICE UNDER LAW—took him back to the night Anton Troy was executed. What a night that was. He would have never guessed then that the next time he'd spend any time on the plaza he'd be disguised as a soiled homeless man.

"There's several cops up here," Sam whispered into the phone.

"Just act like you belong. It'll be fine."

The Great Hall didn't look so great on the diminutive screen of the iPhone. Gray's field of vision was just above waist height, so it was a lot of midriffs.

"Take a right at the X-ray machines near the entrance to the courtroom." In front of the chamber was another security checkpoint. The court didn't have the high-tech stuff, the mantraps or other sophisticated security measures at other federal buildings. Just old X-ray machines and wands. Sam and Arturo wouldn't need to go through the X-rays again since they weren't going into the courtroom.

Down a hallway, Gray could see the bronze gate to one of the more remote entrances into chambers.

As they approached the gate, the screen showed an officer sitting on a chair at his station, looking bored. It was one of the few entrances to chambers, Gray knew from his days running deliveries in the building, that had only one officer assigned at the door.

"You're sure about the passcode?" Sam said into his ear as the feed on the phone showed the officer watching her as she got near the entrance to the nonpublic section of the court.

"It will work," Gray said.

At that, the iPhone clicked off. Gray turned his attention to the video feed from Sam's handbag. The officer smiled at her. The guy's face then turned to concern, and he jumped to his feet. The video went blurry. Gray couldn't make everything out, but the officer and two other figures were huddled around a man who was on the ground. He was having a seizure.

The camera then whipped toward the latticework door. He saw Sam's hand, noticeably shaking, stab numbers on the security keypad.

Gray held his breath, praying that the code hadn't been changed. He exhaled loudly when the door swung open. Sam did a quick turn around, and there was a crowd hovering over the man who'd collapsed. This had been Arturo's idea. If it was good enough for distracting a grocery store clerk and pilfering the register, it was good enough for the Supreme Court.

Sam walked quickly down the hallway and around the corner.

Gray's second iPhone rang again. "Okay, it worked," Sam said. Her voice was breathy, worried.

In a calm tone, Gray said, "You're doing great."

"I don't feel great."

"Just one quick delivery and you're out. Just follow the route we discussed."

This time, Sam didn't kill the line, she put the iPhone in her handbag. Gray kept one phone pressed to his ear, and watched the screen of the other as Sam marched into Justice Wall's chambers. The camera was right at eye level for the secretary and she gave Sam a *what can we do for you* look.

It was time for the distraction. On yet another phone, Gray dialed the number. One of Wall's clerks, it sounded like Audrey, answered.

"Audrey, it's me," Gray said.

She paused a long moment. "Gray?"

"I wondered if you could get a message to Keir?" Gray knew that the call would prompt two reactions. First, it would set into motion whatever protocol agents likely implemented in case Gray ever called. All hands on deck rushing to Audrey's office, which was just off the reception area of Justice Wall's chambers. Second, it would place suspicion on Keir. That part was just for fun.

With three phones in play—one a direct line to Sam, the other the FaceTime feed, the third his call to Audrey—he was afraid a homeless guy using three iPhones on the plaza would draw attention. But he was still invisible to the crowd.

"Where are you? Everyone is looking for you," Audrey said.

On the screen, Sam turned and the camera was facing Audrey's door. Audrey was holding the phone, the cord extended and she was waving wildly to get the secretary's attention, mouthing that it was Grayson. Sam spun around, and the flustered secretary was picking up the red phone, the emergency line.

"Can you get a message to Keir? I don't have a lot of time."

"Sure, let me find a pen." Audrey was stalling.

The camera caught officers running into Audrey's office. With all attention on Audrey, Sam used the distraction to tuck the envelope in Justice Wall's in-box.

Mission accomplished.

CHAPTER 71

Gray clicked off from Audrey, threw the phone on the ground, and stomped on it. He then picked up the other phone and waited for Sam to get back on the line. He was pacing small circles, nervous energy flowing through him. At last, her voice.

"Which way?" She was breathing heavily. On the video feed was the hallway outside chambers.

"Straight ahead. You can do this." His heart skipped a moment when he saw officers running toward Sam, but she moved against the wall and they darted past her. More officers getting to Audrey about the call from Gray.

He wondered how Arturo and his fake seizure were going. Gray felt another stab of worry as the video feed was blocked with an officer charging past Sam and into the chief's chambers, bumping Sam's handbag. Now all Gray could see was the blur of a wall.

On the plaza, Gray saw a gurney being wheeled out the side doors by two EMS workers. Arturo making his escape.

They were so close.

But then Gray heard the sirens on the plaza.

Gray tried not to react as agents flooded the front of the Supreme Court. Agent Milstein and her partner were first on the scene. Men and women in Windbreakers, TASK FORCE emblazoned on the backs, jumped out of black sedans and Suburbans. The agents soon were darting about the crowd. Looking for Gray. They must have tracked Gray's call to Audrey. Things were so Big Brother now.

Gray pocketed the phones and stood confidently holding his sign full of crazy, hoping he'd be overlooked. He turned toward the Capitol dome across First Street, pretending not to notice or care that the task force was doing a sweep.

The agents, Gray counted about ten of them, were going from group to group, asking for identification, studying faces.

More dark sedans pulled to the curb. Soon there would be no hope for escape.

From the corner of his eye he watched Milstein move aggressively through the crowd, pushing off ball caps, jerking shoulders, studying faces. It wouldn't be long before she made her way to Gray.

It was time.

Gray threw aside his sign and pulled out one of the key supplies Arturo had provided: the air horn. He pressed the button and it let out an ear-piercing blast. The plaza seemed to go instantly still.

Then, one by one, some of the protesters, all Hispanic—not your typical activists given the tattoos and scars—began to make a show of running in different directions. Six of them scurrying, Arturo's men. The agents on the plaza gave chase.

Not Milstein. She stood in place, intensely surveying the plaza, seeming to understand that it was a diversion tactic.

Gray tried not to draw attention to himself. But then someone started yelling. "It's him, it's him!" The man was pointing at Gray. It was Vincent, the homeless man.

Milstein stared at Vincent, then had a flash of recognition when she examined the other homeless man on the plaza. She drew her gun and started racing toward Gray, pushing bystanders out of the way. Before he could react, she was right on him, her weapon pointed at his chest. They locked eyes. She could've taken the shot. But something in her eyes told Gray she wouldn't.

Gray turned and hauled ass down First Street, his legs burning, heart thumping. He could hear Milstein shouting at him from behind. Gray darted around the corner where he saw the Dodge van. The back door swung open, and Arturo grabbed him by the shirt and yanked him inside as the van sped away. Before the door closed, Gray saw Milstein sprinting after them. As the distance grew larger, she stopped and just watched as they made their escape.

"We did it," Sam said. She was wired. Arturo loosened his tie. They'd gotten the envelope back in play. The trap was set.

CHAPTER 72

"How do we know the justices will take the bait?" Sam asked as they bumped around in the back of the van.

"We don't," Gray said. "We just have to wait to see if they start driving toward Justice Cutler's house at seven." He looked down at the iPhone, which had two blue dots on a map. In the court's garage, Arturo had popped the trunks of Douglas and Wall's cars and dropped in the phones. They would use the find-my-phone app as a tracking device.

"Where are we going now?" Sam asked.

"The Heights. To get us another ride," Arturo said. "Feds saw the van. And my boys got word that Ortiz is looking for the van too. Gunning hard for me now."

"Gunning for you?" Gray asked. "Just for going to one of his drug dens?"

"You forget about what happened that night Razor was messing with you and your girl? Then I went on his turf. He'll look weak if he don't do something. Once the boss looks weak, he ain't gonna be the boss for much longer. And this thing with me and him, it's been a long time coming." Arturo shrugged. "If it was the other way around, I'd be goin' after him." Street politics.

As Arturo made some calls, Sam turned the discussion back

to the plan. "So, the justices go to Cutler's house, then what? I don't understand the endgame."

"If they come, we'll be waiting for them," Gray said. "We'll see from the trackers if they're heading to Cutler's, and when they're nearby, we'll call the FBI and say Cutler is in danger. That'll prompt a rapid response to Cutler's house. I'll then confront the justices, try to get them to say something incriminating while you stay hidden and film it."

"It doesn't feel right," Sam said. "Too many moving parts. And I don't feel good about putting Justice Cutler at—"

There was the skid of tires and scream of metal on metal, as Gray, Sam, and Arturo launched into the air from the violent crash into the side of the van.

CHAPTER 73

Gray didn't remember hitting the floor. He was dizzy and he must have blacked out for a moment. He saw Sam out cold on the bench that ran along the side of the van, her left arm dangling to the floor. Arturo labored to stand. There was a gash on his forehead.

Gray's head was clearing, and he crawled over to check on Sam. He caught a glimpse in the front cabin and the driver and Arturo's other man appeared dazed, but okay.

That's when he heard the explosion of glass.

The windshield shattered into thousands of pebbles, and the bodies of the two men in the front convulsed to the rhythm of rapid gunfire. Gray dove to cover Sam, grabbing her shoulders, taking her to the floor and rolling them both under the bench.

Arturo stood, back pressed against the side panel, wincing as bullets pierced holes in the back door, light lasering through. Gray's ears felt as though they were going to bleed at the eruption of automatic-weapon fire ripping through the metal interior.

The gunfire went on for what seemed like an eternity, though it was probably only a few seconds. Gray could hear nothing but a high-pitched *beeeeep* in his ears.

Still pressing himself against the wall of the van, Arturo seemed to be searching for something on the floor, his gun probably. Gray stayed down low, unclear about what the hell was going on. The police? But they wouldn't shoot indiscriminately, would they?

Then the van rocked as someone from outside was prying at the back door, which was jammed from the impact.

Arturo looked through holes in the crinkled metal. Gray could tell from his expression, they were caught.

Arturo turned to Gray, dread on his face. He put his hands together like he was praying. No harm in seeking help from the Almighty, Gray supposed. But then Arturo put his folded hands to his cheek, tilted his head, and gestured to go to sleep, like a father telling a child *night-night*. He was signaling Gray to play dead.

Light filled the cabin as the van's door pried open, the block of metal making a loud clunk as it swung wide and hit the van's exterior. Gray, on the floor shielding Sam with his body, did as he was told and clamped his eyes shut. Before he did, he caught a glimpse of a man dragging Arturo out of the van at gunpoint.

Razor Ortiz.

CHAPTER 74

Gray opened his eyes when he heard the car race away. He looked out onto the street. Good Samaritans were daring to come closer. The bystanders called out to them. Sam's eyes popped open, her dilated pupils turned to pins in the light.

"Are you okay?" Gray said the words, but couldn't hear his own voice, his ears still ringing.

Sam stared at him, disoriented.

"We were in a car accident," he said. "We need to get out of here before the police come. Can you move?"

Sam blinked several times, then nodded quickly, seeming to collect herself. She gazed around, a bewildered expression. The wrecked van. The bullet holes. The dead guys up front. Arturo gone.

Gray stood up and suffered a wave of nausea. He steadied himself, arm on the side of the van. With his other arm, he reached for Sam, who clutched his hand and hoisted herself from under the bench, pebbles of windshield falling from her clothes.

They ducked out of the back. People were outside talking to them, but Gray couldn't hear what they were saying. He pushed by, clasping Sam's hand, and they ran down the street, not looking back. Around the corner was a bodega. They went inside the ramshackle building caged in metal bars. The clerk behind the counter, a heavyset Hispanic woman, gave them a lazy glance. Sam with blood caked at her hairline, ripped Ann Taylor getup from earlier. Gray still in his homeless disguise. Nothing a store-keep in Hamilton Heights hadn't seen before. His hearing was coming back, muffled, like people talking under water.

Gray grabbed some Band-Aids, baby wipes, and a bottle of Advil. At the register, Sam pointed to the disposable cell phones for sale behind the counter. "I left my purse. I don't have a phone."

"I still have mine." Gray tapped his pocket, which had a rectangular bulge. He gave the clerk a twenty. She took the bill carefully without touching Gray's filthy hand.

"Can we use the restroom?" Gray asked.

"For employees only," the clerk replied, not looking at him as she dug out the change from the register.

Gray slapped another twenty on the counter.

The clerk hesitated, then pulled a key attached to a large slab of plastic that had EMPLOYEES ONLY! written on it.

"Don't make a mess, and I need the key back," the clerk said.

Inside the restroom, which was surprisingly clean, Sam washed her face in the sink as Gray used the baby wipes to remove the blood and dirt from his face and arms. Sam rinsed the blood from her hair, and pulled it into a ponytail. They'd been lucky, none of their lashes were deep, though both ached from the whiplash and bruises from the crash. Gray popped four Advil from the bottle then cupped his hand under the tap and washed it down. He passed Sam the bottle and she did the same.

"What are we going to do?" Sam asked.

"We need to get to Justice Cutler's house," Gray said. "The challenge in the envelope begins at seven o'clock. If we don't stop them, she's dead."

"But if we go, Arturo . . ." There was desperation in Sam's voice now.

Gray sat on the closed toilet seat and massaged his temples with a hand. He needed to think. Sam was right. If they went to save Cutler, to catch the justices before they struck, Razor would surely kill Arturo. But if they went for Arturo, Douglas and Wall would kill Cutler.

"We need to call the FBI," Sam said.

"And tell them what? We don't know where Arturo is. And they're never going to believe us about Douglas and Wall."

"They may not believe us, but the cops won't take the chance if you tell them Justice Cutler is in danger. They'll make sure she's protected, if only to make sure *you* don't hurt her."

Sam was right. They thought Gray was a killer, so if Gray mentioned Cutler they'd get her somewhere safe.

Gray pulled out the iPhone. He was going to call Agent Milstein. But he noticed that the phone still displayed the find-my-phone app screen. The small blue dots showed the location of Douglas and Wall's cars. Both vehicles were still at the Supreme Court, but that wasn't what captured Gray's attention.

"What is it?" Sam asked.

He held up the phone. "The tracker, there's three dots."

Sam shook her head, not understanding.

"One for Douglas, one for Wall. And one for the other phone."

Sam's eyes flashed.

Arturo had the phone. They knew where Razor Ortiz had taken him. And it was only five blocks away.

CHAPTER 75

Milstein sat behind her desk, frustrated she'd let Hernandez escape. It was a huge risk he'd taken, going to the court. What was he up to? She was frankly tired of thinking about Grayson Hernandez and the rest of it. She scanned her desk. The photos of the victims. She kept them out as a reminder and because she knew they held the key to identifying the killer. Hernandez's theory was a good one, it did look like a game. But not the game he had in mind.

She glanced at the old *Washington Post* stories about the Whitlock case. Her mind flew to the horror show that Kevin Dugan had come upon. His deposition testimony about Susie Whitlock, the girl who'd survived:

> *"She was sitting on a stained mattress on the floor of the unit. Her hair was chopped up."*

Milstein had an urgent thought. Her eyes darted to the photo of Sakura Matsuka, her bludgeoned face. Her cut hair.

She searched for the VCR remote and found it under some papers, then rewound the Dugan deposition footage.

> *"And what about her sister, Kimberley?"*
> *"I didn't see her at first, and then . . ."*

"You wanna take a break?"

"No, let's get this over with."

"You said you didn't see Kimberley at first."

"Yeah, so I start looking about the unit. It was small, filled with junk. Then I saw the large duffel bag."

"And what was in the bag?"

"I unzipped it and she was in there. I saw her tiny head. Then her neck, it was bruised. Then I realized that it wasn't attached to her body, that he'd dismembered her."

Milstein paused the frame. She looked at the photo of young Isabelle Hill dead in Dupont Underground, the bruises on her neck. Milstein clicked the video back on.

"He molested them both. We think he made Susie watch him cut up her sister."

Milstein's eyes jumped back to the dismembered bodies of Ben Freeman's son and his girlfriend.

Milstein felt goose pimples envelope her flesh. Then she heard the ping of her e-mail. She glanced at the computer. It was the information she'd requested from the prison. Video of John Whitlock's visitors. Whitlock's only visitor, "L. Smith." The e-mail contained a link. She clicked on it and up popped a split screen, one of the prisoner, one of the visitor's room on the other side of a glass partition. Whitlock was alone at first, waiting for his guest. Milstein examined his face. In his mug shots from the prison file, he'd had a shaved head and been clean shaven. But in the video his hair was unruly. She examined his face; there was something familiar about it. She held her hand up, covering his mouth. The eyes. But it was the person who'd just entered the visitor's room that answered everything.

CHAPTER 76

Gray and Sam ran the five blocks to the blue dot on the phone, pushing through the pain of the crash. Gray examined the entrance to the auto repair shop. The place probably chopped up more stolen vehicles than performed any legitimate repairs. They ducked past the windows, which had been covered in flat black paint, and hurried to the back of the structure. The blue dot on the phone hadn't moved. Arturo was inside.

There was a window next to the back door. Gray cupped his hands and peered through the glass. Inside was a small room that had a desk, phone, and some file cabinets. The office for the garage, probably. Gray tried the back door, but it was locked. To the left of the door were two large garage doors for the vehicles brought in for repair. One of the doors wasn't closed completely. He could probably fit under the gap. "I need you to stay here," he said.

"I'm coming," Sam said.

"No, I need you here." He looked at the iPhone's clock: 5:50. "If I'm not out in ten minutes—and I mean it, if I'm even one second late—you call Agent Milstein, and you tell her where I am." Gray pulled out his wallet and found Milstein's business card.

Sam looked at her watch. "Why don't we just call her now, we can—"

Gray shook his head and jammed the business card in Sam's hand. He didn't have time to debate. Arturo was in there.

"Wait," Sam said, "I need the phone." Gray had the only phone left. She'd been right, they should have bought another at the bodega.

"I need it. If I'm not back by six o'clock, get back to the bodega and call Milstein."

Gray dropped to a push-up position, then skidded under the gap in the garage door. There was a Toyota with front-end damage, probably the car Razor crashed into the van. Spare parts and tires were strewn about, and the place smelled of oil and grease. A section of the garage was cordoned off by a drop cloth that hung from the ceiling. Gray could see light filtering from behind the curtain. Gray stepped quietly over to the curtain and peered through a gap. There they were. Ortiz and three men. It wasn't like the rest of the filthy shop. A camera was mounted on a tripod, pointed at a bed. Behind the bed, a large backdrop hung from a metal frame. Like a movie set. Gray's attention turned to a metal shelf, the kind you buy at Home Depot and had to assemble. It had boxes of Trojans, a large jug of K-Y Jelly, sex toys. Gross. He realized that this *was* a movie set—a makeshift porno studio.

No degrading sex scenes would be filmed today. But maybe a snuff film. Arturo was tied to a concrete support beam next to the bed. His head was lowered, his chest heaving up and down. Shirt stained with blood. One of Ortiz's men was adjusting a portable lamp, another fiddling with the camera.

As for Razor Ortiz, he was wearing what looked like a green garbage bag with holes cut in it, an apron to cover his clothes, and was ranting at his colleagues. "I tell you to get me a chain saw and you bring me this?" He held up electric hedge clippers. They had an orange base and black handle and a long blade with teeth lining the edges.

A man with greased-back hair said, "They was out of stock. We thought—"

Ortiz hit the man hard in the face. The man stumbled, but didn't lose his footing. Nor did he try to defend himself.

Ortiz powered on the clippers, which made a high-pitched whine, like a vacuum cleaner. "Fuck it, these will do."

Another man, this one older, gestured for Ortiz to turn off the clippers. After Ortiz clicked them off, the older man said, "Ramon, I understand that you want to do this—for Angel—but I think it's a mistake."

Ortiz looked at the older crew member. In an even tone, but with a sadness to it, he said, "This motherfucker killed my brother. For nothing! Then he disrespects me? He's dyin'.'"

The older man nodded slowly, resigned that Ortiz needed this, that nothing he could say would stop him. "At least don't film it. If it gets out . . ."

Ortiz ignored him and powered on the hedge trimmers. They didn't have the roar of a chain saw, but the sound was still terrifying. It would be worse—a chain saw could easily slice through flesh and bone. The clippers were going to take some work. It would be slow and messy.

Arturo raised his head as Ortiz moved closer. If Ortiz had expected fear, blubbering, or begging, he would be disappointed. Arturo gave only a black stare.

Ortiz moved the blade close to Arturo's face, toying with him. But Arturo didn't look away.

This seemed to anger Ortiz. He turned to the man working the camera to confirm he was getting the shot. The man nodded.

It was times like this that tested the measure of a man. Arturo, who faced death with courage, had passed the test. Gray would be damned if he failed.

Gray looked at the clock on the iPhone. 5:54. He had only six minutes before Sam would call for help. He stepped into the bright lights of the room. "Ramon Ortiz," he shouted. Gray held the iPhone in front of him filming the scene.

Ortiz's men hastily pulled guns, and pointed them at Gray. In turn, Gray panned the room, catching them on the video.

Ortiz clicked off the hedge trimmers and stared at Gray. "You know that iPhone don't make you bulletproof, right?"

"No, but you've just confessed to kidnapping. To conspiracy to murder. I got it all. That's enough to put you and your friends here away for life."

The older of the crew moved in closer, gun trained on Gray. He gave a derisive laugh. "Or we could just waste you and take your phone."

Not an unfair point. "The video is streaming to the cloud," Gray said. "If I don't get back with Arturo in five minutes it goes live on the Internet."

Ortiz shot a nervous glance at the older man.

"Release him," Gray said trying to sound confident. "You do that, and the video is destroyed."

The men darted looks at one another, not sure what to do. There was no streaming, no cloud, no team ready to release the video, of course. Gray prayed they wouldn't call his bluff. They hadn't shot him yet, so that was a good sign. Gray looked at Ortiz. "Doing this isn't gonna bring Angel back."

Ortiz's face reddened. "Say my brother's name again, and I'll string you up next to your friend."

Gray held the iPhone, continuing to film.

Razor turned to Arturo, who was looking more alert now. Ortiz seemed to be calculating his next move, deciding whether he believed Gray. Deciding whether Arturo was worth the risk.

"If the video goes live, you're all going away for a long time," Gray said. "Let him go and it never sees the light of day. You have my word."

"Your word," Ortiz scoffed.

"I mean it. I got no problem with you."

Ortiz looked to the older member of his crew again. The older man didn't say a word, but it was clear his view on the matter: walk away.

The other men kept their guns on Gray, but their faces betrayed their worry that Gray had them on video committing multiple felonies.

"Only four minutes left before this goes public," Gray said. "Decide."

Ortiz pressed his lips together. He clicked the starter on the clippers and marched toward Arturo, who was standing erect now.

"Don't!" Gray shouted.

Ortiz moved the clippers near Arturo's face again. Arturo didn't back down.

Ortiz made a fast arc with the clippers striking the cement beam, the teeth clacking against the concrete, echoing through the garage. Threads of rope securing Arturo flew into the air.

Arturo pushed himself free, and was now face-to-face with Ortiz.

The guns previously directed at Gray were now on Arturo.

Arturo started to speak, but stopped himself.

Ortiz said, "You best get the fuck outta here before I change my mind."

"Let's go," Gray said, keeping the video on them.

Arturo and Ortiz held a stare for a long moment. Then Arturo said, "Nice to see you again, Ramon."

Ortiz smiled wryly. Arturo then walked slowly to Gray.

Ortiz turned to them both. "Hernandez," he said. The sound of his name still sent a chill through Gray the same way it had that night with Lauren.

"Yeah?" Gray said, the iPhone still pointed at Ortiz and his men.

"That video ever gets out, there ain't gonna be much of a future in the pizza business. Or for its owners."

"Don't you threaten his family, motherfucker," Arturo shouted.

Ignoring Arturo, Ortiz looked at Gray. "It's not a threat."

Gray believed him.

"And Alvarez," Ortiz said, as Arturo and Gray paced backward out of the room. "This ain't over."

Arturo gave an exasperated smile. "It never is," he said.

CHAPTER 77

Sam's face lit up when she saw them run out of the garage. *"Thank God!"* She threw her arms around Arturo, then Gray. "You had only thirty seconds left before I was gonna go make the call."

Arturo smacked Gray on the back. "Ponyboy don't need no thirty seconds, he's a fucking badass." For having been worked over and almost dismembered, Arturo was in good spirits. Gray thought perhaps shock was making him loopy.

Once they were a safe distance from the garage, Arturo pulled out his phone.

"You're not gonna call your crew to have them go in there, are you?"

"Not gonna lie, I was thinking about it. But, nah. This shit's gotta stop somewhere." Arturo put the phone to his ear. "But I assume we need a way to get to the justice's house?"

It took Arturo's men thirty minutes to arrive with two motorcycles.

"Bikes?" Gray said.

"Thought it would get us there faster since we can ride around traffic. Also good for escapes," Arturo said. "What's wrong? You forget how to ride?" Arturo smirked. Sam smiled too.

"I'll be fine," Gray said, though he wasn't so sure. If you grew up in the Heights, you knew how to street bike. But it had been years since Gray had ridden solo.

As Gray familiarized himself with the motorcycle, Arturo and Sam talked to the guys who'd delivered the bikes. The men handed Arturo two bandanas, the guns. Gray checked the time. It was 6:35 p.m. If the justices proceeded with the game they'd be leaving in twenty-five minutes.

"We need to get moving," Gray said.

Arturo continued talking to his men, taking his time, not a care in the world. Gray made eye contact with Sam, hoping she'd get the hint and urge Arturo to get a move on. Arturo said something to the men, who laughed. A tricked-out Impala then pulled up and retrieved the men.

Arturo climbed on the other bike. "Don't worry, we'll beat them there," he said. "You want to ride with me or Pony?" Arturo asked Sam.

She climbed on the back of Arturo's motorcycle. "Not even a close one," she said.

The two motorcycles then tore off into the night.

CHAPTER 78

Justice Cutler's estate in the exclusive Avenel neighborhood in Potomac, Maryland, bordered a thick throng of mature trees and was perched on a hill behind an iron fence. No neighbors nearby. The justice was somewhat of a recluse. Divorced, no children. Gray had a stab of guilt that they were using her as bait. They hid the bikes in the trees that lined the fence on the side of the place. Gray gave Arturo a boost, and he cleared the tall gate, then opened a side door to let them in. Easy enough. They decided that Gray and Sam would hide out front, while Arturo would cover the back.

Gray and Sam stayed low in the brush, a spot that gave them a line of sight to the front door. The moon occasionally made an appearance from under the clouds, casting a silver glow over the damp grass. Sam tested the phone Arturo had given her to make sure it was ready to film. Gray stared at his phone. Two blue dots were just minutes away.

"Justice Wall is way ahead of the chief's car," Gray said.

"What if they don't say anything incriminating?" Sam said. "What if you can't subdue them both?"

Gray didn't answer. They were rhetorical questions.

"I think we should call the cops now," Sam said.

"If I call too soon, it won't work."

Sam opened her mouth to protest, then closed it. Then: "You

can't let them get in that house." She tightened her lips. "Please, make the call."

Gray gave in. He dialed 911, reporting an intruder at Justice Cutler's home. He also sent a text to Milstein.

Headlights swung around a bend and Wall's car pulled up to the front of Cutler's estate. Gray wondered if Wall would scale the fence, but Wall simply stopped at the intercom right outside the iron gate. From the brush Gray couldn't hear what Wall said, but the automatic gate creaked open. Gray realized that Wall wasn't planning a surprise attack. He was coming in the front door as a colleague. Gray glanced at the phone. The chief's car was still a good five minutes away.

Wall pulled his sports car to the long drive and around the half circle in front of Cutler's porticoed entrance. He stepped out of his car quickly, looking flustered, agitated. Pretty brazen going to the front door. But that was the genius of the plan. Play the colleague stopping by for an unexpected visit to discuss a case.

Gray looked at Sam, who had the phone's lens directed at Wall. Gray steeled himself, then stepped out from the brush, a gun trained on Wall.

"Don't go any further," Gray called out.

Wall turned. His eyes wide.

"Don't move," Gray said, louder now. He was having a hard time holding the gun steady.

The porch light clicked on. Justice Cutler appeared at the front door.

"Don't worry, Justice Cutler," Gray yelled. "The police are on the way. It's not what you think."

Cutler looked out at Justice Wall. "I'm so sorry, Peter. He made me call you both."

Gray didn't understand.

Headlights beamed from behind, another car coming through the gate. That's when Gray saw it. The mass behind Cutler, and the reflection of the steel blade pressed to her throat.

Gray held the gun, not sure what was going on. He heard the car come to an abrupt stop behind him, and he made a quick look, the gun still on Wall. Gray then felt a jolt of electricity, like the one that had brought him to his knees in the garage attack. He had a sickening realization that it wasn't Wall and Douglas who'd been caught in a trap. He struggled to see who had jammed the stun gun in his side, but saw only the butt of a gun coming down on him.

CHAPTER 79

When Gray came to he had a terrible thumping in his temples. His head thick with sounds. It was hard to breathe. He had tape covering his mouth. He tried to move, but his wrists and ankles were bound to the chair with plastic ties, disposable restraints. The blur was coming into focus. Three chairs lined up next to him in the elegant dining room. Three Supreme Court justices—Cutler, Wall, and Douglas—tied up. That didn't make sense. Douglas and Wall were the killers. The man at the front door with the knife at Justice Cutler's throat, Gray was sure it was the chief. But, wait, then who was in the chief's car? Who hit him? He wasn't thinking straight. The blow to the head, his mind was playing tricks. Gray started to lash about, but the plastic restraints were tight. He needed to calm down.

Then another shockwave shredded through him. Arturo. No. *No!* His old friend was spread out on the dining room floor, his shirt stained in red. And another surge of dread. Where was Sam? Maybe she'd escaped. Gone for help.

Gray's body stiffened when he heard slow footsteps on the creaky hardwood.

It didn't make sense. Who?

The figure entered the room. He was tall with a scruffy beard. Wild eyes.

Vincent.

The homeless man who'd taken up residence outside the court. He didn't look at his captives, instead he just paced about, a caged animal.

Gray's thoughts swirled. All of this orchestrated by a homeless man with mental disabilities? How would he even get into the Supreme Court unnoticed? Why? And where was Agent Milstein? It shouldn't be taking this long.

Did Gray hear sirens? Or was it still the ringing in his ears? Then he smelled it. Smoke. He glanced at the others. Douglas and Wall started making sounds through their gags. Justice Cutler's head snapped up, like she suddenly regained consciousness. They saw it too. The orange glow from the hallway outside the dining room.

Vincent had started a fire.

CHAPTER 80

Milstein and Cartwright raced down the George Washington Memorial Parkway, the sedan's blue light flashing from the dash, Milstein careening on the shoulder through traffic.

"It'll be a waste of time if we crash and don't make it there alive, Em," Cartwright said, his knuckles white on the armrest.

In the rearview, Milstein saw more police lights. She'd been debriefing the full task force on her theory—showing them the footage of Whitlock and his prison visitor, which resolved any doubts—when a text arrived from Grayson Hernandez. Dozens of agents were now racing to Justice Cutler's estate.

Traffic came to a stop. Milstein laid on the horn, and cars parted a path as the sirens from behind drew closer.

Cartwright was talking to someone on his mobile, but it was hard to hear with all the horns and sirens. She heard him say something about a fire. They needed to get there before it was too late.

CHAPTER 81

The smoke was growing thick in the hallway. Fire alarms were beeping loudly. Vincent was muttering to himself, still pacing. Like he was waiting on something. Gray and the others sat helpless, bound up, watching the smoke wisp into the room. Arturo was still on the floor. Gray thought he saw the smallest of movements from him, but maybe it was just wishful thinking. Where was Sam?

Then Vincent stopped suddenly. He looked to the doorway. Through the smoke, a figure emerged. A backlit feminine form. She wore a business suit. And a ski mask. She carefully pulled off the mask. She shook out her long locks, then looked at them. What little breath Gray had in him was stripped from his lungs.

Lauren.

CHAPTER 82

Lauren looked dismissively at Gray, then the others. She walked up to Vincent and spoke softly to him. She stroked his back gently as if trying to calm him down.

She then faced the group. Gray had always considered Lauren one of the most beautiful women he'd ever seen. But standing before him, eyes dark with hate, she was the definition of ugliness.

She walked up to the chief justice, and yanked the tape covering his mouth.

"Lauren, what are you?— I don't understand. What is—"

"You *still* don't know who I am, do you?" Lauren said, her voice tinged with disgust.

The chief gave her a bewildered stare. "I don't under—"

"I kept thinking, surely he'll understand. He'll remember Amanda Hill was the piece of shit's lawyer. That Ben Freeman was the agent who testified in the suppression hearing that helped free him. But you're just too much of a fucking narcissistic *asshole* to get it." It was Lauren who paced now. Vincent gazed at her, his expression one of sorrow.

"Why?" the chief said.

"They got to watch their loved ones die the way *I* got to watch my sister die," Lauren said.

The chief's face showed a glimmer of recognition. "You're one of the Whitlock girls?"

Lauren raised her hands: *No shit.* "You know, I put so much thought into this. What would make you suffer the way I did. What would hurt more than killing you. So you could experience the pain we experienced. But a selfish son of a bitch like you has no wife or kids. Far as I could tell you have only two things you love even re- motely as much as you love yourself. Your career and your dear old friend."

She nodded to Vincent, who walked over. Bile reached Gray's esophagus when he saw Vincent pull a knife from a sheath at his ankle.

"I thought it would be so fitting to make it look like it was you," Lauren continued. "Use your pitiful competition against you. Take away your precious reputation, your career. But the feds were too slow on the uptake, even as I tried to spoon-feed it to them. Quill pens, for fuck's sake, and they still didn't get it!

"Then that fucking reporter learned who I was, and was going to ruin everything." She looked over at Gray. "And, of course, your little charity project got in the way." She bore no resemblance to the woman he knew.

The chief finally spoke. "Lauren, I'm sorry about your sister. I'm sorry for what happened to you."

Lauren's face reddened, her jaw set.

The chief said, "I've relived that ruling over and over. And if I had to do it again, I wouldn't have let him out. I was young. I thought it was my duty—it was justice—to follow the law, no matter the cost."

"You and your fucking justice games." Lauren gave a nod to Vincent, who moved toward the chief, knife gripped in his hand.

"*Please*, I was just following the law," the chief repeated. More desperation now. "I'm sorry," the chief said. "It was twenty years ago, a mistake. I'm *so* sorry."

Lauren put a hand up to stop Vincent. "You're violating your own rules, chief."

The chief gave her a quizzical look.

"You know, the lessons you taught your minion." She looked

at Gray. He'd once told her the rules he'd learned from the chief justice. Lauren looked at the chief again. "*No apologies*, remember?"

"Please," the chief pleaded.

"But that's not my favorite little nugget of wisdom." She nodded at Vincent, who glanced at Douglas, then twisted around and drove the blade into Justice Wall's chest.

"*No mercy!*" Lauren screamed violently in the chief justice's face. She then got near Wall's face. Wall's eyes were wide, an expression of shock. Lauren said, "My skin crawled every time you touched me. You couldn't possibly think I wanted you."

Douglas let out a sob, and Lauren then roughly slapped the tape back over his mouth.

Gray had a moment of clarity. Lauren wasn't at the condo that night to see Gray, she was there to see Wall. Lauren knew that Dora Baxter was having an affair with Wall because *Lauren* was having an affair with Wall. And she never saw the chief justice talking to Amanda Hill before Hill was murdered. Lauren was trying to cast suspicion on the chief. When Gray told her the FBI was focused solely on the Whitlock case—that they were close to a big break in the investigation—she must've panicked, knowing it would lead to her. She needed to blame someone else before they found her. Gray recalled the day before she faked her own abduction, her insistence that the FBI should be focusing on the clues she and Gray had provided them, and not the Whitlock case.

"Watch him die," Lauren said to the chief. "*Watch him!*" There was madness in her voice now.

Wall writhed in the chair, a repugnant gurgling from his throat filling the room.

Gray sucked for air, his chest pushing in and out. The room was a haze of smoke now. Gray's heart plummeted when he saw Lauren and Vincent coming toward him.

He squeezed his eyes shut. Bracing himself.

But no blade came slicing into him. Instead, he felt a latex-glove-covered hand on his bound wrist, and another on his right hand. He started to struggle, closing his hand to a fist. They weren't going to stab him, just yet, anyway. No, they wanted his prints on the knife. Vincent pried open Gray's balled fist, and Lauren wedged the knife's handle into Gray's hand. Once his palm gripped the knife, they released their hold and Lauren carefully threw the weapon on the floor. They were going to make it look like Gray stabbed Justice Wall.

Lauren glowered at Gray. "I knew you'd believe those papers came from the envelope. That you'd come running to Cutler's. The hero, proving he was worth something, that you belonged."

Lauren was about to say more to Gray, but stopped at the sound of sirens in the distance. Lauren looked at Vincent. "You need to do it."

She stood in front of Vincent, bracing herself.

The man spoke. "I don't wanna hurt you, Susie." He had a lisp. Despite just plunging a knife into a man's chest, there was a gentleness to him. "You're my baby sister."

"Johnny, it's okay. You need to do it. It's the only way to save me."

Vincent, or Johnny, or whatever his name was, gave a reluctant nod.

Lauren braced herself again. Vincent then punched her in the eye. She stumbled backward.

"Okay, good. Now the mouth. Not so hard, though."

Vincent punched her again. Lauren walked over to a mirror that hung over a bar cart filled with decanters. She nodded at her bloodied face as if it would do. She then walked over to Gray and scratched deep into his arm. She did the same with his face.

He realized what she was doing. Evidence of a struggle with him. DNA under her nails. She looked Gray in the eyes for just a moment. He thought he'd see some remorse, some sadness, but there was nothing.

The chief justice and Cutler were coughing through their gags now. Wall was still.

Lauren looked at Vincent. "I need to go. You know what to do. Just like we went over. No one can leave here alive. I'll be at the storage unit so they can find me."

"I'm worried, Susie. What if I mess up?"

"Look at me," Lauren said. She clenched Vincent's chin in her hand and turned his face to hers. "You took your meds?"

Vincent nodded.

"Then it's just like you did at Christmas at the train station. Just follow my instructions one at a time. You have the list?"

Vincent nodded again and pulled out a folded sheet of paper from his coat pocket.

"I need you to do this to protect me. Can you do it?"

Another nod.

"Say it, Johnny."

"I can do it. Just follow the list."

"I love you." She kissed him on the cheek, then disappeared out of the fiery house.

CHAPTER 83

Gray choked back the terror as the room enveloped in smoke. Lauren had all the bases covered. The killer Grayson Hernandez's final acts of carnage, acting on his obsession with the Supreme Court, killing three justices, aided by his childhood friends. Physical evidence to back that up. And a fire to destroy any other evidence. Vincent would kill Gray and untie him to make it look like Gray died in a struggle with Justice Wall. Vincent would then kill the others and make his escape. Lauren—Gray's prisoner—would be found alive, beaten with Gray's skin under her fingernails. Suspicion averted. Lauren's vengeance-laden plan a success. Gray wasn't clear what that plan was, but she and Vincent were siblings, that much he understood. The Whitlock kids from that old case. Piecing things together, it seemed that Lauren had intended to send a message to the chief justice before framing him, but apparently there had been too much attention on the scheme. She'd mentioned that a reporter had discovered her real identity. She needed a fall guy. He wondered if that was her plan from the start. She'd never cared about Gray. She was just using him. The coldness in her departure confirmed it all.

He closed his eyes again, feeling heat blanketing the room. *Just do it already, Vincent,* he thought, his heart thumping. *Just get on with it.*

His eyes shot open to the sound. A struggle. He had a swell of hope when through the smoky haze he saw Arturo clasping Vincent's wrist, trying to wrestle the knife away from him. Arturo's torso was covered in red. He'd been shot or stabbed, but he clawed and scrapped like the brawler he was.

Vincent came down on Arturo's head with his fist, again and again. But Arturo kept a grip on Vincent's wrist, trying to loosen his grasp on the knife. Both were tall and muscular, but Arturo was severely injured. Arturo shifted his weight, swinging Vincent's wrist like a baseball bat, and both men crashed to the floor.

Gray rocked his chair. Maybe if he kept it up, the wood would give, the bindings would loosen. But the chair was solid, the zip ties tight. Gray kept jerking side to side until he toppled over.

Arturo kept his grip around Vincent's wrist and the two men thrashed about on the floor, colliding into the bar cart. Heavy decanters fell, shattering on the hardwood floor. The room was growing black with smoke, and Gray heard cracking wood. More coughing from the others. The floor was actually the best place to be right now.

Arturo managed to get on top of Vincent, straddling him, his hands not letting go of Vincent's wrist.

Gray, still bound to the chair, bucked, inching closer to them. Maybe, just maybe, he could help his friend. He lashed about, skidding along the floor.

Vincent was still on his back, Arturo sitting on top of him, still holding Vincent's wrist. But Vincent didn't let go of the knife. Vincent was still writhing about, and managed to twist the blade toward Arturo. With his hand that wasn't pinned to the floor, Vincent grabbed Arturo's shoulder and started pulling Arturo toward the steel point. He was trying to impale him. Arturo turned his torso just as he came down on the knife, stabbing through his shoulder, eliciting a wail of pain.

Gray was right next to them both now. Arturo was slumped over, semiconscious. Gray skidded closer on the floor that was slick with blood and liquor, littered with broken glass. Vincent shoved Arturo off of him. Vincent stayed on the floor catching his breath. This was Gray's only chance. He slid closer, cocked his head back, and head-butted Vincent.

Gray saw stars, but forced himself to do it again. This time he saw black. When he came to, Vincent was still. But then he saw Vincent's hand, feeling for the knife.

Vincent continued to feel about, finger painting in blood, trying to locate the blade. Gray tried to move, but he was exhausted, muscles aching, head fuzzy. Vincent's fingertips were on the knife's handle now. And then he had the knife again, firmly in his grasp. He jolted up, and made eye contact with Gray.

Then came the explosion of shattered glass, and Vincent collapsed. Arturo was on his knees, the neck of a broken decanter in his hand. Vincent staggered to his feet, the fire radiating behind him. His hair a mess, eyes wild, and clothes drenched in alcohol, he looked like a madman. Vincent clutched the blade, a look of resolve on his face. Arturo then charged Vincent. He crashed into him, sending Vincent flying toward the flames. When Vincent hit the floor of the hallway, there was a bright flash of yellow and orange. Vincent then screamed in agony as the alcohol on his clothes accelerated the blaze that now consumed him. It was a small eternity until he stopped moving, as Gray gagged on the smell of burning flesh.

Arturo crawled to Gray. He retrieved Vincent's knife from the floor and slid the blade under the plastic tie securing Gray's wrist, cutting it away. From there Gray cut through the rest of the bindings. Gray saw a folded sheet of paper on the floor. The list Lauren had made for Vincent must have fallen out during the struggle. He scooped it up and jammed it in his pocket. There was no time to untie the justices. Gray dragged the chair constraining Douglas, while Arturo pulled Cutler to safety outside. It was clear that Justice Wall was gone. Maybe they could make it back in for his body before the fire ravaged the rest of the place.

Police lights now illuminated the front gate. "Sam, where's Sam?" Gray said desperately.

Gray looked at Cutler's home, which was ablaze. He turned to the groan of the iron gates of the estate that opened and a band of agents rushed onto the grounds, guns drawn. He saw Agent Milstein and her partner. Milstein ran to him.

"It was Lauren Hart," Gray said, his voice in rasps, "and a man named Vincent, or John, her brother. They—"

"We know, Grayson," Milstein said. "Where are they?"

"He's dead, but Lauren escaped." But he cared little about them now. *"We need to find Sam!"*

"The woman?" Justice Cutler said. Her face was smeared with blood and soot. "She was in the house. When they brought you in, she was unconscious. The man carried her to the back."

Gray started to run toward the blaze, but two agents grabbed him by the arms restraining him. He struggled to tug free, but he was weak. Every part of him ached. That's when he saw a figure already at the front of the house running into the blaze.

Gray tried again to break free, but Milstein gently placed a hand on his shoulder. Her partner kept hold of Gray's arm, sorrow in his eyes.

An explosion shook the earth, and the mansion's windows shattered, smoke billowing out.

Tears streamed down Gray's face as the roof collapsed. The loud wail of a fire truck filled the air.

His best friends, the three amigos.

Then he saw it.

The figure, a silhouette against the flames, came staggering from the house. And he was carrying someone.

CHAPTER 84

Beating Gray there, a paramedic took Sam from Arturo's arms, racing her away from the fire that roared close and hot. Gray reached Arturo, who had collapsed on the ground.

He cradled his old friend in his lap. "You're gonna be okay. Help is here. You're gonna be okay." Gray screamed for another medic.

"No, I'm not," Arturo said. He gave a contemplative look. Then a faint smile. "A fire—like the book," he said, a hint of amusement. A scene from *The Outsiders*. Gray stared at his friend. Arturo's tough and weary face morphed into his fourteen-year-old one, sitting in group therapy, refusing to answer questions about the book, everyone in the room seeing the pain in his eyes. Then, a sad ten-year-old on Christmas Eve.

Arturo coughed, and blood shot out of his mouth over his cheek. Gray wiped it away.

"Hey, Ponyboy," Arturo struggled to get it out. "I need to say something to you."

Gray said, "I swear, if you say 'stay golden' "—the famous line from *The Outsiders*—"I'm going to kill you myself."

Arturo let out a breathy laugh. Before his eyes rolled to the back of his head, he crammed something into Gray's hand. Paramedics pulled Gray away, and he looked on in shock as they maneuvered Arturo onto a stretcher and whisked him away.

Gray looked at the item in his hand.

It was a battered old Pokémon card.

CHAPTER 85

Gray ran to the gurney where Sam was stretched out with an oxygen mask over her face. She reached for his arm.

"I'm so sorry," he said. "I should have never brought you into this."

Sam said something, but he couldn't make it out. Then she slowly pulled down the oxygen mask. "Stop being a pussy, and go get that bitch."

At that, Gray remembered Vincent's list, the instructions Lauren had given her brother. Gray pulled the paper from his pocket and unfolded it. It included a numbered list. Step-by-step instructions. About going to Cutler's house to force her to call Chief Justice Douglas to lure him to the estate. Then the same for Wall. Subdue the justices one at a time. Gray realized that if the justices had seen the envelope, it would have meant nothing to them. Lauren must've originally come up with the game to frame or taunt the chief justice, then used it against Gray.

When the chief arrived first at Cutler's house, John Whitlock overpowered him, then Lauren must have taken his car. The list also gave instructions about killing each of them. Matter-of-fact murder. The last item on the list: "If they haven't found me by Friday, make an anonymous call from the phone I gave you and tell them to look for me at U Store It on River Road." Gray recalled what Lauren said to Vincent: *I'll be at the storage unit.*

Gray took in a deep breath and collected himself. He ran to the side gate and found the motorcycles where they'd hidden them. A fury was burning in his chest now. As he climbed on the bike, he saw Milstein running toward him.

"What are you doing?" she shouted over the roar of the bike and commotion of the army of federal agents and fire fighters on Justice Cutler's estate.

"I know where she is." Gray stuffed Vincent's list in Milstein's hand, pulled back on the throttle, and sped off to find Lauren Hart.

CHAPTER 86

The wind lashed Gray's face as he weaved around cars, horns blaring after him, but he didn't let up until he saw it. A large, faded fiberglass sign: U STORE IT. A self-storage place. It was surrounded by a barbed-wire fence. There was a keypad near an automatic gate so customers could come and go to the small metal cells where they kept the leftovers from their lives.

He parked the bike near the front gate and considered how he'd get inside. He could climb the fence, but the razor wire would tear him to shreds. He could wait for someone to visit a storage unit and trail after them, but that could take hours. Then he saw the Dumpster, lodged next to the fence, overflowing with cardboard boxes. He ran to the container and began scaling the trash spilling out of it.

At the top, he balanced precariously on a large cardboard box. His body ached from the car crash and violence with John Whitlock. He was running on pure rage. He estimated the distance from the Dumpster over the barbwire. He thought of one of his father's rules. *No fear.*

And he made the leap.

He cleared the fence, but landed hard, a clumsy stumble, skinning his knees. Gray ran though the facility, which had two large buildings. One structure had a single door, which Gray presumed led to small interior storage units. The other building had several exterior doors, units accessible from outside. He saw the chief justice's silver Audi, the loaner Gray had used during the term, parked in front of one of the exterior doors. The car Lauren or John Whitlock had used to run down Dora Baxter. He ran over and stopped in front of the unit. He took in a breath, then turned the handle on the door. It was unlocked.

Inside was dark, but a section in the back was lit by weak fluorescents. He stepped quietly toward a radio that was crackling. A police scanner, he realized. He thought he heard the dispatcher say "U Store It." The agents were on the way. On top of the scanner, five feather quill pens. The signatures Lauren and Vincent had left at the crime scenes. Under the pens, a receipt for the storage unit. What caught his eye was the name at the top of the papers. Gray's name. She must've rented it online with his credit card. She'd thought of everything.

Gray hoped he'd find Lauren handcuffed, the poor victim waiting to be saved, but he didn't see her. He lost his breath at the sight of an axe that was leaning against the corner. He thought of the couple from Union Station. It reminded him that he wasn't dealing with Lauren Hart, brilliant young law clerk. He was confronting a vengeful, twisted killer.

That's when he felt the presence behind him.

Gray's body then convulsed as thousands of volts shot through him. Temporarily paralyzed, his neck snapped violently back with the force of a sheet of plastic yanked over his face. He sucked in and the bag nearly touched the back of his throat. He weakly clawed at the plastic, but felt another jolt of lightning in his side.

He was being pulled to the ground, the bag tight around his face. He fought it, gasping for oxygen. Things were starting to blur. His body and mind retreating.

He thought of Arturo and Sam and their bravery tonight, and then his father. He willed himself to find the strength to not give up. Launching backward, he felt the break of cartilage as his head slammed into her face. The grip on the plastic loosened, and he lashed his head back again, then ripped the plastic away.

In the shadows he saw her, hands red as she moved them from her face. Sirens were in the distance.

"It's over, Lauren."

She just stared at him. A long silence. Then her expression turned remorseful. She spoke softly. "It was in a storage unit like this that he did it. We were so young, we didn't even understand what he was doing. I still smell him on me."

She looked off at nothing. Gray decided to just let her get it out. He needed to keep her there until Milstein and the troops arrived.

"We were just running to the store," she said. "Our big brother was with us, so nothing to worry about, right?" She sobbed, her face awash in blood and tears. "He said he had candy in the storeroom. Then he hit Johnny with a brick."

"But you got through it. You survived, you've been so successful. Wouldn't your parents want you to—"

"My *parents*," she spat. "My birth mother took a fistful of pills after Justice Douglas let him go free. She left me. I was five years old. Of course, a cute little girl had no problem getting adopted. But Johnny . . ."

Gray needed to stall, the agents would be there soon. "Why now, after all this time?"

She stared at him with an intensity he couldn't describe. "Because I didn't think any of it was real. My adoptive parents, in all of their affluent overprivileged wisdom, made me think it was all in my imagination. Years of shrinks and meds, and they let me think it wasn't real. They thought a high IQ and money could solve all my problems, everything would be just fine. Didn't even tell me I had a brother. They said the sweet boy who I dreamed about was a figment of my imagination." She let the stun gun fall to the floor and began sobbing again. "But when they died when I was in law school, I went through their papers, and I learned the truth. And I found Johnny."

She was a killer. Probably a sociopath. She'd hurt so many people, but he had the urge to comfort her.

Gray saw strobes through the cracks in the walls now. It would be over soon.

"You didn't deserve what happened. And your parents should

have told you the truth. But those people you hurt, they were innocent, just like you."

"I'm sorry, Grayson." More tears. "I'm sick." She fell into his arms and held him tight. He remembered how this felt before. Her body shuddered as she cried.

"They'll get you help," he said.

The door burst open and flashlight beams and red lasers filled the aluminum storage unit. Gray pulled away from Lauren's embrace. He then stepped in front of her, raising his hands, trying to prevent the agents from coming in guns blazing. He felt her hand briefly on his back. He was then blinded a moment by the lights. He kept his hands raised high.

Then the shots rang out.

Pop, pop, pop.

Gray braced himself, but he wasn't hit. He twisted around and saw Lauren, an expression of shock on her face. The axe in her hand. She collapsed to the cement.

Gray stared at Agent Milstein, whose arm was still extended from taking the shots.

EPILOGUE

Grayson Hernandez walked up to the lectern in the well of the U.S. Supreme Court. He wasn't intimidated by the marble columns that encased the room or the elevated mahogany bench where The Nine had been known to skewer even the most experienced advocates. It had been two years since he left his clerkship and already he had made a name for himself. He'd joined a public interest firm where he represented the poor and needy in impact cases. He glanced at Justice Cutler, who was now in the center seat, confirmed after Edgar Douglas had retired in the wake of his abduction and the death of his best friend. Cutler's scowl seemed to grow even more pronounced after the attack, but she held the hint of a smile for Gray under that harsh stare.

Gray turned briefly to the spectator section. His parents were in the reserved seats. Next to Mom and Dad, Miranda was holding Emilio's arm as if to keep him from wiggling. And there was Sam.

He was about to turn back to the bench when someone in the gallery called out, "Kick some ass, Ponyboy." It prompted tittering from the spectators, and Gray saw Arturo getting a lecture from an officer.

The press had made much of Gray's first oral argument— feature stories in every major newspaper—so he was only half surprised to see other familiar faces in the wings. Keir gave him a nod, Mike a thumbs up, and Praveen an admiring gaze. Even Agent Milstein and her partner, Cartwright, were there.

Gray collected himself, then turned back to the justices and began his argument.

"Madam Chief Justice and may it please the court. Some may think that the tenants of Stonewalk Gardens should be happy that the government took their land, paid them to leave the so-called blighted area; that they should take the relocation money offered and never look back. But it shouldn't be the government who decides where these good people live. This is their home. And no one has the right, good-intentioned or not, to force them to move away from the place they love, the people they love. No one has the right to make them outsiders . . ."

ACKNOWLEDGEMENTS

To my wife, Tracy—my rock, my life, since I was sixteen years old.

To my children, Jake, Emma, and Aiden, the other joys of my life, who keep their dad on his toes. (And, Em, you finally got the serial killer you wanted in this book.)

To my agent, Lisa Erbach Vance, and the team at the Aaron Priest Literary Agency. Lisa, I continue to marvel at your literary insights, sound judgment, and the best representation an author could ever hope for.

To my editors, Pete Wolverton and Jennifer Donovan, for making *The Outsider* the best it could be. It's an honor to be guided by such able hands. Also thanks to the many hardworking professionals at St. Martin's Press, including Joseph Brosnan, Paul Hochman, Justin Velella, Bill Warhop, and Allison Ziegler.

To my law firm, Arnold & Porter. I've spent most of my life at the firm and am the better for it. My days large including with our tight-knit Supreme Court and Appellate t Theodore, Lisa Blatt, Stanton Jones, Reeves Anderson, F as advocacy, and Sally Pei—whose legal acumen, creati go to my other and sense of humor always inspire. Th Kat Lindsay, John longtime friends from the firm: Deb art. and Rob Weiner, Massaro, Evie Norwinski, Sheil who have supported my writi

To my writer pal Barry Lancet, as well as the other great friends I've made through the International Thriller Writers organization.

To you, readers. I never forget that you are giving me and my stories precious hours of your life, and I do my best to live up to that privilege.

ABOUT AUTHENTICITY

This is the part in my books where I separate fact from fiction, somewhat.

 The Supreme Court is indeed like a small town. The high court employs not only The Nine, but more than four hundred others whose office is a marble palace located just behind the Capitol dome at One First Street, Northeast, Washington, D.C. As I note in the novel, beyond the courtroom and justices' chambers, the building houses a full police force, a marshal's office, a clerk's office, a curator, a press office, a public cafeteria, a gift shop, and a breathtaking library. I should note, however, that there is no marshal's "cube farm" filled with messengers like Grayson Hernandez, though there are marshal's aides who perform various tasks, including sitt͚ su-
behind the bench to fetch things for the justices during ora͚
ments.   or take)

 It is true that every summer thirty-six law clerk gal careers.
embark on what most will consider a highlight of o the nation's
And the one-year clerkship is truly an entr Justices were law
most prestigious legal jobs. Three of the ing bonus for clerks
clerks themselves. The $400,000 law $300,000, but the en-
I mention is not accurate; it's actu n included interviewing
ticement is sure to tick up. M s, articles, and first-person
former clerks as well as r

accounts of the job. I drew substantially on the work of the leading scholars in the area, Professors Todd Peppers and Artemus Ward, as well as Edward Lazarus's *Closed Chambers*, a somewhat controversial account of Lazarus's year as a law clerk.

As for the responsibilities of a clerk, I believe the "five tasks" Lauren Hart describes pretty accurately summarize them. The clerk "happy hours" are real; the First Saturday events are not. I also made up the famous "envelope." Clerks I've spoken with note that they can't imagine that a justice would bring his or her clerks on a trip like the jaunt to Martha's Vineyard in the story. I was also told that a justice would *never* work while eating in the justices' opulent private dining room.

On a more serious note, my novel suggests that the law clerks lack diversity. Nearly twenty years ago, Tony Mauro, the esteemed Supreme Court correspondent for the *National Law Journal*, was the first to systematically study the demographic profile of Supreme Court law clerks, finding that fewer than 2 percent of the clerks were African American and even fewer were Hispanic. Mauro continues to study and write about the issue. While *The Outsider* is a thriller and I have no intention of preaching, Mauro's work did help me think about what it would be like for a poor Mexican American who attended a low-ranked law school to be thrust into the clerk community.

As for the primary setting of *The Outsider*, the Supreme Court building is as majestic as I describe, a Roman temple filled with marble and mahogany. I've had the privilege to represent clients in a few numerous cases before the court, to sit at the long table just a few places from the justices, and to get behind-the-scenes tours of the building. I've done my best to capture the feeling of being in the novel. If you are ever in Washington, D.C., I highly recommend you visit the building. It is open year-round, and admission is free. If you are unable to visit, I recommend Fred and Suzy Maroon's book *The Supreme Court of the United States*, which contains more than one hundred beautiful photographs of the building.

The court is a place of order, as I note in the novel—from the justices being seated in order to the most junior justice designated as note taker and doorman, when the justices are in their secret conferences, to the quill pens given to advocates. Speaking of the pens, which obviously serve as a plot point in the novel, the court started the practice in the 1800s when Chief Justice John Marshall gave pens and inkwells to lawyers appearing before the court.

The book also references several Supreme Court decisions—some real, some not. The *Korematsu* case, which upheld the internment of Japanese Americans during World War II, and *Buck v. Bell*, wherein Justice Oliver Wendell Holmes made the offensive "three generations of imbeciles" remark are, unfortunately, real decisions. So is *Plessy v. Ferguson*, which upheld the separate-but-equal doctrine. All are considered low points in the court's jurisprudence, but I hope readers do not forget the many high points.

The school-speech case about the rapper in the opening pages of the book is based on a real case that the court declined to review. Friends of mine represented the student rapper, and Adam Liptak of the *New York Times*—a storied reporter and former First Amendment lawyer himself—wrote an insightful piece on the case that I relied on for my scene. The Anton Troy death penalty case is not real, though it was inspired by actual legal challenges concerning the drugs used in lethal injections. Also, Lauren Hart's recitation of my fictitious chief justice's opinion criticizing the death penalty is drawn largely from real dissenting opinions in two recent death cases, as well as the exceptional analysis of the cases by Adam Liptak.

The *Filstein* case about the government's drone policy is fictitious, but drawn from articles by Jeremy Scahill. And the *Wakefield Estates* eminent domain case and the *Jando* search-and-seizure case also are not actual cases, though someday variations of the issues in those cases could well reach the high court.

I reference past justices, including Justice William O. Douglas (a justice from 1939 to 1975), whose quote opens the book. Some dispute that Douglas referred to clerks as the "lowest form of animal life," and Douglas's former clerks have defended history's harsh assessment of their boss. No one, however, defends Justice James McReynolds (1914–1941). Retired Justice Sandra Day O'Connor (1981–2006) noted in her book *Out of Order* that McReynolds was a "self-professed anti-Semite who behaved badly to Justices Brandeis and Cardozo, who were Jewish." Clare Cushman, managing editor of the *Journal of Supreme Court History*, wrote a fascinating article about McReynolds's law clerks, relying on letters written by these poor souls during their clerkships. In 1938, one clerk wrote his mother about the difficulty of spending time with "a man so small that no matter how hard he tries, will never become as big as his position."

Justice Horace Gray (1881–1902) was in fact the first justice to hire a law clerk. And the anecdote about Justice Thurgood Marshall (1967–1991) writing "not yet" on his medical file passed on to Richard Nixon is purported to be true, among so many other great Marshall tales.

I did not mention sitting justices in *The Outsider*, but there were a few things I borrowed from their lives. For instance, in his nomination speech, the current chief justice, John G. Roberts, remarked that "I always got a lump in my throat whenever I walked up those marble steps to argue a case before the court, and I don't think it was just from the nerves," a statement I modified and attributed to the chief in *The Outsider*. Like my chief, Roberts also used sign language to swear-in a group of deaf lawyers to the Supreme Court bar.

I also drew from Justice Elena Kagan. During her confirmation hearing, then Solicitor General Kagan was asked about the solicitor general being referred to as the "tenth justice." Kagan said that she thought the "justices think of the solicitor general more as the thirty-seventh law clerk." If you've finished *The Outsider*, you know the significance of that reference to the story. Several justices, including Justice Ruth Bader Ginsburg, serve as judges in the Shakespeare Theatre Company's annual mock trials, which I also reference in the novel.

Finally, you may recall my character Justice Wall's speech at Georgetown about growing up with his friend the chief justice. Here, I was inspired by a real speech Justice Samuel Alito gave at an end-of-the-term celebration held by Georgetown University Law Center's Supreme Court Institute. This is the second book where I've appropriated events from the institute's annual party—I hope they invite me back.

Outside the Supreme Court realm, D.C. State is not a real institution. And sketchy Hamilton Heights is not an actual D.C. neighborhood. I love D.C. and the surrounding area—all three of my children were born in the District—so I didn't have the heart to single out a particular neighborhood.

Errors are all my own. The fictitious criminal elements in the story aside, I hope to have given readers a glimpse into an institution that I greatly admire and truly believe is the finest our government has to offer.